R O B E R T   O L M S T E A D ' S

SOFT WATER

"When morning comes, it will be Sunday and
Asel will have breakfast ready when Phoebe
wakes up. They'll unlock the door and have coffee on the front porch, where they can watch the
last leaves of the season on the hills that rise up
across the river, where Asel can look out on the
meadow that surrounds the house and see
whoever comes down the road long before they
see him. While he sits there, eating birthday
cake, he'll put off again his decision to leave her,
though he knows he must go. He knows he must
leave this place to save her from what will
come."

Also by Robert Olmstead

R I V E R   D O G S

SOFT WATER

ROBERT OLMSTEAD

SOFT WATER

**VINTAGE
CONTEMPORARIES**

VINTAGE BOOKS
A DIVISION OF RANDOM HOUSE
NEW YORK

A Vintage Contemporaries Original
First Edition, May 1988

All rights reserved under International
and Pan-American Copyright Conventions.
Published in the United States by
Random House, Inc., New York,
and simultaneously in Canada
by Random House of Canada Limited, Toronto.

Library of Congress Cataloging-in-Publication Data
Olmstead, Robert.
   Soft water.
   (Vintage contemporaries)
   I. Title.
PS3565.L67S64 1988   813'.54   87-45925
ISBN 0-394-75752-1 (pbk.)

AUTHOR PHOTO © 1987 BY DAVID TOBIN

BOOK DESIGN BY BARBARA M. BACHMAN

Manufactured in the United States of America
10 9 8 7 6 5 4 3 2 1

TO MY MOTHER,
AND FOR MY FATHER, WHO LOVED HER
IN HIS OWN WAY

How to Cross a Swift Dangerous Stream—There are four ways to cross a dangerous river or stream. Pack or Weight fording—Pole fording—Rope or raft fording—Animals must swim—the outfit (Duffle) won't spoil by a wetting—the chief point is to get the grub rations across and keep it dry. (This must be done). . . . But in all fords remember it is the fool who never turns back. If the water feels too strong, return while you can, for a glacier stream has no mercy.

—*Francis H. Buzzacott,*

THE COMPLETE AMERICAN
& CANADIAN SPORTSMAN'S
ENCYCLOPEDIA OF
VALUABLE INSTRUCTION

PART ONE

STREAMS

An Indian Method in Winter—of killing wild game, wolves, bears, etc. . . . take a piece of flexible steel or whalebone and bend it into a small circle, securing it with sinew, this they insert in a ball of meat, flesh, fat and blood and allow to freeze . . . these they throw out on the snow or ice about the haunts of animals; coming along they find them and being hungry, ravenously devour them. The heat of the stomach soon melts the frozen parts, the spring coil straightens out piercing the stomach, causing agony and death which in due time ensues. . . . I have often assisted in the preparation of these killing balls, and witnessed their fearful results.

—Buzzacott

1

A S E L watches wrestling on Saturday nights. He likes
it when Verne Gagne goes for the sleeper hold. He jumps
out of his chair and slaps his thighs with both hands. Then
he cranks his arms around, one across his chest and the other
upright with the hand cupped as if it's on someone's skull,
as if he's doing it himself. He imagines that it's him putting
Jerry Blackwell into slumberland and that it's his partner,
Mad Dog Vachon, lying outside the ring, blood running down
his face and pooling on the concrete, black and shiny.

"Phoebe, come here," Asel says. "Verne's going for the
sleeper."

But Phoebe can't hear him. She's in the kitchen with her
headphones on. They are the kind that wrap around the head
and have tiny speakers that fit inside the ears. She has a song
she keeps playing over and over again. It's an Emmylou Harris
song. She hears something new every time she plays it. She
hears something new about how hard it is to kill off the ghost
of a no-good man. At certain times in the song, she presses
her fingers into the palms of her hands and at other times,
she spreads them wide and tilts her head back, her braid so
long that it curls up at her feet, snug and warm on the floor.

Verne Gagne lets go his hold on Jerry Blackwell and whips
him into the ropes. Everyone at the Hartford Civic Center
is on their feet. Asel can hear them. He wishes he were there
too, so his voice could join the others in urging Verne on to
victory. Verne gets his hands on the chair that Blackwell used
to open up Mad Dog's head. He holds it in the air and turns
round and round. It's a folding chair, made of steel and wood.
It will make quite a dent in Jerry's noggin when it comes
crashing down. But Verne isn't that kind of guy.

"Break it," Asel whispers and Verne does. He breaks it
over his knee and drops the halves over the side, where they

land on the concrete next to Mad Dog's head. It's Verne's
way of telling Mad Dog that he's going to kick some ass.

Verne goes back to work on Blackwell. He grabs his arm.
It's the arm Blackwell broke two years ago in Atlanta. Verne
knows this. He turns the arm as if he's wringing out laundry,
twisting it around and around. The ringside announcer says
it's a testament to Blackwell's experience and training that
he doesn't sustain a spiral fracture. Meanwhile, Blackwell's
partner, Ted Grizzly, climbs to the top of the turnbuckle.
He intends to catapult his body into the air and pounce on
Verne, maybe drive an elbow or a knee into Verne's back.
Maybe hurt him in a bad way. An injury that could end his
career. Paralyze him a little bit.

"Verne, look out," Asel yells. He knows Verne can't hear
him because Verne's in Hartford and the match was fought
Thursday night of last week to a sellout crowd that went
home days ago, but he yells anyway.

Mad Dog's face fills the television screen. For a second
Asel thinks that Mad Dog must have heard him, that his words
roused him from his unconscious state. He thinks Mad Dog
is coming into the room. Blood runs from a razor cut to the
right side of his forehead. It's a neat incision that would lead
you to wonder how he got it if you hadn't seen the chair
come down on his head with your own eyes. Mad Dog crawls
up the ring apron and grabs Ted Grizzly's ankle. It's enough
to knock him off kilter just as he is about to leap from the
ropes. Ted Grizzly goes into a somersault with a half twist,
barely missing Verne, and knocking the referee out cold as
a cucumber with the point of his elbow.

"Phoebe, you've got to see this," Asel yells as all four
wrestlers begin hurtling off the ropes, their huge bodies criss-
crossing in the middle of the ring, a hairsbreadth apart.

Asel steps back and looks down the hall.

He can see that Phoebe is still listening to the tape. Her
eyes are closed. Her black hair is drawn tight, and shines in
the light over her head. Asel looks back to the television in

time to see Verne and Mad Dog pull up short, allowing Ted
Grizzly and Jerry Blackwell to collide in the middle of the
ring. Verne sets the sleeper hold on Grizzly while Mad Dog
sends Blackwell into an atomic drop, compressing the ver-
tebrae in his spine. The referee wakes up in time to give the
three count. The Hartford Civic Center is bedlam. Mad Dog
takes a bite out of Blackwell's ear.

Asel is happy for them. He shuts down the volume and
goes into the kitchen for a coffee. Phoebe's school stuff is
on the table in front of her. She has a stack of papers to
correct but hasn't gotten after them yet. Her blue marker is
still capped, next to the stack. Asel sets the water to boil and
sits down beside her. They sit like that until, after a while,
Phoebe takes her headphones off. Asel moves his mouth as
if he's talking but he doesn't say anything. She looks at him
for a second and then moves her mouth. He's not sure but
he thinks she's telling him to go to hell. The pot begins to
blow steam.

Asel makes his coffee and sits down at the table again. He
drinks coffee all day and all night, catching a few hours' sleep
here and there. It's a habit he picked up in Maine when he
was a boy. Sometimes it gives him heartburn, but only when
other things are on his mind.

Now he stays awake every night until after Phoebe has
gone to sleep and if he does sleep, he gets up before she
does. He makes sure of it. He has done this ever since they've
lived together. At first it bothered her and she tried to stay
awake with him but she couldn't. She kept a diary the first
few months, trying to chart his habits to see if there was a
pattern to them, but she couldn't stay awake and he wouldn't
tell her one way or the other, so she gave up.

She still remembers, though, their making love in the early
morning, so early that she considered it to still be the day
before. She'd wake to his touch, but after a time, she began
to lose track of that too and it became a long dream she would
have every night, whether he came to her or not.

When she was still of a mind that she needed to know the truth, she came to rely on small things, the smell of the sheets and the shape of the pillow. She'd search them out, needing to know before she started her day. She'd be most certain when she'd wake up and feel the wetness between her legs. She'd then close her eyes and try to remember what it had been like and she'd touch herself where she imagined he had and she'd imagine it had been good and then she wouldn't want to get up and take her shower. She wouldn't want to start her day.

On those mornings she'd call to him and when he came into the bedroom, she'd say, "You made love to me last night," but he'd only look at her, not moving, not giving a sign. They'd stand like that, Asel in the doorway, so close to the bed he could touch her face, and Phoebe half under the sheet, wishing he would. She'd reach out a hand, grab him by his shirttail and pull him to her.

"You were very good, you know," she'd say, and then he'd finally let himself touch her. They loved each other very much and they still do.

"T H E R E ' S   more cake in the cupboard," she says.

Asel looks at her. It's a birthday cake for someone named Benjamin. It's a box cake with white frosting. It says how old Benjamin is, four. And there is a horse in each corner, and they're all connected by lassos. A month ago she brought home one for a girl named Mary. Phoebe gets them at Jeanne's Pastry Shoppe, where she stops in the morning for coffee on her way to school. They were ones that had been ordered but nobody picked up. Jeanne marks them down so they're a good deal. She's famous for her apple turnovers too.

"What are the papers about?" Asel asks.

Phoebe looks at the wall in front of her. She's tired. She wants to go to bed, but she hates to sleep on the weekends.

She likes to stay up as long as she can, enjoying the hours that will eventually take her into Monday. She admires Asel for living the way he does. Since they moved to New Hampshire, he seldom knows what day of the week it is. He hasn't had a steady job but that's because she wants him home and besides, they have what they need.

"They are sentences the kids wrote on a story called 'Gift of the Magi.' It's a story about a man who sells his watch to buy his wife a hair clip and she sells her hair to buy him a watch chain. They are really two fools, but I still like the story anyways."

"Is it a story I should read?" Asel asks.

"Only if you want to. Like I say, they are fools and the writer feels as if he needs to show how foolish people in love can be."

Asel thinks about what she has said. He tries to make sense out of it, but he can't. He thinks about the story. It seems a shame that people would do those kinds of things. He can tell she's tired by the way she talks and by the way she stares out in front of her. In a while, he'll make her go to bed and then he'll check each sentence for a capital letter and a period and then draw a happy face and write the word *good* with an exclamation mark after it, as he's often seen her do.

"So why do you like the story?" he asks.

"Because once I have finished reading it to them, I unknot my hair and let it fall down. The children can reach out and touch it from where they are sitting. They pass it around the reading circle until each has held it in their hands. It becomes very important to them. They make pledges to not be so foolish when they grow up. Sometimes they cry. It's a good lesson for them to learn. Then I have them practice their sentences. They work hard to write good ones."

Asel decides he will read the story. He has been reading for quite a while now, ever since Phoebe taught him when they started living together. Reading has become one of his favorite ways to pass the time. He keeps stacks of magazines and newspapers throughout the house, so something to read is always handy.

"Go to bed," he tells her. "You can't even keep your eyes open."

"I know. I am tired. I'll go if you come sit beside me until I fall asleep."

Asel takes her hand and they both stand up. She follows him down the hall to the bedroom. He takes her clothes off, letting them fall to the floor, and then she gets in between the cool white sheets. Asel sits down in the rocking chair next to her and folds his hands.

"I got a new kid," she says. "I have to watch him like a hawk. He eats stuff. He eats coins and paper clips. He'll pluck a button off your sweater and eat that too. Mostly metal, though. He goes for metal."

Asel rocks quietly in the chair next to the bed. She takes his hand and puts it on her head. She likes him to hold it there until she falls asleep. She tries to coax him into getting in with her, into sleeping when the rest of the world does, but she can't do it.

"It's better this way," he tells her. "I can't sleep like that. I get flat on my back and I'm no good. I'm worse than a turtle. It takes me longer to right myself. I'm just no good that way."

He feels her head nodding under his hand and he knows she understands. He strokes her head, feeling the part in her hair.

"They have to X-ray him once a week," she says, her words soft and distinct as she begins the swim into sleep. "It could be worse. I read about kids who eat themselves. They start by chewing on their fingers and arms. They can't help it. They constantly have to chew and gnaw at their bodies."

Asel thinks about beavers and rats that have to do the same thing to keep their teeth from growing long, only they do it to wood. He wonders if anyone ever thought of giving the boy a piece of pine.

Asel takes her hand and her sleep seems to come over him too. He can feel himself walking out of a wood, the trees thinning and the small animals stepping aside to let him pass. She says a few more things, but then she's quiet and he's alone with her. Pulling a comforter to his chest, over the walnut grip of the revolver he wears under his left arm, he puts his feet up on the bed and lets his head go back against the chair. He will sleep a little bit and then he will wake up to walk about the house, checking the locks on the windows and doors. He'll draw faces on the kids' papers and write the word *good* with an exclamation mark after it.

But for now he dreams his mother and father come down to pat him on the head. His father chucks him under the chin and his mother runs her dry red fingers across his cheek. The four of them in the room together.

Outside, a fog settles in the valley. It brings out moisture on the floors and walls and woodwork. When morning comes, it will be Sunday and Asel will have breakfast ready when Phoebe wakes up. They'll unlock the door and have coffee on the front porch, where they can watch the last leaves of the season on the hills that rise up across the river, where Asel can look out on the meadow that surrounds the house and see whoever comes down the road long before they see him. While he sits there, eating birthday cake, he'll put off again his decision to leave her, though he knows he must go. He knows he must leave this place to save her from what will come. When he thinks about it, he's reminded of the man and the woman in the story and he doesn't think they're so foolish after all.

2

W I N T E R comes to the meadow in a billow so thick it can choke you off, and leave you dead or crazy if you give in. It runs up the windows and hammers at the hay bales that bank the foundation. It stays there outside the house, willful in the way it rests quietly throughout the day, smooth and even, taking on the lay of the land it covers and then kicking up when the sun is gone. Asel is thankful that Phoebe is home and sleeps in the bed beside his chair. This night, he thinks of his father again and how, when he was a little boy, his father used to set him down on the floor when he got home from work and tickle his feet. He'd then get down on his hands and knees and rub his face in Asel's belly, growling like a bear and pretending to ravage him. He'd open his mouth and squeeze him with his teeth, making him laugh. Averell'd run in from the other room and jump on his father's back. Their sister'd come into the house and yell at them to stop before they broke something, no matter how small, because they didn't have very much.

Later, when Asel was still a boy and Averell was a man, Asel went from the potato fields in Caribou, where he'd been working, down to live with Averell in Jackman. Averell'd become an outfitter, guide and taxidermist. He set up hunting and fishing trips into the backcountry. He needed Asel's help, because his knees were beginning to knot up with arthritis and he'd gotten a bad case of the croup. It was from wading too many spring runoffs with a fly rod in one hand and the other gripping the arm of a sport who could tip over any minute and be lost when his flotation vest didn't do what the Coast Guard rating sticker claimed it would. Waders fill up quickly when they go under, and it becomes a helluva thing to drown for trout. Losing customers that way wasn't much good for business, either.

· · ·

O U T S I D E the snow is beginning to act up again. It plays in the wind, dusting against the house like handfuls of sand shot from a gun. The sash weights clatter and thud inside the casings. The house yawns and creaks with each gust. Asel dreams his father is eating him again and it's something he likes. The children laugh while Averell rides their father's back, holding his collar in one hand, raising the other high in the air and kicking his feet the way broncobusters do.

It goes on like this until Asel's mother picks them up in her arms and holds them against her breast. She makes cooing sounds to each one, even to his father, who lies in the crook of her arm and stares up into her face. Then it becomes day and the children stand on the bank of the Saint John, the sky flaming red behind them as the sun rises from the ocean. They wave to their mother and father, who push off from the land in a canoe and pull with deep strokes into the flow that takes them away. They are beautiful on the water, like something to be kept hidden away because it isn't right that it should be on this earth or any other.

They become smaller and smaller, but they never disappear. They hold the unfolded point between the fog and the river that's still there now, so long ago and so far from the bedroom where Asel dreams in the chair with Phoebe asleep in the bed beside him.

A while after they leave the land, Asel wakes up to the sound of another strong wind. Since he slept, a new snow has come. It shakes the house and at other moments leaves it more quiet than it has ever been. He takes the comforter from his lap and spreads it over the bed to help keep her warm. He steps into his boots and walks about the house, moving his hands to feel the drafts that come through the electrical outlets and from around the windows. The curtains lift and settle as the wind sweeps by.

At times the cold air gains such weight that he can hold it with almost enough purchase to lug it back outside where it belongs. He makes his way to the kitchen, moving slowly through the dark rooms, his hands still in front of him, passing from his knees to his shoulders, up and down through the rising thermals.

And the drafts still come into his body, white plates at fixed altitudes. They slice round his knee or thigh or belt and then suck together behind him for one last go at his back, before finding some warm hole to shimmy down or scatting up the chimney and out the flue.

He makes coffee and puts a log in the stove. He stands at the kitchen door and looks out its window. Tails of rime ice are clipping off in the wind, long feathers nipping back and tumbling away in the darkness. He takes his coffee to the bedroom and sits down beside her. He slides his hand under the covers and finds her hand, holding it and feeling it go strong inside his own as if to answer him.

He thinks hard and again they come back to him. They come to the room where he sits. He can only remember a few things because they died on the Saint John when he was a boy. His mother couldn't swim and his father loved her too much to let her go down alone, so they were found wrapped in each other's arms, a sight so beautiful in death that all who saw them grew quiet and distant.

And he knows he remembers crawling inside his father's baskets and his father finding him there and, with one hand, lifting him out by the back of his shirt or his heel. His mother cooked on a cast-iron stove, its nickel and porcelain gleaming in the hot red light that came from the seams where the stove had been fitted together. Winters, she kept a stew going in a black kettle. Panfish, rabbit and out-of-season venison were added daily, by Averell before he took off on his own. The taste and color changed in ways that were hard to tell, a new stew every night.

It was Asel's job to keep stovewood piled in the box. He

carried it in, a stick at a time, liking the sound of the thud it
made when he dropped it. He remembers having a sister and
how when the news came she passed out on the floor and
that by the time they were split up and farmed out to different
families, her hair had gone as white as a snow goose and was
falling out of her head. He never saw her again after that and
is certain he never will, because even as a boy he knew she
wouldn't make it.

Asel was sent to Caribou to live with a man named Borst,
a submariner fished out of the North Sea in '44, after a depth
charge coughed up his U-boat. Borst and his crew manned
the pumps for three days, living on uncooked food. By the
time they were picked up, his fingers were so turned he was
never able to straighten them again. He finished the war a
prisoner, driving an earthmover in the construction of Loring
Air Force Base, saving his pay and learning English.

After the Third Reich bellied up he became a citizen and
a potato farmer, a grower of Kennebecs and Katahdins. His
wife came over to be a citizen too, and they started a family
and took on wards of the state to work the farm, orphans
and idiots, boys who'd been gelded so they couldn't make
more of their own kind. The only cost to him was their room
and board.

Asel was spared the knife by being sent straight to Borst's
house by way of a neighbor who already had too many mouths
to feed. He went with a basket of clothes and his father's
1910 copy of Francis H. Buzzacott's *The Complete American
& Canadian Sportsman's Encyclopedia of Valuable Instruction,*
which he couldn't read but had to have.

Borst was a niggardly man with a long nose and a shiny
forehead. He kept his wards hard at it throughout the year
working in the fields and potato houses. They cut seed, plowed,
planted and cultivated. Then, in the fall, they picked behind
the digger as potatoes spilled from the ground. When the
crop was in, Borst hired his boys out to other farmers and
kept the money for himself.

Asel hated the man, but there was little he could do. Sass or foolishness earned a swift cupped hand to the side of the head, something the older boys were already paying for with a loss of hearing.

The first time Asel got laid out by Borst's right hand, he was ten and trying to catch a skunk with Reinhold, Borst's older son. Reinhold was six and his brother, Dirk, was three. Both of them were old enough to enjoy whatever mischief Asel and the idiot boys were up to and then squeal to their father when things got out of hand.

Asel and Reinhold cornered a mother and her kits coming out of the cellar. The plan was to sweep down on them with horse blankets and snatch them up, skunks being as prized by boys for pets as they'd always been. When the two made their lunge, Reinhold went down and came up with a faceful of skunk spray, his eyes hot and tearing and the rest of him drenched in stink. The other boys laughed and Asel laughed too, but when Reinhold ran and told his father, the laughing stopped. Asel got knocked down, picked up and knocked down again. Borst cursed him in German and then left him on the ground. Reinhold got dragged by the ear into the house, where he soaked in tomato juice the rest of the day.

Asel tried to even up later by throwing a skunk in the outhouse a few minutes before Borst was known to take his daily shit, but one of the idiot boys went in with the lime bucket and the revenge was played on him, much to his pleasure to be a part of things. Borst laughed from the porch as he watched the boys spend the morning moving the outhouse, filling in the pit and planting an apple tree while the boy who got sprayed ran around flapping his arms. When they were done, Asel got knocked down again, learning the lesson that revenge knows its own time.

That night the idiot boys tried to comfort him. They'd come to look up to him because even at ten he was the hardest worker and always had a kind word for each of them. While they talked one of the boys found Buzzacott's book in Asel's basket. He opened it to the sketches on page six, scenes and incidents in the author's career. Pointing to each one, he read the words under each picture: trapping, Antarctic expedition, Arctic expedition, sealing, infantry, South African Zulu War, cavalry, whaling, camping with Indians, Spanish-American War, duck shooting and fishing. The other boys pulled close, the tallest one holding the lantern over their heads so they could see. The boy who'd read seemed as surprised as the rest of them at the words that came from his mouth.

When Asel thought of Buzzacott, he thought of his own father, a man who surely could have done all those things. And he told them so. He told them that Buzzacott had been his father and he'd written the book before he died.

The boy turned the page and kept reading. It was a picture of the largest civil camp ever erected, accommodating eighty thousand guests. There were immense tents for resting, dining, cooking, sleeping, barbering, smoking, doctoring and shitting. It seems Buzzacott was big on keeping the bowels open and Asel told them it was so.

Each night after that, he and the boys listened to the words from the book. Some nights they made the boy read again the lists of wing flies, hackles and palmers suitable for trout and salmon. They gazed at the photos of Wyoming and the Tetons. The tallest boy liked to say, "I bet ol' Buzzacott wouldn't take no shit from Borst." Asel told him his father certainly wouldn't and it made them feel good.

As time went on, it became Asel's job to tend the team of Belgians, Lion, a sorrel gelding, and Sal, a bay mare, both with flaxen manes, tails and locks. It angered Borst because they stopped working for him and worked only for Asel. When Borst came around they got hot and worried, pawing the ground, but for Asel they stepped right out, laying their ton and a half into their collars and treading smoothly across the ground.

He grew to love the two horses and they responded in kind. The summer's work went more quickly, and the nights he led them down to the stream and stood them in the cooling water became the most peaceful times of the life he'd lived up till then. It was Lion and Sal who saved him from Borst in all ways.

That last fall the price of potatoes jumped sixteen cents. Borst pushed the boys harder than ever. They could take it, but Lion and Sal couldn't. Their hooves began to split and crack. Asel stayed up nights treating them with pine tar— pine oil and lanolin. He checked for punctures in the frog and heel and when he found them, he soaked them in iodine. Finally they both came up with bowed tendon and wouldn't be able to work for a long time, maybe not ever again.

Asel worked late that night, only this time to keep them from being shot or sold. He held ice packs to their legs and then fired them with a hot point to make heat in an attempt to increase the circulation. He worked slowly, not wanting to rush the treatment and not wanting to lose touch with the horses.

Borst's younger boy, Dirk, came into the barn. He spoke German first and then English, telling Asel that his father wanted to see him in the house. Asel crossed the yard from the stable to the porch. The ground was hardening under his feet and there were potatoes still left in the fields, waiting on the threat of frost, a black frost, that would turn them dark and soft.

Borst told Asel he hadn't decided what to do with Lion and Sal, but he did want him to go in the morning to look at a team of Percherons a man down the road was trying to sell. Asel knew of the team. One was weak and the other had a hard mouth. He was relieved that Borst was thinking about buying another team. He knew the Percherons could be had cheap and that they'd last long enough to give Lion and Sal a chance to heal. He walked back to the stable, breathing deeply the chill air, and looking into the harvest moon, full and high. When he got back to the stable, though, he knew in no uncertain way that Lion and Sal wouldn't see the

morning. Dirk was laid out behind them, his head caved in,
a mark left by the studs and calk of a shoe, curved and in-
delible where the bridge of his nose had been.

S O   that's when Averell's knees were breaking down and
he had a case of the croup so bad he thought he had a can-
cer and gave up his smokes. He called on his brother to
take over the guide work, while he continued to outfit and
do his taxidermy, which was already backlogged two years.
Borst threatened to report Asel as a runaway if he left, but
he went anyways, hitching a ride out of town a week after
Lion and Sal were dragged into a back lot and bulldozed
under.

Working for Averell was a good deal while it lasted and
it lasted a long time. Asel stayed in the woods year-round,
ranging from Jackman to Millinocket and as far north as Quebec, though how often he left the country, he never knew,
there being no black line of bars and dots on the forest floor,
only the height of land, where the mountains stretch out in
long high rolls and rivers begin to run north to the Fleuve
Saint Laurent.

The property of the Great Northern Paper Company was
his purview, land that can be measured in hundred-thousand-
acre units, land where it's easy to die if you don't have any
business being there.

Asel never knew it, but Averell told the hunters and fish-
ermen that he was simpleminded in the ways of life, that he
was an orphan and they weren't to provoke him by talking
of the outside world. Averell told them he was saving him
from the draft and that if they agitated him by trying to cut
through his ignorance, he'd track them down and kill them.
After he'd said it, he'd smile and nod his head as if he liked
the idea of tracking someone down and doing him in. He'd
nod his head in a cockeyed sort of way as if he might have
been just foolish enough to keep his word.

Those stipulations made an outing with the boy all the more appealing, especially since Averell kept his brother somewhat ignorant of the fish and game laws in terms of bag limit and the way one hunting season might be allowed to drift into another.

In turn he told Asel that the sports weren't to be trusted, that when he felt he had met up with one who could be, that was the time to worry the most. Averell told him they were babies who'd wander off and get lost and hurt, maybe shoot themselves, or worse yet, shoot him. They were babes in the woods and if ever one of them babies so much as got hurt, let alone died, it'd mean the electric chair for Asel, words that have a way of impressing a young boy's mind.

So Asel took this to heart. He determined he would give up sleep so he could watch them. He'd stay awake, tending the fire and drinking coffee. If they were awake, he'd talk to them and if they were asleep, he'd talk to himself. He'd talk into the night to hold off the possibility of death, his own and theirs, keeping tight the circle of life. When they were gone, he'd sleep for days at a time, dreaming of Lion and Sal and his mother and father.

For the sports, the experience was worth coming back time and again. They considered Asel to be the last of a breed, a woodsman nonpareil who quoted often from Buzzacott on the don'ts and ifs of camping, hunting and fishing. He told them how to cure their diarrhea and constipation. He could recite from memory such piscatorial selections as "The Old Bass Ground," "The Salmon Leap," "When the Bull-Heads Bite" and everyone's favorite, "That Trout."

Spending a week in the woods with him gave them heart enough to go back into the world, to break unions, shut out competition and make the rent. They paid Averell handsomely and lauded Asel with gear from Abercrombie & Fitch, Orvis and L. L. Bean. But the more guns, compasses, fly rods, knives and Hudson Bay blankets he received, the more he distrusted them in the woods. Finally, he just stopped opening the bundles and packages they brought and stacked them against the cabin wall.

Things finally went bust. The hunters stopped coming and Averell missed the fall rendezvous just before deer season. Asel waited around as long as he could until finally he was running low on provisions. He secured the cabin, stashing what he valued, which wasn't much, under the floor and inside tree trunks. He packed a basket, strapped on his .44 and made the three-day hike out to Route 201.

There he hitched a ride into Jackman on a pulp truck with a man named MacDougall. He found his brother's place, but it was boarded up. He asked at a house down the road and they told him it'd gone up for back taxes and Averell had up and moved out in the middle of the night. So Asel turned around and went back to the woods, where he stayed alone for three years.

"Y O U slept," she says. "I was awake while you did. Come into bed with me for a while. You don't have to sleep. You don't have to stay either. Come for a while, though."

The room is still dark, but the dawn is close. The snow still carries on outside the house, whirling and howling across the meadow.

"I have to finish my coffee."

"Then you will come," she says. "When you finish your coffee."

Asel sets his cup on the floor, kicks off his boots and slides in next to her. She reaches a hand inside his shirt and holds it to his chest.

"Your heart is pounding. It feels like it's coming right through your chest."

"Something always happens inside me at this time of night."

She unbuttons his shirt and strokes him where his heart is, her fingers tracing the sling of his holster. She brings her hand to his face and lets it trail along his beard.

"It's a storm," he tells her. "A bad one. You might not have school in the morning."

"I'll stay here with you. I'll cook you breakfast and make you fat. What would you like?"

"Eggs, bacon and apple pie."

"Then that's what we'll have," she says softly, drawing herself into his body. "Stay with me till morning. Stay here beside me."

"You know, sometimes I try to figure it all out and I can't."

"It's like that," she says. "Sometimes you want to run a needle and thread through, then pull it all together like smocking, but it doesn't work that way. I think it's more like an onion. Skin upon skin. Layer upon layer."

"Onions are sweet when you boil them."

"Yes, they are," she says, pulling his shirt open until she can get her face high on his ribs.

"Once you get down inside them, though, there's nothing. Maybe a tight fold or two."

"That's something," she says. "That's all you need," and then she's quiet.

Asel lies there with her until she falls asleep again and then he gets up. He sits in the rocker, puts his feet on the bed and his head back, trying to sleep the same way he did before, trying to bring his mother and father back to him, but he can't. He doesn't worry, though, for he knows they'll come to him again on some other night. If they don't, he's content because he knows that someday he'll go to them.

3.

B Y the time Asel got back to the cabin, his clothes were frozen solid. He'd been back in the woods for only three months since Averell'd disappeared and already he'd gone and almost gotten himself killed trying to cross a pond on green ice. He had to smash a channel in water up to his chest until he got to the bank.

His clothes bent at the knees and elbows and a little bit at the waist, but no place else. He got himself near the woodstove and laid his body into it, sending a hiss and a billow of steam rising into the air. He reached down, laying the palms of his wool mittens on the hot black iron, sending up more steam and the stink of wet wool. It was two hours ago and still daylight when he went through the ice. He never once thought about dying, just getting himself home and hugging the stove. Only now did he realize the possibility of death and cursed his stupidity for not simply skirting the pond to get to the other side, where he wanted to be.

When he was able to move again, he shucked his clothes and hung them to dry. He dressed and built up the heat in the stove. This night he'd allow himself some of the precious kerosene to have a lantern, to clean his guns in the soft golden light and reconsider his decision to spend the rest of his life in the woods, a decision, as he now saw it, that could have abrupt and painful consequences.

He went to the table and spread a cloth over the top. He broke down the .44, first drying, then oiling its parts. The smell of gun oil from the spout can rose in his head, clearing his mind and at the same time making him more angry with himself. After reassembling the piece, he loaded it and set it off to the side. Then he started on his rifle.

For a while he wondered about Averell, where he'd gone and why he hadn't left word. He knew he'd been left behind before, and he hated the feel of it and didn't want to live it out again. He cursed his foolishness and then he cursed his brother for skipping out on him the way he did. He thought about how nice it'd be to find Borst and do to him what he'd done to Lion and Sal, but he knew he wouldn't. He didn't think it was in him to determine the length and breadth of another's life. He wanted nothing to do with such things and was saddened at the emptiness left by his vengefulness.

From the far corner of the cabin came a scratching noise. Mice were at his larder, making their way into the small store of food he'd brought back in with him, food Asel couldn't find in the woods or waters where he now lived. He slid his hand across the table, wrapping it around the walnut grips of the revolver.

The first mouse disappeared before the sound cannoned off the walls. The second and third went too as the noises rolled together, drumming inside his head. Then another noise came inside the other, one he didn't recognize, somebody pounding on his door, and then it stopped. Asel yelled out for whoever it was to come in but he didn't move from where he sat. He only turned down the lantern and pushed it away so he was out of its light.

"I said, come in," he yelled again.

The door swung open, but there wasn't anyone there. He waited, not moving from where he sat, but palming his revolver in one hand and a speed loader with six shells in the other, confident he wouldn't need them but ready anyways.

"I'm coming in. For Christ's sake don't shoot."

An old man stepped into the doorway, his hands out in front of him and his palms up. He grinned at Asel and his gums were pink and shiny. Not a single tooth was left in the old man's head. Asel smiled back, almost laughing. The old man let his hands fall, but kept grinning, all the while concentrating his milky blue eyes on Asel's right hand.

"I didn't come at a bad time, did I?" he said. "I mean, you

haven't decided to go crazy just this very minute, have you? I wouldn't want to imposition you if you have."

"No. Come in. If I was, I'm not now."

"Good. Good. I wandered a little far tonight and needed a place to stay."

Asel stood up, knocking the table with his legs. He pulled another chair across from his own and pointed to it. The old man moved over the threshold and closed the door. Instead of sitting down, though, he went straight to the stove and stood with his back to it, rolling gently on his heels, to and fro, as if drunk on the heat.

"Can I get you some food?" Asel asked.

"No, I wouldn't think of it. Just a little warmth."

The old man held his hands clasped behind him. He let his head go back and closed his eyes.

"Let *me* share my supper with *you*. Your cupboard looks a little bare and I've found indoor hunting not that awfully good."

Asel smiled when he saw the pink gums again. The old man's mouth was the mouth a baby would have.

"Oh, the hunting is pretty good. It's just that there isn't much left for the pot," Asel said, setting the revolver back in its holster and strapping it on.

"No, Asel, I don't suppose there is."

"You know my name."

"Yes, I do. I had dealings with your brother before he got run out of town."

"You know my brother."

"Yes, I do. He was into a man named Weinberg for quite a sum of money. Ol' Weinberg's a Jew in more ways than one. He was coming after his money with the sheriff, so your brother up and left in the middle of the night."

Asel sat down at the table. A little bit of him felt good to know the details of Averell's leaving, but not enough to discount the pain he felt over his brother's and his own misfortune. The old man went outside and then returned with a pack and a Winchester. From the pack he took out bread, cucumbers, tomatoes, salami and foil packs of mayonnaise and mustard. He made up sandwiches for both of them, commenting on how handy the foil packs were. Asel ate slowly, enjoying his sandwich. He hadn't had vegetables in a long time, though in season he'd gotten his share of dandelions, fiddleheads and fern fronds. When the old man finished his second sandwich, he went back into his pack and came up with apples, candy bars and a set of dentures wrapped in a plastic bag. He slipped them in his mouth and then cut wedges of apple and ate them.

"Did he leave the state?" Asel asked.

"Oh he might've done that, or he might be just moved down the highway. He didn't get out with much. I imagine he's had to take a job to live."

Asel picked up an apple and bit into it. He tried to remember the last time he'd eaten one, but couldn't.

"It seems hard to figure you'd wander in," Asel said.

"Yes, I guess it does. Well, the truth is, I didn't. I came by snowmobile. I left it down the trail. I didn't know your opinion of them. Some people aren't too fond of them. Your nature buffs and all. You aren't a nature buff, are you?"

"What brought you, anyways?"

"Business. I deal in fur and I've come to make you a little proposition."

"I'm listening."

"All right, then. I'll get right to the point. I'll start you up and you sell to me. It's that simple. You never have to come out unless, of course, you want. But I'll come by with what you need, give you what money's left in cash and take out your furs. You've got good territory here. It hasn't been trapped since you've been here. You'll do well. Better than the other boys I got spread about the state."

"I don't know," Asel said. "I'll have to think on it."

It intrigued him to think there might be others like him

in the world. The old man reached out his hand and smiled, opening his mouth wide and clicking his teeth.

"You've got to trust somebody, if only a little bit and for only a little while," he whispered, taking Asel's hand and holding it tightly, with a grip more powerful than it seemed he could have in him.

Asel shook his head and smiled too, making his hand go strong inside the old man's.

"I knew you'd see it my way," the old man said.

For the rest of the evening he talked to Asel about what'd been happening in the world. He told him that LBJ had gotten his tit caught in the wringer and that a man had walked on the moon, which convinced Asel that he was a liar, but he still liked him. Later that night, before falling asleep, the old man got back to the topic of trapping.

"You do know trapping, don't you?" he said.

"I've never done it on a big scale," Asel told him, "but I have studied up on what Buzzacott had to say about it."

"Buzzacott? I knew him as a kid. If you ask me, the old fart never even stepped in the woods," he said, and then he fell asleep.

Asel stayed awake that night and watched the old man sleep. In the morning they hiked down to get the snowmobile. When they got back, the old man fried eggs and bacon for them. He'd brought along provisions for a month, a range of traps and vials of bait scent. For the next three days he educated Asel as to the secrets of taking furbearers, while helping him to set a trapline he could cover in two days' time.

The dawn of the fourth day he prepared to leave, telling Asel he'd be back in a month with supplies and to pick up furs.

"Leave them hang from the eave and I'll do the same with your stuff in case you're not here. Some people prefer it that way. Whether they're in camp or not, they don't like to be bothered."

"We'll see what happens."

"Yes we will. And by the way, that habit you have of not sleeping. It's a good one. You should keep it."

Asel missed the first three rendezvous, as he was working his trapline. He had a good number of sliding ring-and-chains he used at the foot of otter slides and where the banks were undercut by water. He worked them deep in the swamps and bogs that fed the waterways on their run to the river. He worked dens, paths and runways with #1 through #4 New-house Standard wire traps, taking prime mink, fox, otter, coon and beaver.

When the fourth rendezvous rolled around, he was there to hear the old man's snowmobile, its engine whining up the trail.

"Long time no see," the old man said. "Smells like you've been into a little skunk lately. Unless, of course, you've got a woman stashed somewhere."

"No woman. It was a skunk."

"The goddamn things. If only the prime furs could be so stupid. Hey listen, I've got some news for you. We have a new broker. His name is Beecher. He's taken your brother's place. He's a good man. Quite curious about you."

"Nothing to be curious about."

"No, you don't understand. He thinks he owes you a little something for the way things seemed to shake out with your brother and all. He thinks you got shafted. Abandoned. Left holding the bag."

"It's no concern of his," Asel said. "I think I liked it better when I didn't get any news."

"Fair enough," the old man said. "I'll be on my way. I just wanted to tell you that my stake in you is paid up and you've been earning money. Good money too. What do you want done with it?"

"Give it to that man, Beecher. Tell him to hold my money for me."

The old man looked up. He could see something in Asel's eyes. Something he'd seen in the old-timers who lived in the

woods. It comes into a man who knows how to hold a living
thing under his boot and club it to death, a man with old
wounds that only aggravate from loneliness. Eyes that get like
curtains that let through light and nothing else and, after a
time, not even light. Seeing Asel that way made it all right
with him if they didn't cross paths too often, though it pained
him.

"That Beecher's a fair one," the old man said, not being
able to think of anything else.

T H R E E   years in the woods can do things to a man
and worse things to a growing man. Buzzacott had plenty to
say about rut and scent, but always in terms of how it can
get killing done. He never talked about what's to be done
when a man gets into his season.

It came on Asel the morning he couldn't push the door
open to check his trapline. The snow was too deep. Not going
was a decision that bothered him. He knew he could have
unfastened the hinges and taken the door down, or easier
yet, he could have gone out the window. He told himself he
should load shells and that it would make him feel better.

He took his tool kit from where it hung in the rafters and
set up shop on the table. Heat radiated from the woodstove,
making the room warm and dry, a haven in the lap of cold
and snow. Asel sat down, hooking his feet under him in the
rungs of the chair. He counted out two hundred cartridges,
a hundred each for his rifle and .44-caliber. He then decapped
the pins and resized, changing dies when he came to the .44s.
Loading shells was work he enjoyed, so he took his time,
more time than was needed. He reprimed the cartridges,
being sure to seat the primers at the bottom pocket of the
shell and polishing each one as he went.

When he finished the priming and polishing he got up and
went to the window. It was a dark day, heavy and gray with
clouds that rolled out, one into another. There would be no

sun to filter through the tall pines into his site, no light or warmth to ease the winter. He didn't mind because the loading of shells calmed him. He'd let the work stretch out, maybe stop for a while and fix himself something to eat, something with macaroni and tomato sauce.

Asel went to the corner of the cabin furthest from the woodstove and opened the box that held the cans of Hercules 2400 smokeless powder. He took the last one back to the table and started in again. This time he had to set the charge, seat the bullet and crimp the mouths, contracting them .02 inches smaller than the diameter of the bullet. By the time he finished the .44s, he'd run out of powder. He went back to the corner and found only a few grains in the bottom of the box. He'd have to make sure the old man brought him some on his next trip. He looked to the gear piled against the wall. He'd see what the sports had left him from back when they still came, when Averell still ran the business. Maybe one of them had brought in a can of powder, something useful for a change.

Taking down packages and slitting them open, he found more gear than any one man could ever use. There were fly-tying kits with packages of chenille, flank feathers, bronze turkey quills and strung marabou. There were bucktails, kip tails and zonker strips and seven kinds of fur. And everything came in fourteen colors. He found fillet knives, binoculars, sharpening stones and decoys. There were rods and reels and all manner of camouflage outfits, archery equipment, gloves, waders, polarized sunglasses and a pocket multitool that could be eleven different things, but there was no Hercules 2400.

Asel started on another pile. This time he hit a stack of magazines. He couldn't read them but he figured he could at least look at the pictures, so he cut the twine that held the first bundle. The top of the pile was picture magazines, *Look* and *Life,* the edges chewed away by mice. Further down he came to *Sports Afield* and *Popular Mechanics.* Under those came new delights, magazines rife with pictures of naked ladies.

The pages were full of women sprawled and frolicky. They lay on beds and across bearskin rugs, black bear, polar and grizzly. Some were in the desert and some were in the snow. There were black women, and white women, fat ones and skinny ones, old ones and young ones. There was one he took to be pregnant and even one without a leg. Asel tore her pictures out and immediately threw them in the fire. He didn't think that a woman without a leg should be in such a magazine. He determined that it couldn't have been her idea.

Asel went to the other bundles and cut them open too. His private stack grew every time he put the hide slitter to the twine that bound them. Some of the bundles had been eaten through by the mice and nests were built in the cores. And the surrounding pages were stuck together, pasted as they were by mouse droppings. He held them over a kettle of steaming water, slowly peeling back the pages of half-eaten women. After a quick look, he threw these in the stove too until it roared and the pipe glowed cherry red. Before he knew it, it began sucking air, causing its sides to heave and pop. He opened the door and watered down the inside just before the firebox was ready to cave in on itself.

Asel went back to the bundles. There were six wooden crates, the property of the Charboneau brothers, Roddy and Blaze. They last came north before Averell blew town and when they left said they wouldn't be back for a few years and to keep an eye on their stuff. It was business as usual to Averell and Asel. One time they had a married man from New York bring his lover along. He paid dearly so Averell wouldn't take any other parties while they were there. Asel spent that week sleeping under the stars when he found out the man's lover was another man. They were a nice couple, though, avid hunters.

Asel spread open the multitool and snapped the first Charboneau crate's steel bands with the wire cutter. He then pulled the staples and took off the lid. Inside were forty .38PPK Walthers, the serial numbers drilled out. The other crates held the same, except for the last one, which was chock full of ammunition and spare clips.

He was uneasy about them being in the cabin, but there was little he could do. He decided to think about them later and until then be content that he'd found the extra ammunition. Hefting one of the guns, he worked the mechanisms until satisfied. With the palm of his hand, he sent home a loaded clip and then emptied it, firing a tight pattern into the logs on the opposite wall, breathing deeply the smell of powder and flash and feeling the shots echo inside his head. He put the lids back on the crates, keeping out the one gun for himself as a spare and a hundred rounds of ammunition. That done, he went back to his ladies.

By the end of the week, Asel was exhausted. He feared that he was in danger of starving if he continued the way he was going for the rest of the month. He was afraid someone would pass through in spring and knock at the cabin door. When they heard no sound, they'd break in and find only the hardest parts of his body still alive, still moving across the floor.

It became evident to him that carrying on with so many women at once could kill him. It was sapping his strength. Some of these women he didn't even like. He began to feel his spirit diminish. The only solution was to give them up and return to the life he'd been living. Otherwise, it'd be the end. The old man would find him reduced to an idiot and he'd have to be turned over to the state of Maine and they'd take out the small piece of his brain that made him bull and give him back to Borst.

He set up a schedule by which he could wean himself from all the women he shared his cabin with. He began by cutting himself back to four times a day and reducing that number by one every week. When he got down to twice a day, he worked toward doing away with the magazines, thereby re-

ducing the temptation to commit such whorish behavior. The
first to go were any that had even so much as been fouled
by the mice. These he stacked by the stove to be fed in with
some sense of measure, knowing better than to risk another
chimney fire. The next bunch to be weeded out were all those
not in glossy color, the black-and-white ones on cheap paper.
This helped him reduce his pile by two-thirds. The last third
went according to lack of beauty and modesty, ladies he'd
never consider marrying.

By the time he was down to once a day, he only had three
of them left and, strangely enough, had regained his strength.

He began to hunt again and tend the traps, each day going
out early, snowshoeing through the deep snow along the
frozen streams and down to the marsh, taking muskrat, mink,
fox and otter. In the afternoon he skinned, scraped, cleaned,
dried and salted what he'd caught, bundling his hides for the
old man at the end of the month. He was going to make it.

One night he sat by the stove on the stack of discards,
cleaning fat from his knives and sharpening them. The magazines he sat on were ones he hadn't opened since he put
them in the pile to feed the stove and the one for that night
sat on the table in front of him.

He drew the last blade back and forth across the hard
Arkansas stone to take the wire edge off. Honing oil covered
his hands. It was good, he thought, that he was down to only
a few, because he was starting to run short on oil. He craned
to look at the cover and tried to remember who waited for
him inside the pages of tonight's.

He shaved a patch of hair from his forearm, testing to see
if the blade was sharp enough, then went to the water bucket
and ladled four cups into the coffee pot. He washed his hands
and face. He ran his fingers through his hair and tucked in
his shirt.

He allowed a tablespoon of coffee for each cup of water
and then one for the pot. He put it on the stove and waited
for it to boil. When it was done, he removed it from the heat

and settled it with an icicle he broke off the outside eave. Pouring himself a mug, he sat back with one of his last magazines. It was one with a page in the middle that folded out to a third again its size. Starting on the first page and turning one at a time, he got near the middle and then started from the back, saving the foldout for last.

As he went, he touched his fingers to his mouth to wet them, so it'd be easier to turn the pages. He took pleasure in the many beautiful women, looking as if they were from exotic lands, surrounded by expensive goods. He wondered if Buzzacott had known such women in his life of adventure.

Asel closed the magazine and poured another cup of coffee. He then sat down and took up his magazine again, this time going directly to the center. She was at a desk when he saw her, feet up and her dress unbuttoned. Her eyes held him in such a way that he folded the page to hide her nakedness. She smiled at him and he believed that her mouth was moving. He couldn't bring himself to fold her out again. He let the magazine fall shut and drop against his chest. It was then he decided that when spring came, he'd cache what gear he couldn't pack out and leave the woods. He'd find someone for himself.

I N March when the old man came for his furs, Asel told him they'd be the last pickup. The old man told him that'd be fine with him because he knew he was dying and wanted to spend the rest of his days in Mexico.

Asel studied the old man. He looked at his feet, up his body and back to his face. His gums were still pink and he still smiled.

"What do you mean you're dying?" Asel said.

"Dying. At the point of death. Ceasing to live. Finis. Kaput."

Asel knew what *kaput* meant. He'd heard Borst say it when he put down Lion and Sal.

"I don't get it," Asel said.

"Ain't nothing to get. It's adios amigo."

"Can I fix you something to eat?"

"That would be fine, son. I'd like that."

Asel and the old man went into the cabin. They ate flapjacks, eggs, bacon and potatoes. When the old man had his fill he pushed back his chair and looked about the room, then back at Asel.

"It's stuff that was left by others," Asel said.

The old man nodded and then picked up Asel's last magazine. He folded the center out and then quickly closed it back down so that only the lady's face was visible.

"She's beautiful," he said. "I guess I don't blame you for leaving."

Asel looked into his coffee cup. He'd never spent time with someone who was leaving him. They'd always just up and left without letting him know.

"Old man," he said, "I bet they've got women that pretty in Mexico."

"I doubt it. To me, she looks like one of a kind," the old man said, looking up at Asel, the blue in his eyes so faint it was almost gone.

And then he said, "Much like yourself, son. Much like yourself."

I T   took Asel a week to pack the extra gear into a cave a mile from the cabin. When he was done he sealed the entrance with boulders and for the second time in his life he made the three-day hike out to Route 201, and caught a ride in a van with two boys whose hair and beards were as long as his. They asked him where he was going and he told them Jackman. They said that's cool, but they were on their way to Canada and if he wanted to come, he was welcome. He thought that to be a nice thing for them to offer, but he told them Jackman would be just fine and that was all that was said the rest of the ride.

Asel got out in front of Averell's old place. It was newly painted and the taxidermist shop had been expanded. A man sat on the front porch. He was huge in the belly. It covered his belt and almost made it out to his knees it was so big. Asel stood on the ground looking up at him.

"You're Beecher," he said.

"That's right. And you're Asel. The old man told me you'd be coming."

"How is he?"

"He's dead. He got as far as Chicago. They're mailing him back. It's nice that you'll make the funeral."

"Have you heard from my brother?"

"No. I haven't. Can I get you something to eat or drink?"

"No. I'd like to wash up, though, and get some sleep."

"We have a room for you. It has no windows and we installed a dead bolt on the inside of the door. The old man said you'd want it that way."

A woman and two children came out onto the porch from the house. Asel looked at her and he was reminded of his mother even though the woman didn't look anything like her.

"You are a bit of a rich man, Asel," Beecher said. "You have your fur money and the old man left you all of his money. I have it in a separate account in my wife Ellie's name."

Asel shook his head. He didn't want to hear what Beecher was telling him.

"You hang on to it for me," he said, and then he turned his back to them and sat down on the porch, the butts of his rifle and shotgun clunking on the boards.

Beecher kept talking. He told the old man's story. He said the old man had been a friend of Averell's and that's how he knew about Asel being up in the woods. His sons enlisted, and then died in Tet, so he gave up his name because he was ashamed he'd let them go.

"I see," Asel said, nodding his head, but not understanding.

"He didn't want you getting mixed up in it so he kept your secret. He figured it was his right to keep you out. Their dying ended his family and you were the only one he had left. He wanted you to get everything he could give. He knew you'd have a rough road ahead of you."

Asel liked the story because he liked the old man, but he wasn't sure what it was all about.

T H E old man's ashes came at the end of the week. Asel and Beecher took them to a knoll and buried them without a marker. It was as the old man wanted. The job done, Beecher put his hands on Asel's shoulders.

"Asel," he said, "I'm taking you down to Skowhegan. My cousin George Gilbus is a contractor there. He knows the situation and will treat you right. You go today because people around here are starting to ask who you are. We're afraid the kids may say something. People are suspicious because we get so many hippies coming through on their way to Canada. Big George is from New York State. He's a bit of a desperado too."

"The old man. He told me they walked on the moon."

"Yes, they did. It was quite something."

"He said they landed on the moon and it screwed up the weather."

"Well, yes, that's one thing we know for sure. The weather has changed. Predicting it will be the wave of the future."

Asel thought about that. For the most part the weather seemed to be pretty much the same from one day to the next. It was a safe bet to say that the weather tomorrow will be like it is today.

When it got dark Beecher and Asel got in the flat black Impala and left for Skowhegan.

4

B I G George Gilbus and his sidekick Cutler were on the lam. As the story goes, they fell asleep one night, drunk, and the kettle of water Cutler kept on the burner to humidify the air cooked out dry. It started to melt, liquefied by the heat that rose up from the 1932 Hotpoint deluxe electric stove the boys had rewired that morning.

The fire that ensued burned down four hundred acres of prime Adirondack State Park. For Big George's wife, it was the last of the last times. For Cutler, it was the end of his stay in paradise. He'd already tangled with the park authorities on a number of occasions. In the past, they'd taken umbrage over such things as the location of his trailer, his septic system, and his ignorance of fish and game laws, most specifically the taking of fish by use of high explosives and army ordnance he'd acquired from a buddy in the National Guard.

Cutler would have snuck out from under this one too if not for the fact that he put in for a pay voucher to cover the hours he and Big George spent helping to combat the flames that engulfed the ranger station and tourist center. Both men were convinced that Rockefeller himself had the troopers hot on their trail, pounding over the New York State Thruway and up and down the Northway, setting out roadblocks, checkpoints and bulletins.

Their first stop was at Big George's house. It was empty except for a note from his wife tacked to the wall with a tenpenny nail. It said, "I read it in the papers. Hasta luego!" She'd even swept the floor and washed the windows.

Big George and Cutler loaded every tool they could into the Dodge Power Wagon and hightailed it for the woods of Maine, where Big George had a cousin, Beecher.

After hiding out in Jackman, they moved on to Skowhegan,

where they started a cash and barter construction company. They moved into an abandoned Esso station and set up housekeeping. There was room for them, their equipment, the pickup and a small woodshop. They kept the windows covered up and the truck inside the first bay.

Cutler built a frame and platform on the high lift. It held his box spring and mattress. He raised it two feet off the concrete and left it there for a bed. He liked it until one night Big George raised him up to the ceiling and yelled, "Fire." Cutler rolled out over the side and dropped through the air to the floor below. Halfway down he righted himself like a cat would, and landed on both feet.

"You son of a whore," he said, doubling his fists and dancing on the balls of his feet, which must have stung like hell. "You son of a whore. I'm going to take you down a peg or two."

Big George sat up in bed and looked at his friend, slowly shaking his head.

"Jesus, Cutler. That was remarkable how you did that. I never saw a man do what you just did. I've seen roofers come out of the sky like that and get all busted up, but not you. You're a regular free-fall artist. I have decided that whatever you do to me will be a small price to pay for what I have just witnessed."

"Now that you mention it, it was really something, wasn't it?" Cutler said, letting his hands fall to his sides.

"I wouldn't shit you, old buddy. Never saw a man do what you just did."

"Good for you, George. I'm happy for you."

The next morning Cutler padlocked the hand valve on the compressor. He then hid the hacksaw blades and the key to the acetylene and oxygen so Big George wouldn't have any way to cut the lock. Later in the day, Big George asked him where they were hid in case he needed them when Cutler wasn't around, but Cutler still wouldn't tell.

Every night as they'd pull up, it was Cutler's habit to jump out of the moving vehicle and run up the overhead door so

Big George could pull in. Big George'd shut down the rig and Cutler'd run down the overhead door, clattering it along its tracks. Then Big George'd step out onto the oil-stained concrete floor, slam shut the door of the Dodge and pull open the door of the Frigidaire, which was always stocked with beer.

Soon word got around as to how the two men had come to be in Maine. Big George's cousin swore on a stack of Bibles that he hadn't told a soul. George knew *he* hadn't told anyone and Cutler swore he hadn't breathed a word of it to a soul either, living *or* dead. He said he was certain and for Cutler to say he was certain was enough for any man to believe him. It didn't matter, though, because people didn't care how they'd come to be in Maine. If the truth were to be known, most people probably admired them for coming into the state under the circumstances they did, being as how they'd left a bit of New York State charred.

As far as women went, both men were beyond the age of need. They neither had the energy nor the ambition to go out and track them after a full day's work. They tended to talk about their mothers and how they should have loved them more when they had the chance. They made plans about jumping in the truck one day and taking the risk of driving west so they could put flowers on the dead women's graves. They'd drive through Quebec to Montreal, maybe catch an Expos game. They'd buy flowers from a girl on a street corner and then descend on New York State by cover of darkness like bandits in the night. Cutler was certain he knew a back way into Churubusco. After so much talk, they finally decided to go.

Friday afternoon they shut down the job. They planned on leaving that night for their trip back home. As they approached the station, there was an unfamiliar car parked by the pumps. Big George drove by two or three times before he recognized it as his cousin Beecher's black Impala.

Cutler jumped out and ran up the door while Big George

rolled in. Asel and Beecher slipped in behind the truck, nearly taking the closing door across the tops of their heads. Big George opened the Frigidaire and handed out beer to everyone.

"I have business with you, George," Beecher said. "I want you to train this man in your craft. I'll pay half his wage. In return, you have to teach him, work him and keep him under wraps."

"Now hold on just a minute. I don't know a damn thing you're saying. You don't even say hello to me. I'll tell you what. You go to the store and buy some grub for the weekend and hole up with us. That will give you time to explain everything. Me and Cutler can't just walk into this thing blind. We got a business to run and we don't take charity cases. Besides, we were getting ready to leave on a little vacation."

"That's right, Beecher. Me and George, we're hung out to dry here a little bit, if you know what I mean. Stay the weekend like your cousin says. We'll stay too."

"I'll stay, but why the hell do I have to buy all the food?" Beecher said, feeling as though there would be no easy way to get around the problem.

"Don't be that way," Big George said. "We have been taking our dinners down the road where we did a little work in exchange for suppers. It's the kind of place where you eat from the same kettle, the same loaf. We can't go waltzing in there with you and your friend here. There would be questions to answer and you know that neither me nor Cutler are too clear-minded. He ain't a damn hippie, is he?"

"Nor a beatnik," Cutler broke in. "I won't live with no beatnik nor a hippie. Neither of them are clean."

"Tell Cutler he isn't a beatnik or a hippie, Beecher. Tell him he isn't."

"Jesus Christ," Beecher said. "His name is Asel and he's in a little trouble that is no cause of his own. He ain't a beatnik and he ain't a hippie. He's a guide, an authentic Maine guide. Now shut your goddamn mouth, you little pipsqueak."

Asel drank the beer Big George'd given him. It was cold in his hand and he liked the way it felt in his throat. He rocked forward on his feet, thinking there might be trouble.

Beecher raised up his shoulder and puffed out his chest, trying to make himself look big. It scared off most people, but not Cutler, because Cutler always took them out at the knees. He didn't care how big they were. To him, Beecher was just some big goddamn cuckoo flower even if he was George's cousin.

Cutler hunched down and began to skirt Beecher. He didn't like Beecher moving in on them the way he did. He wanted to knock him down and gouge his eye. The thought took hold and began to have an importance all its own. Beecher could feel it coming.

Cutler rose up on the balls of his feet, only to feel two arms come around him and clamp his own flush against his sides. Something hard jabbed him under his left shoulder blade and he stayed there, not being able to move.

"Let him go, Ace," Big George said. "We're all friends here. You and me will talk while good cousin Beecher goes for groceries and while good friend Cutler washes his face so he can go too."

Asel let go of Cutler and stepped back. The four men stood looking from one to the other.

"Go wash your face," Big George said, and Cutler went over to the hose. When he came back Big George put an arm around him and pulled him close.

"That's better, isn't it?"

"I don't like getting manhandled," Cutler said, looking at Asel.

"You go. You show Beecher where the grocery store is."

"Come on, Beech."

Beecher and Cutler raised up the overhead door just enough to slip out underneath it. They got in Beecher's Impala and drove off to the grocery store. Beecher would use the pay phone to call home. Cutler and Big George didn't have a phone. They had a bulletin board where people could leave messages if they needed work done.

"So what have you got in there, kid?"

Asel pulled back his coat. He unholstered his revolver and handed it to Big George.

"Nice," Big George said, ".44 Blackhawk. Good gun. Now I'll tell you, if you're smart, you're going to give Cutler a little something to soothe his ruffled feathers. He doesn't like to be manhandled."

Asel looked up at Big George and nodded his head. He knew it was the right thing to do. "Fair enough," he said. "I don't need enemies."

"Cutler would probably prefer a little piece of your ear, but if not that, something out of your kit would be fine. The trick is, you're going to have to make him think that it isn't a present. You're going to have to give him something without giving it to him."

Asel nodded, more as a way of moving the conversation along than out of agreement.

"Now tell me what's going on here," Big George went on. "I don't have to know a lot. Beecher is usually right on the mark when it comes to others. If he wants me to take care of you, that's okay."

Asel told Big George about how he'd been in the woods these past years and how he hiked out and Averell was gone. He told him how Beecher moved in and took care of him the second time around and about Beecher thinking he owed him something but how it wasn't true.

"Beecher's like that. He takes in strays. He always has. It doesn't seem as though Beecher owes you anything, but if he says so, then he must be sure in his head that he does. Beecher's word is good enough for me. Consider yourself part of the crew. Just remember, we stay fairly tight-lipped around here. A lot of people do it by nature, but me and Cutler are more or less forced into it. We don't mind."

Big George gave Asel a tour of the station while they

waited for Beecher and Cutler to return. He showed him the
bays and the grease pit. He took him to the upstairs storage
room and into the office. He showed him the men's room
and finally the one bay they'd sheeted in with plywood that
they used for a combination kitchen and bedroom. Big George
took Asel outside to show him the bulletin board. They had
constructed a roof over it and hung a tiny door with a window
to protect it from the elements.

"People are able to open the door and leave messages,"
Big George said. "It's why we don't need a phone."

Big George was satisfied that Asel would be good to have
around. He considered him to be someone who'd keep his
business tight to his vest. He liked the way Asel moved and
he liked the way Asel's eyes were wide awake while the rest
of him seemed a little tired.

"We got a big job coming up. We'll need an extra hand.
It's the parsonage, the church and the house next door. A
new reverend is coming in. A real spark plug. The people of
the congregation picked up the house to turn over into a
day-care center. They've got a government person who's coming in to run the show."

Asel didn't like to hear that it was a government person.
It reminded him of Borst and the idiot boys. Big George
could tell it made him uneasy and he liked that.

"Don't worry about it. We're told she's from an outfit called
VISTA. College students, mostly. It's something for the ones
who can't be soldiers or hippies. More likely it'll be some
refugee off a commune who won't admit it, but would rather
get back inside daddy's checkbook. Probably sick of raising
bean sprouts by day and sneaking cupcakes by night."

Big George started to laugh. If Cutler had been there he
would have too. They would have carried on into the night
until it hurt to laugh anymore.

The bell in the office rang. Big George looked out to see
Beecher's Impala pulling in by the pumps. He and Asel went
out to help carry stuff in.

"Now Beech," Big George said. "We're all set here. You hit the road. There'll be no need to send money. We'll make out fine."

Beecher started to talk but Big George held up his hand to stop him. He then smiled and lowered his hand to take Beecher's.

"Don't be such a stranger from now on."

Beecher was grateful. He got back in the car and pulled onto the highway. It dawned on him that Big George had sprung him for the weekend. He turned the car around. He figured he'd go down to Old Orchard for a few days and maybe have some fun.

The next morning, Asel's education began. The trip Big George and Cutler had planned to take to their mothers' graves was forgotten. Cutler pulled chairs up to the desk in the office. He put on his baseball cap and rolled up his sleeves. Big George set out the coffee pot and a box of cinnamon doughnuts. Cutler broke open a deck of cards and began riffling them in his hands.

"Now we see what you're made of, Ace. We're going to play a little high-low-jack. Also known as Old Sledge, pitch and all-fours. You might have heard of it. It's a card game for three. Sometimes it can be played in partners but given how there's only three of us we'd have to resort to floating partners which is a concept I don't think you're ready for. Now, the object is to win, of course. To do that you have special scoring points. The highest trump, the lowest trump, the jack, the ace and the ten. Now, these can change during the course of a game and during the course of a hand. There are special hand signals and I *know* you're not ready for them. Highest and lowest scores share the pot. All right, let us begin."

As the morning went on, Asel was obliged to go into his kit and put up his belongings one at a time. Cutler's mouth hung open and Big George's forehead went deep with lines as they watched him come up with knives, compasses, guns,

ammo, loaders, tackle, rods, first-aid supplies, candle lan-
terns, cook sets, binoculars, hatchets, a meat saw and a machete.

By noon, he was cleaned out except for the Ruger and
already into his future earnings. Big George and Cutler held
a conference in the grease pit. They decided that the game
would be chalked up as a learning experience. They told Asel
he could have his gear back, but after that it would be dog-
eat-dog, destructive and ruthless competition without self-
restraint. Asel agreed to this and felt bound to play a few
more hands so they could win things legitimately, maybe a
clutch knife, or the machete. Asel thought that would make
them feel better about the kindnesses they'd directed his way.

Asel began to win. At two o'clock, he and Cutler owned
it all, the business and everything. At four o'clock, things
changed such that he and Big George owned it all and by
seven o'clock that night, he was the sole proprietor. Big George
and Cutler were tapped out. They didn't have any more to
bet. They sat back and looked across the table at Asel, for
some sign.

"It ain't right," Cutler said. "It just ain't right."

"Well, it happened," Big George told him. "You and your
goddamn card games. Sometimes you think you're so smart,
Mr. Cutler. Well, you got your tit caught in the wringer this
time."

Asel remembered the old man saying just such a thing
about someone else. He looked at the men. He said, "That
sure was dog-eat-dog, wasn't it? I won everything. Everything
for keeps."

Asel smiled and then he began to laugh. He lit a match
and began burning markers. The other two men began to
laugh with him. Cutler took out his Zippo and helped burn
up the slips of paper. They jumped up and clapped each other
on the back. They sent cans skittering across the floor, spilling
out stale beer and Cutler's cigarette butts.

"We'll do good together," Big George said. "We'll do a bang-up job. Now Ace, tomorrow around eleven, a few of the local boys get up a game in bay two. There will be the selectmen and the constable, but don't you fret, it's just a way that Cutler and me have of keeping tabs on those boys. They're the town's finest and it's strictly penny-ante stuff."

5

A MONTH later, Cutler fell in love with the Reverend's wife the first time he laid eyes on her. She was a beautiful woman with white hair. She wore shorts that drew up the backs of her legs, the tendons behind her knees, parallel, long and thin, when she bent at the waist to set tomato plants in the black ground.

In her garden, she was planting cucumbers, carrots, lettuce, onions, peppers and dill, along with the tomatoes. She moved her hands slowly, looking at them after each procedure, running her fingers along the palms of one, the back of the other. She held the handle of the hoe as if it were the long, delicate neck of a bird, easing it into the ground and pulling gently, lifting and separating the earth to make perfect seedbeds.

Cutler, Big George and Asel watched from the roof. They had all the Reverend's work, the whole complex, as he liked to call it. The buildings needed shingling and siding. Windows were to be replaced, a garage built and an annex for the Headstart program that would begin in a few months.

Whenever she moved it changed each man in a small way. Big George forgot a little bit more about how much he hurt inside from his wife hitting the trail when he needed her most or at least more so than all the other times. She made Asel think of his mother's hands and the way they'd move the soap over his body when he was a boy. For Asel, this was hard to understand because he didn't know the easy explanations and if he did, he wouldn't trust in them. And for Cutler, it was true love.

"Big George," he whispered. "What kind of a woman studies her hands that way?"

Big George shrugged and told him to watch what he was doing. His courses of roofing were dropping off the chalk line and making a mess of the job.

Cutler went back to work, but at lunchtime he came down off the roof and told her how she should put wooden matches under the pepper sets because they liked the sulfur tips. Then he took up her hoe and began setting the plants for her.

"These will make them hot peppers," he said, taking off his cap and rubbing his forehead with his dirty hand.

The Reverend's wife smiled and nodded her head. She handed more matches to Cutler as he went back to setting the plants in the holes he dug. Big George and Asel sat on the peak of the parsonage roof, leaning back against the chimney, eating their sandwiches. When Cutler finished with the pepper plants he explained to her how the tomatoes, Romas and Beefsteaks, would do better if they'd been settled in a slurry made of water and cow patties that had laid in the field at least a winter. She smiled again and nodded her head. She held out the package of carrots. Cutler shook the tiny seeds into his hand and broadcast them inside a square where the dirt had been cuffed back. He made a joke about the seeds needing to be planted right side up but she didn't laugh, she only smiled and handed him the lettuce seeds, which he planted next.

Big George and Asel watched from the roof. They watched her walk barefoot in the spots left by Cutler treading through the soil in his workshoes. Finally Big George turned to look at Asel.

"The beauty and the beast," he said.

Asel thought for a moment and then without looking back to George he said, "What's that?"

"It's a story. It's a story about an ugly man and a beautiful woman."

Asel didn't say anything else. He could see it was a fair description, though he didn't know how the story went.

By the time the boys were through with lunch, Cutler had finished planting the garden. Asel and Big George came off the roof for nails and the Reverend drove up in his white Brougham.

"I see you have met my wife," he said. "She was concerned about the weather. She just got in a few days ago from Atlanta where she was helping the new mission to transfer in."

"I helped her get a start on her vegetable garden," Cutler said, pumping the Reverend's hand. It was a habit the Reverend had, shaking hands every time he saw someone.

"Good," the Reverend said. "Sowing the fields. It's God's will to work the land."

"I hope God looks kindly on roofers," Big George said, "because it's going to rain. Right, Mr. Cutler?"

"Yes, Big George. God loves roofers. I know in my heart he does."

"God helps roofers what helps themselves," Big George said, clapping Cutler on the back between his shoulder blades. "Up you go, my little friend, closer to heaven."

Cutler went up the ladder with a bundle of shingles, though Asel'd already stockpiled the roof with enough shingles for the final push of the day.

"Reverend," Big George said, "do you have a minute?"

"Just a minute," the Reverend said, "I have to get the missus started on practicing her signs for Sunday's sermon. I'll be right out."

Big George stood in the driveway and waited. Against the sun he could see Cutler and Asel laying shingles toward the ridge. The dull knock of their hammers was not in synch with their hand movements. The sound came slower than the motions of their swinging right arms.

The Reverend came back out. In his hand he held a roll of hundred-dollar bills.

"I believe this is what you wanted," he said, handing them over to Big George.

"Yes, that's right, it's time to make a draw. I'll write you a receipt."

"No need now. We'll take care of it later."

The Reverend shook Big George's hand and turned to go away.

"Reverend. What did you mean about the signs?"

The Reverend looked at Big George. Several times he opened his mouth as if to speak, but didn't. Finally he motioned for Big George to follow him. They went to the back of the house, where the new picture window had been installed overlooking the river. The Reverend stopped inside the shadows and pointed up toward the window. Inside, Big George could see the Reverend's wife moving her hands into shapes and patterns, spreading her fingers and drawing them across her body. She'd then hold her hands up, sometimes cupping them, sometimes putting them together, sometimes using only her fingers.

Big George wanted to tell the Reverend that his wife was quite good at the hula dance, but the look on the Reverend's face made him think it was a serious business.

"Malvine is deaf and mute," the Reverend said, still looking up at her through the window. "In my line of work, it's created problems. She is the burden the Lord has placed upon me. I have made cripples walk, I have cured the cancers of the body and I have chased out the devil from young girls' bodies, but I can't bring words out of that beautiful mouth."

Big George didn't like listening to this. He felt it was something that was none of his business. More than anything he wanted to be back on the roof.

"Reverend," he said, "it can't be all that bad, now can it?"

"You don't understand. If only I could have made her speak. We'd be over the top now, George. I'll tell you, it's created quite a few problems. During the last mission they saw it as a chink in the armor the Lord has given me to wear against evil. It's created problems, especially among the ladies. My healing power became suspect, though I must say that to the men of the parish, a woman who couldn't speak was a miracle unto itself. That's a little joke, George. I find that humor is nutriment, much like the good word."

"Oh, I like humor too, Reverend. I find it tends to make people laugh."

The Reverend turned to Big George. "Oh, yes," he said. "I think I know what you mean."

Big George took a handful of roofing nails from his apron and rattled them around in his hand. He looked back up at the Reverend's wife. Now she'd incorporated her whole body into the movement of her hands. He felt drawn in by them as they threaded the air, weaving words about her face and neck. It was as if she were talking to him and him alone.

"So now we're in Maine, George. We've decided to back off on the healing for a while. Play it down and beef up the 'mysterious ways' aspect. We have a good shot at local TV and maybe a few radio spots. The radio stuff is quite novel. She'll do the text in sign and then I'll read it. You get what I'm driving at? It's a switch on what's normally done."

Big George nodded and walked away, leaving the Reverend in the trees watching his wife. He went back to the ladder, hoisted a bundle of shingles onto his shoulder and climbed to the top of the roof, where he stayed the rest of the day.

That night back at the garage, Big George took Cutler off to the side and told him everything he'd learned from the Reverend. Cutler stood looking at the floor without saying a word. From the kitchen, Asel could see Big George moving his hands in the air as if he were trying to snatch flies on the wing. Cutler's face was pinched and drawn. At different points in the conversation he slowly shook his head back and forth.

When Big George was finished talking, Cutler took the padlock off the hand valve on the compressor. He tied two lines to the handle. The first one straight out and the other he looped back around the pipe. He played them out to his bed on the high lift. He then took his shoes off and crawled inside the covers. He pulled on the first line, opening the valve. The compressor kicked in, raising his bed to the metal rafters on a column of steel. The second line he tied to his wrist. He'd use it when he was ready to come back down.

. . .

A S E L came to love the construction work. His time in
the woods, though only a few months past, seemed like another life to him, a life lived by someone else. He liked the
way Big George kept him tired as much of the time as he
could. Asel had no choice but to sleep and for that he was
grateful. For Big George, it meant keeping the young man
under wraps so's he wouldn't lose him to drugs or bad women.
It meant keeping his word to Beecher, who in turn was keeping his word to a dead man.

Cutler took to listening to the radio every Sunday afternoon when the Reverend translated the sermon from his
wife's sign language. Cutler imagined her standing there beside her husband, her hands floating in the air saying strong
and elegant things, powerful things about the fires of hell and
the sin that dwells in the breast. He lay in his bed ten feet off
the concrete as the beauty in her hands came through in the
Reverend's words. One Sunday he swore he heard his name
included in the benediction, but then he wasn't sure if he'd
willed it into his brain or if he'd dozed off for a moment and
dreamed she'd said "Cutler," with her hands close to her face.

O N the fourth of July, Beecher came down from Jackman
with his wife Ellie and the kids. He hugged Asel for a long
time and then held him at arm's length.

"You've trimmed your beard and cut your hair," he said.
"You look good."

"I feel good," Asel told him.

Beecher clapped him on the back and then turned him
around so Ellie and the kids could get a look. They smiled
at Asel and each one shook his hand. Ellie gave him a kiss
on the cheek and told him he looked like he was filling out.
She told him he looked like a real buck and Asel's face went
red with embarrassment.

Then they all pitched in, taking from the back of Beecher's Impala a hibachi grill, a bag of charcoal, lighter fluid and coolers filled with beer, lemonade, hot dogs, potato salad, beans and a bottle of whiskey. There were bags of rolls, chips and pretzels. Jars of mustard and relish and a plastic tub full of diced onions. Beecher reached into his breast pocket and pulled something out, keeping it hidden in his hand until Cutler smiled and reached out an open palm. Beecher let fall into Cutler's hand a bottle of celery salt.

"I knew you wouldn't forget it, Beech," he said. "It's what makes a hot dog, you know. It really brings out the flavor."

Cutler thanked Beecher again and then went into the station.

Big George threw open the overhead door, got his hands on Cutler's radio and brought it inside. He turned it up so loud that only noise came from the speaker but that was good enough for him. Beecher called Asel over to the car. He pulled out another of Asel's satchels that'd been left at his house in Jackman. It held winter gear, the rest of his reloading tools and a new five-pound can of Hercules Blue Dot 2400.

Asel looked up at him. Beecher shook his head and told him he hadn't heard anything from Averell. Asel thanked him and took the satchel inside to where he kept his belongings.

It was cool in that part of the garage, cool and dark. He sat down on his cot and thought about how alone he felt, yet didn't have a right to. He was safe in the company of his friends. He'd been so tired before and now he was rested and, in a way, living inside a family again. But it wasn't his family. His family was missing or all dead. Maybe he'd go and find out which.

The bell in the office rang. He looked out to see the Reverend's Brougham pulling in next to where the pumps had been. The Reverend and Malvine got out. Then Malvine stuck her head back in and pulled the seat forward. Someone handed her a cake box and then got out too. It was a young

woman with a long braid that fell below her knees. Asel drew
air into his lungs and held it there for a long time. The
Reverend kept a hand on her shoulder while he introduced
her to everyone who was standing there. Asel heard him say
her name was Phoebe and she was the VISTA worker.

"Women. Can't live with them. Can't live without them.
Ain't it the truth." It was Cutler's voice coming from near
the ceiling where he lay stretched out in his bed high over
the floor.

"I wouldn't know," Asel said, craning his neck to see out
the window.

"I thought I was over them, but I'll tell you straight out.
You probably haven't noticed, but I've got a real thing for
Malvine. She's gotten inside me and I can't do anything about
it. I'm telling you straight, Ace. I'm in a bad way." Cutler's
voice got louder the closer to the floor he came, as the column
of steel disappeared into the floor.

"No, I hadn't noticed," Asel said.

The kids came into the bay. They told Cutler that Big
George said to give them a ride on the high lift. Cutler told
them to get lost. They said Big George warned them he'd
say that but not to take no for an answer. Cutler told them
all right he'd do it, but there'd be no farting around. Being
able to bitch at Beecher's kids seemed to cheer him up. They
climbed aboard and he ran the valve, sending them to the
ceiling and back down again, over and over, yelling, "God
damn it, don't be hanging over the side or you'll fall on the
floor and crack your head open," and then he'd mutter, "Probably crack the concrete too."

Asel watched for a while and then went outside. The women
were grilling hot dogs and setting the table. He watched
Phoebe until she turned and smiled at him and then he ducked
around to the back of the garage, where the other men were
building a cannon out of a steel drainpipe. The Reverend sat
on a truck tire watching Big George and Beecher work. They

had a six-pack with them and the bottle of whiskey. Asel went to where they were and sat down. He positioned himself so he could watch them and still see the women.

"We belong to a syndicate of holy men," the Reverend was saying, looking around the corner of the garage and then taking a nip from the bottle. "We have forty-seven parishes across the nation. There is one of us currently doing the Lord's work in each. Dues are steep. They run five thousand dollars a year. We are a pentecostal, evangelical nonsectarian denomination. There's one guy in Arkansas who's a real comer. He gives out green stamps that can be redeemed for valuable religious items. As you can imagine, crosses are a real biggie. He has one model that holds two penlight batteries and when you clutch it to your breast they light up our savior's eyes. We believe in just about everything. Our thinking is that's the safest way to go. One thing we don't countenance, though, is handling vipers and strychnine cocktails."

The Reverend took a longer drink this time, holding the bottle up, letting gravity help. He then hiked his trousers and sat down on a stack of bald tires. He flicked at his pants legs with the backs of his fingers and started talking again, the sound of his words thick in his mouth.

"The syndicate makes it nice. They have a legal service, major medical, life insurance and a retirement package. The life insurance is what gets the boys on retreat rolling in the aisles. Whenever it comes to the floor for discussion the whole place busts up. You know what I mean? Talking about life insurance being in the business we're in when we work for the greatest actuarial of them all.

"Right now, we're looking to put our money into unborn thoroughbreds. There's quite a few tax advantages to that. The boys at headquarters, though, tell us that computers and frozen cow embryos are the wave of the future. What line of work is it that you're in, Mr. Beecher?"

"Furs, Reverend. I'm in furs."

"Oh really. My wife Malvine loves fur."

"That's nice, Reverend. Watch it there, you don't get those white pants all black from that tire."

The Reverend jumped up and tried to look at his rear end. He turned, making three tight circles, clutching at the back of his pants. Big George and Beecher started to laugh. The Reverend stopped and looked at them and then he laughed too.

"You looked like a dog about to bed down," Beecher said.

Asel could see Malvine looking at them and moving her hands. Ellie turned toward him too. She looked at Malvine's hands and then yelled out at the top of her lungs that dinner was ready and everyone headed for the picnic table.

W H E N   night came Big George rolled the bottom half of a fifty-gallon drum out in front of the first bay. He stacked kindling inside and lit a fire. Its light and warmth drew everybody close. Cutler sat in a wheel rim with his back against the block wall of the station, a kid on each leg. Phoebe had Asel help her bring out a sofa from the living quarters for the Reverend, Malvine and Ellie. Then she got a milk crate for herself and Asel tipped a wheelbarrow back onto its handles and reclined in the box. Beecher and Big George stood next to each other, towering high above the rest of them. At times they tipped a little, bumping into each other, and had to right themselves or topple over.

"This surely takes me back," the Reverend said. "It reminds me of the tent days, going from town to town. We packed them in boy, we sure did. The old folks came from miles around. They'd camp right out in the night. We'd roll up the flaps and they'd be a hundred deep, as far as you could see, hot and steamy. Sometimes it'd rain. Believe me, it doesn't take much to bog down a wheelchair.

"That's where I met this old gal," he said, squeezing Malvine's knee.

Phoebe rapped her knuckles against the side of the crate to get everyone's attention. She began to move her hands through the air, making quick, sure signs. Malvine smiled and then she said something back, all the while nodding her head with the pleasure of a good idea showing on her face.

"We have decided to teach you a song," Phoebe said. "It's 'Michael, Row Your Boat Ashore.' "

"I know that one," Cutler said.

"But you don't know how to sing it the way we are going to teach you."

"Phoebe, I don't know if this is appropriate," the Reverend said.

"Sure it is," Cutler told him. "We're game. Me and the kids will learn it. You go right ahead."

"Mr. Cutler, please don't interfere."

"Lighten up, Reverend. You only go around once in this life."

"I hope you're wrong," the Reverend replied.

"I heard that, Reverend. Don't be so down in the mouth. You got a good job and a beautiful woman."

"I'm glad you see it that way, Mr. Cutler."

Big George gestured for Asel to get the whiskey bottle and pass it around. Everyone drank from it, except for the kids, the Reverend and Malvine. Big George took a long draw and let out a whoop and Beecher pretended his drink was mouthwash, swirling it from cheek to cheek and gargling before he swallowed.

"You go ahead, Miss Phoebe," Big George said. "Now that me and Beech have conquered gravity, we'll give it a whirl."

Malvine looked at Phoebe for the go-ahead. Phoebe nodded and as Malvine got up and moved to the fire, she told the rest of them that Malvine had trouble reading their lips in the dark and often felt a little left out. She asked the Reverend to confirm this and he did with a single solemn nod of his head.

Phoebe started singing and the kids joined in. Malvine's hands could be seen in the light from the barrel, her diamond ring sparkling with the colors of flame. Big George and Beecher looked on, over her shoulders, one working his right hand, the other his left, while they held their beers in their free hands. Cutler stood opposite her behind the kids and worked as hard as he could to make his hands go like hers. Asel could see the Reverend. His eyes were closed and his hands were together as if in prayer. Asel then turned to look at Phoebe and was struck by how beautiful her skin was and how she sang and moved her hands, giving more meaning to words than they could possibly have.

"God damn," Ellie said, and they all turned to see what she was looking at.

Over the town, six miles to the south, they could see silent bursts of reds, greens and blues, mushrooming in the sky. Some were like blossoming trees and others like lilacs bursting open and spinning off in all directions.

"That was a whistle," Beecher's oldest said.

Then five of them went off on delayed fuses, each one a bigger spread and a brighter color than the one before it. After that, some were just lights and played out much like you'd imagine falling stars would be if you could get that close. Then came a dud. It went up straight, turned around and rocketed back to earth, lighting up a stand of pine with a thousand shards of color before going out.

"Back to the drawing boards on that one," Cutler said, and everyone who heard him laughed.

Beecher tipped toward Big George and suggested they trot out their cannon to provide the missing sound effects. Big George looked at Malvine. She held her folded hands in front of her face, the backs of her thumbs lightly touching her red lips. He could see in her eyes every color that was lofted into the sky. He then looked at the way the others studied the sky and, turning back to Beecher, he told him he didn't think it was needed and Beecher agreed.

· · ·

T H E   three men sat alone on the sofa, Big George in the middle. It was early in the morning and still as dark as the night can get. The embers glowed in the barrel, red and hot like those used to forge steel.

Beecher and his family were on the road to home if not there already. The Reverend, Malvine and Phoebe were back at the parsonage. The whiskey and beer were about gone too.

"Did you see, Big George, the way she was perched up on those high heels, her ass higher than a wooden Indian?"

"I saw. It looked to me more like she had an ice pick stuck up her rear. I don't mean that, though. I think she's a fine woman."

"No. No, Big George. You don't understand. See, it's the way it tilts her pelvis forward in such a fashion. It strengthens her muscles down there."

"Jesus Christ, Cutler. You're talking about the Reverend's wife."

"She's a woman first, George. She's a woman first."

Asel thought about Phoebe. She'd worn sandals and when she walked she seemed to lie back, stepping out on strong legs, her rope of hair behind her, swinging free from her body.

"I'll tell you another thing I like about her," Cutler said. "She's proud of her chest. She's a woman who's proud of her chest. She's got a body makes women jealous. She's a real baby doll."

Cutler got up quickly and went into the garage. He came back with what he called his emergency whiskey bottle and opened it. Each man drank to Cutler's savvy and forethought, his regard for the future, knowing its ways and stashing a whiskey bottle for when it came.

"I *am* a cunnin' bastard," Cutler said, pleased with himself. "I am that, a cunnin' bastard."

Big George handed the bottle back and forth, taking a drink on each pass. Asel and Cutler didn't mind it, being as his length and girth warranted the extra hit.

"You know what I'd do if she were mine? I'd butter her feet like a cat, so she'd never stray from home."

Big George held up the bottle in its passage. "Listen here, Mr. Cutler. You're headed down the wrong road and I know because I've been there. You'd best keep it in your pants and I mean it."

"I know that, but I've got my own ideas. They haven't quite jelled yet, but I know there's more to it."

Asel stood up. Cutler and Big George looked at him. He went to the wheelbarrow and moved it as close to the fire as he could and tipped the handles back to the ground. He sat in the seat it made, leaned forward and placed his elbows on his knees. The other two men leaned forward too until their heads almost touched, the glow of the fire beneath them warm and red on their faces and on their necks where their collars opened. They stared down into where the fire had been and where now only tiny waves of heat shimmered and danced, hovering, just over the embers.

Cutler spoke again, saying, "The first woman I ever had made me get down on my knees before she'd love me." And then in a whisper, he said, "Man, she could roll her belly."

Big George sighed. "I only had one woman," he said. "She gave me up and I can't say as I blame her for doing it."

Cutler said, "I could have had a lot of women, but I'm not that kind of guy."

Asel listened to the men and thought about Phoebe. In his mind he saw her walking across a meadow, her hair swaying gently behind her. She wore a white sleeveless blouse and jeans, cut off high on the leg. Much like she wore tonight. And then he dared to remember that at times in the night, while everyone was talking, he turned her way and she was looking at him and smiling.

The whiskey bottle began to go around again, each man drinking his even share until it was inside him and bringing on its own kind of sleep. As Asel dozed off inside the wheelbarrow, the last thing he remembered being said was, "Marry a virgin, boy. Marry a virgin."

6

A W E E K before Christmas, the Reverend left a message on the board for Cutler to stop up when he got home from work. The snow was heavy, but Cutler had no problem busting through in Big George's 4 × 4. The Reverend was at the kitchen table with a ledger book, running tallies by candlelight. Cutler let himself in and stood by the refrigerator, treading his feet up and down, letting the snows come away from his legs, and melt on the floor. The Reverend's pinkie rings were red and blue and his hands were fish-belly white.

"Mr. Cutler, so good of you to come by," he said, closing the book and opening his Bible.

"Good evening, Reverend. I see you've taken to the good book for the night."

"Yes, yes. I read when I can. Do you read the good book, Mr. Cutler?"

"I did, Reverend, up until me and George got burned out back in York state. I must have read it a hundred times or more. I never liked the ending, though. It was a stirring enough finish but it seemed like an awful waste, if you know what I mean."

"Yes. Well, I have been reading Job, Mr. Cutler. Have you read Job?"

"I'm not sure, Reverend. Is that his first name or last?"

"Some would say, Mr. Cutler, that Job was unduly punished. His sin was not proportionate to his misfortune. What do you think of that, Mr. Cutler?"

Cutler crossed the room to the table. He sat down opposite the Reverend. He folded his hands and hooked his boots in the rungs of the chair. He could tell the Reverend was pleased with whatever God had dished out to this fellow named Job. To Cutler the Reverend seemed comfortable in the knowledge that this man, Job, got the shaft.

"Job," Cutler said. "Could you spell that for me? No matter. About the Bible, Reverend. After a while I was forced to pull out some of what I considered to be the less important pages and use them to plug draft holes around the windows. By God, even as I sit here I know just where those particular pages went. I had a radio set up there that was putting out the most ungodly hum you can imagine. So what I did was knot up several of those pages and slide them in amongst the tubes. It made them sit better. After that, it came in clear as a bell."

The Reverend squeezed his hands tight. Blood came into his knuckles and fingernails, making them go from white to pink and then red. Cutler fished a cigarette from his breast pocket and lit it. He drew the smoke deep in his lungs and then flicked the ash into his pants cuff.

"You mind if I smoke, Reverend?" he asked.

"Mr. Cutler, you know better than to use the good book the way you did," the Reverend said, mopping at his forehead with a long white handkerchief.

"Damn straight, Reverend. You're telling me. It wasn't a week before the whole place went up in a ball of fire. My eyebrows didn't grow back in for a month. No matter, though, by then we were across the state line."

"Mr. Cutler, about the ratio of sin and punishment. Was God just in what he exacted from Job?"

Phoebe came into the room. Cutler stood and took off his hat. She smiled at him and then she opened the refrigerator.

"Hello, Cutler," she said. "Has the storm let up or is it getting worse?"

"Oh, it's getting worse, I suppose you'd say, but for me, it doesn't make much difference. I can get around in all conditions."

"That's good," Phoebe said. She closed the refrigerator and stood beside the Reverend. She tapped him on the shoulder with a pickle fork, letting the tines pass close to his ear.

"She's almost ready. She wanted me to tell you that."

"Sit with us, Phoebe. Sit with Mr. Cutler and me."

"No, I'm going back to my apartment. I have to clean the gun Asel gave me. An animal has been leaving footprints outside my window. I've decided to shoot it."

"You do that," Cutler said. "You plug it right between the eyes. Then me or Ace will skin it and cook it up for you."

Phoebe laughed. Her hair shook behind her in long movements that worked their way to the floor. She gave Cutler a hug.

"Tell Asel there's candlelight service next week and I'd like for him to go with me."

"I sure will. I'll make a point of it."

Phoebe hugged him again and went down the hall to the back of the house, closing doors and latching them behind her.

"Mr. Cutler, I'm trying to come to grips with the issue of Job. Deep in my soul, I struggle with what is on earth, what is in scripture and what is in the heavens. Do not get me wrong. I know in my heart and soul whose side I'll come down on, but I am required to engage myself. I am required to wrestle these things out so others will not have to."

"All well and good, Rev. Let me make my contribution. Before me and Big George teamed up, before I was alone in the woods, of my own choice mind you, I was in the service up in Anchorage. You might say I fought my wars in Alaska when it was still a territory in '55. It was nothing to see a man with a pistol or a bowie knife strapped to his leg. I carried one myself. A Ruger Blackhawk much like Ace's only mine was a .357. But don't get me wrong. It'd still put quite a dent in you. Now listen close, Reverend, this is a complicated story and I don't want to lose you."

Cutler lit another smoke. The yellow lights of a snowplow beamed through the windows and swept across the room. It geared down to make the climb up the hill and then the sounds and lights disappeared into the blizzard.

"One night me and a boy from Baton Rouge went into town. I love to say those words, Baton Rouge. You should have heard him say them. God, they sounded pretty when he said them. Go ahead, say them."

The Reverend said the words, Baton Rouge. Cutler was a little surprised. He heard something in the Reverend's voice he hadn't heard before. The Reverend sounded like the boy from Baton Rouge. He said them just the same way.

"It was his birthday and to top it off, he was getting short. He only had a few weeks to go. So me and him go into Anchorage and let me tell you, in them days it was a wide-open town."

"Sodom and Gomorrah," the Reverend said.

"No, Anchorage," Cutler said. "Fort Richardson across the inlet."

The Reverend shook his head and drummed a finger on the Bible. He started to speak, but Cutler broke in before he could.

"I get you. You mean you've been to places just like it. I'll bet you have, doing your mission. Anyway, they had girls behind the bar. You throw a silver dollar in the can and they start singing. Late at night, them same girls would take their clothes off, but that's a different story. You got a cold one, Reverend? All this talk makes me dry."

The Reverend went to the refrigerator and found a beer.

"Take out three or four there, Reverend, it'll save you trips," Cutler said.

"So me and this kid sit down with a couple babes from Seattle. They try to get me to buy a round but I won't. Old Cutler'd been down that road before let me tell you, Bub. But you see, the kid from Baton Rouge hadn't. He didn't know no better. I told them girls I'd buy a round on condition they drink what I drink, but they wouldn't. You know what I'm getting at, being as you've done time in Sodom and Gomorrah. Those girls weren't drinking nothing but water.

"Well, 'What the shit,' I says to myself, 'if that kid wants to be a fool, I can't stop him.' You know what I mean, Reverend. Don't you?

"About that time another fellow starts singing 'Reenlistment Blues.' I'm telling you even to this day, that song gets down inside me and brings out stuff that scares the living shit out of me. I told that boy to stop, but he wouldn't, so I was forced to go over there and knock him ass over tea kettle. All hell broke loose.

"The bartender pulls a pistol. It was a little snub-nose .38 and he starts to come after me with it. You catch what I said, Reverend? He come after me with it, the damn fool, like he thought it was more effective as a billy club. I tell you, the fools in this world.

"I pulled that Blackhawk and I held it right to his forehead. I said, 'You want it that bad, mister, you come ahead 'cause I'm loaded for bear,' and then I ripped him across his nogging with the barrel. I laid him out like a dead tuna."

Cutler slumped back in his chair and shook his head. He drank down his beer and he thought about the bartender stretched out on the floor, a knot already rising from his brow.

"Mr. Cutler, please wait a minute. I must talk to my wife," the Reverend said. "I'll be right back." The Reverend got up from the table and went upstairs, leaving Cutler alone. Cutler kept telling his story.

"So about that time, the troopers show up. They were called territorial police. Now mister," Cutler said, pointing his finger where the Reverend had been, "there was no little bastards on that department. They didn't believe in little men, I'll tell you. They picked me up by the seat of my pants and threw me in the slammer. I give 'em my belt and shoelaces. They told me they had guys that tried to kill themselves. Can you believe it? I can."

Cutler went to the refrigerator. He found some more beer

stashed in the vegetable drawer. He sat back down again, spinning off a cap as he did.

"The next day I got back to base. That kid from Baton Rouge was in his bunk. His face looked like ground beef. His cheeks was busted open and his eyes were blackened inside his head. He looked like death warmed over. You see, what happened was, them girls conked him on the head and then went at him with their shoes. After that they took his money."

Cutler sat back in his chair. It tired him out to go back to Alaska after so many years. He had a movie of a salmon he caught up there. It burned up in the trailer. His projector and his movie melted down to a sodden lump. Cutler'd liked to play the movie when he'd been home alone. He'd liked to listen to the nicker of the cogs as they wound the tiny pictures through the guts of the machine.

"You can't imagine what a woman's shoes can do to a man," Cutler whispered.

The Reverend came back into the kitchen.

"Mr. Cutler, I have a favor to ask you. My wife would like to go to Freeport tonight to do some shopping. She's promised our relations Christmas presents from the L. L. Bean store. She feels it would be appropriate as we now live in Maine. The problem, Mr. Cutler, is that I am a poor driver in the snow. Our car is equipped with studded snow tires, but frankly I haven't mastered the art of turning into a skid to gain control."

"I can understand that, Reverend," Cutler said, now standing with his hat held to his chest.

"As much as I hate to burden you, I think you can see the situation I'm in," the Reverend said, closing the Bible and pushing it aside. "What I would like is for you to drive her to Freeport. You seem quite competent in the snow."

"That I am, Reverend. I've been turning into skids all my life. The trick is timing. You have to set your course im-

mediately and then you have to worry about overcompen-
sating. You also have to know when to dive for the carpet."

"Yes, well if you are amenable, then that is what we would
like you to do. I will go get my wife."

Cutler went to the refrigerator. He filled his coat pockets
with bottles of beer. Freeport would take a good three hours
in the snow. He would stop back at the station and pin a
note on the bulletin board. He wouldn't be back until the
morning. Cutler looked up from the refrigerator. He could
hear the sound of heels clicking on the hardwood floors. The
Reverend and his wife came into the room. She had on a
white sable coat and white shoes. She wore a white fur hat
that towered above her head and white pearl earrings. She
held her hands in a white muffler. For a moment, Cutler
found it hard to stand.

"You look quite stately in your furs, ma'am."

The Reverend's wife studied Cutler's lips while he spoke.
She looked confused and then Phoebe came into the room.

"She says for you to call her Malvine," Phoebe said. "You
don't have to be so formal. She'd also like for you to move
your lips more and look at her when you talk."

"Malvine, then, it is," Cutler said, looking up at her and
showing every word with his mouth as he spoke.

The Reverend handed Cutler the keys to his car. It was
in the garage that he and Big George had built in September.
The four of them stepped out onto the porch. A foot of snow
had fallen on the land and more was coming. The 4 × 4 was
in the driveway, but Cutler chose to ignore it. On the note
he'd tell Big George where he'd left it. Cutler turned to the
Reverend.

"The point I was getting to in my story, was that the kid's
name was Valentine. The kid from Baton Rouge was named
Valentine."

The Reverend stood on the porch in the light of the open
door. He watched the Brougham back down the drive past
Big George's 4 × 4.

"Valentine," he whispered to himself as the red lights on the car's wide rear end fishtailed up the hill and out of sight. "Valentine, what the hell does that mean?"

"Like Valentine's Day?" Phoebe suggested, clapping him on the back and going inside, closing the door behind her.

O N Christmas Eve Phoebe and Asel went down to Trinity Lutheran for candlelight service. The Reverend had canceled his own. Cutler and Malvine hadn't returned yet from Freeport. They had car trouble and then another big front moved in. Big George had gone to Beecher's house in Jackman.

The moon was ringed in a circle of light that came down to where they were, bluing the snow at their feet and in the high banks that lined the walks. They walked along, her hand resting lightly in the bend of his arm. Asel breathed deeply, sending puffs of air into the night and then walking through them as they hung there. It reminded him of Lion and Sal tramping across the low black ground on an autumn evening, lathered, and late for supper. He could feel her hand at his arm and slowed down, wanting this walk to last as long as it could.

"You look handsome tonight," she said.

"Thank you." He wanted to tell her how beautiful she was, but he couldn't bring himself to say it and then she spoke again.

"Do I look beautiful?" she said.

"Yes, you do. You look beautiful."

"That's good. I want so badly to look beautiful. I'm tired of wearing ugly clothes. I bought these new today. They were on sale but I would have bought them anyways."

Asel and Phoebe came to the church. On the front steps was a stable. Inside was Jesus and his mother and father. One step higher, the Wise Men stood, holding presents for the baby. At the top of the steps, real men were shaking people's hands as they walked in the door.

"Under my skirt, I have a new petticoat and under that, tights, and under them, a body stocking," she said.

Phoebe held Asel back so she could look at the stable. Other people passed by them smiling and nodding their heads. She turned and looked up at him.

"Under my skirt, I have a new petticoat and under that, tights, and under them, a body stocking," she said again.

"You sure must be warm, then," Asel said smiling.

"I am," she said, pulling his face down to hers, kissing him and then leading the way up the stairs and into the soft light of candles that bathed the nave, where they sat holding hands during the service and then, after it was over, they went back to the station together.

Late that night, closer to what is morning, Phoebe lay quietly, her body tight to Asel's. She began to cry softly and when he asked what it was, she told him it was nothing. She told him she was all right. It was just something she'd been thinking about and now it was okay. She moved closer, her body insistent, her shoulders bare against his skin.

The two of them stayed together until after the new year, when Big George came back from Beecher's place and Cutler and Malvine were able to make it back from L. L. Bean with presents for everyone.

7

P H O E B E   went downcountry in the spring. She went to a job interview for when her stint in VISTA was up. It would be her first real job since leaving the university. She was tired from working with kids who suffered constantly, kids who had to fight off bouts of impetigo and the flu. She wanted out for a while. She wanted to work with kids who got three square meals a day, and whose skin wasn't always sallow and dirty.

A few nights later, when the men got back to the garage, there was a note from her on the bulletin board. It was for Asel. She wanted to let him know she was back and she wanted him to come by so they could talk. Certain words in the note were underlined. The men studied it, each one taking a turn at figuring out what it meant.

"You must wash up before you go," Big George said.

"I'm not going to wash up. It never made any difference before."

"It's different," Cutler said. "See how she underlined these words. You listen to Big George and you wash up."

Asel went into the second bay and stripped off his jeans and shirt. Cutler sat on the hood of the truck, aiming the hose at him. Big George threw him a chunk of Ivory and then got beer from the refrigerator. He laid his elbows on the hood and drank while Cutler blasted Asel with the spray and then shut it down so he could soap up.

"Make sure you get the concrete out of your hair," Cutler said, "and watch out you don't leave sawdust in your belly button. Wash your privates too."

Asel made his body slick with soap, matting his black hair against his chest and stomach. He ran his hands along his legs and arms and thought about otters skimming down a riverbank into black water in the shadows of long-needled pines.

He drank from his beer, tasting the soap in it that washed from his moustache through to his lips.

Big George and Cutler watched. The nozzle of the hose dripped water down Cutler's leg and into his shoe, but he didn't seem to notice. Big George looked at Asel and then into his hands. A thumb he hit a day ago began to throb. The nail was black and he wondered if it had hurt like that sometime before, and if it had, why he hadn't noticed it.

Asel soaped his hands and then worked the lather into his scalp. He looked up into the steel trusses that held the roof. He could feel his hair fall away at the back of his head as he drew it into a ponytail and worked it in his fist. He then stopped what he was doing and looked back at his friends. He could see Cutler perched on the hood of the truck, holding a beer between his legs, his pants leg and shoe now black with water from the dripping hose. Big George was cradling his thumb in his hand, against the cold side of his beer can.

Cutler raised his arm and blasted him in the chest. A soapy froth burst from his body, white and full. Asel held his arms out and then clamped them to his body. He crossed them, squeezing them tight to his chest, driving his fists into his biceps, his elbows into his ribs. He turned slowly against the spray until he was rinsed.

"I can't go," he said. "I don't know why, but I can't."

"You go," Big George said, staring into the windshield, his voice soft and coaxing. "You go and listen to what she has to say."

P H O E B E was sitting on the porch when Asel got to the Reverend's house. She stood as he climbed the steps and he could see her move inside her dress. They held each other and she became small against his body.

"Sit down," she said. "There's so much to tell you. I have a job for September at the Robbins School in Keene, New Hampshire. It's the sixth grade. It's near where I grew up. I bought a house too. It's on a dirt road near a river west of Keene. It's cheap. The owner will hold the mortgage. I can afford it on what I'll be making. I'll be able to get a car too, but not much more than that."

"If you need money," Asel said, "I have a lot that Beecher's holding for me."

"No that's not it. I will be fine. Are you thirsty? Let me get us something to drink."

She stood up and went in the house. Asel leaned back against the porch railing, his chin cupped in his palm, her smell on his hands and face. Phoebe came out with lemonades for them. She passed him one and then she sat on the top rail above his head, resting her back against the pilaster. They sat quietly, staring off in different directions. The sun worked hard to give up its last light in the heavy spring air.

Asel plucked at the front of his T-shirt, pulling the wetness away from his chest. He brought his knees up and rested his arms on them. He would miss her when she left. She was the person he loved most in the world and now she was leaving. The thought of going along was too risky. He had a good situation. Big George was wise to his predicament and Asel trusted him. He would have trusted Phoebe the same way if she were a man, but she wasn't. Trust and love were two different things.

He wouldn't go. He sucked in his guts and slowed his breathing. He began to steel himself for his decision, already beginning to shut down the reaches in his mind. Phoebe turned and rested her feet on the top of his head.

"When I was a little girl, my mother told me I should never ask for what I want because sometimes I couldn't have it."

Asel thought about this. It seemed like the smart thing to say to a kid to get them off your back. He tried to remember something his mother told him before she died, but he couldn't. Buzzacott recommended reading the twelfth chapter of Hebrews in such situations, but he hadn't tracked it down. He'd ask the Reverend about if he got the chance.

Asel thought about his mother again. He tried to see her face, so he could maybe make her mouth move in his head. He tried to remember the sound of her voice but he couldn't.

Phoebe made her toes drum lightly on the top of his head.

"It means the wanting becomes more important than what you want. It's really quite simple."

She let her foot down into his lap. Asel wrapped his arms around the calf of her leg and pulled her knee against his face.

"You come too, Asel," she whispered, and then she could feel him nodding his head, his beard soft and full against her skin.

T H E rest of that summer they'd go down to the river late at night where there wasn't a soul. They'd take off their clothes and walk out into the water. When it got too deep for Phoebe, she'd get on his back and he'd keep walking, her one arm around his neck and the other across his chest, her long hair trailing out behind them in the black water. She'd ride with her chin on his shoulder, her mouth close to his ear. He'd feel her smallness, light and warm against his back.

Without a word, he'd bend his knees and they'd go under to see the moon through the glassy water and come up again, sucking in the dark air and laughing out loud. Then Asel'd spin in place until Phoebe's hair surrounded them in the slow-moving current.

She'd float to his front and lock her legs around his waist, her hands on his shoulders, and they'd be quiet and listen. Soon would come the snap of bat wings feeding on the night hatch, the night birds' call and the splash of heavy fish rising and sounding up and down the river.

They'd stay that way until their bodies were pale and their smiles tight across their faces. Then Asel'd carry her back to the bank, where they'd pull their clothes on over their wet bodies and then walk home without talking.

. . .

P H O E B E handed Asel an envelope.

"Inside there's a bus ticket and a phone number. Call that number when you get into Keene. They will get the message to me that you have arrived. I'll come to get you."

Asel took the envelope. He folded it in half and slid it into the back pocket of his dungarees. He wanted to get in and go with her now, but he felt he had to hit the fall rendezvous one last time in hopes that there was a sign from Averell. Maybe one of the sports had shown up with word, maybe a fisherman or bird hunter.

"Come as soon as you can," she said, raising herself up on her toes so she could get her arms around his neck. Asel took her braid in his hand. He wrapped it around his wrist six times and then held her at the small of her back until she was in the air.

"If you change your mind," she whispered, "I'll understand."

Asel had not thought about changing his mind until she mentioned it and then it became a possibility. He wondered if in a way she was telling him to change his mind. He wondered if he should stay on until he found Averell. He would think about it and maybe he would not go when it came down to it. Maybe he should stay on with Big George and Cutler until things changed.

"You take these," he said, bringing out a satchel and a duffel. They held clothes, the hand tools Big George had bought him and his long guns. "It's probably too much to bring down on the bus."

This made Phoebe happy. She took it as confirmation that he would be along.

"Now remember, when you get into Keene you call that number and they will get a message to me that you have arrived. It will take me awhile but you wait right there for me," and then she said, "You come soon. People disappear when they get too far away."

She kissed him again and then got in her car and left. He stood there watching until her car was gone from sight.

Asel went back into the station. Big George and Cutler were breaking out a new deck of cards. They didn't say anything to him. Asel didn't speak either. He had old feelings of being alone. They reared up inside him, making him feel gray and hollow. He sat down at the table and Cutler dealt him in. Asel started to shut down little pieces of himself. Others he set aside in his head, not knowing whether to cancel them out or just temporarily tie them off.

Finally, Big George reached out and clamped his right hand around Asel's forearm. There was enough power in the grip that Asel thought any second he'd be lifted off his seat and snapped in the air like a wet towel.

"You're safe with us, boy, and you'll be safe with that girl. You're young. You do what you have to do, but if you ever need me or that cross-boned son of a bitch sitting across from you, you know where we are. You hear me? You do what you can do."

Asel smiled. He knew George was right. He knew he'd go.

"I'm going back in for a while, George. I'll hook a ride with someone passing through, but I'll be back."

T H E   third bay was deep and long. It was partitioned off from the rest of the garage with plywood walls. The floor was carpeted and a new woodstove cast dry ambient heat throughout the space. Clothes were picked up and all gear was stowed so there was nothing to trip over in case one of them had to get up in the night to take a piss.

Big George slept on a mattress and box spring that had been framed high off the floor so when mornings came it was easier on his knees getting out of bed. Cutler was parallel to

him, in the bed he'd built on the high lift. He kept it at the
same level as Big George's bed, though he could go clear to
the ceiling if he wished. The only light showing in the room
was a small red bulb, half the size of a dime, that indicated
the coffee maker was set to go off at six.

"Big George," Cutler whispered softly. "Somebody is in
here."

Big George was already awake. He reached over and tapped
Cutler on the shoulder to let him know he'd heard it.

"Beecher's dead."

"Ace, it's you," Cutler said. "What the hell's going on?"

"Beecher's dead. It will appear to be an accident, but it
was two sports from Boston."

Big George and Cutler sat up. Both reached out to turn
on the lamp, but it wasn't there.

"Don't move. No lights. I'll say what I have to and then
I'm gone. Beecher can be found on the east side of Allagash.
I left a map with Ellie. It will look like he shot his leg off
and then took quite a tumble."

"What about the two who did it?" Cutler said.

"They won't be found."

"Ace," Cutler said.

"You two leave it alone. Just leave it alone. I'm going now.
You get Beecher before he gets eaten up too bad."

There was a quick movement in the room. Cutler went
for it while Big George went for the wall switch, but when
the lights did come on, the only thing he could see was Cutler
standing alone in his undershorts with his hands held out to
his sides.

PART TWO

RIVERS

At such times they remain quiet seemingly lifeless and because they exert so little energy they require but little and it is during activity only that they consume quantities of food.

It is the inclination to go into deeper and consequently warmer water in the fall, that has doubtless been the factor in developing that migrating instinct in the species that run "down stream in fall" and "up stream in spring."

—Buzzacott

8

"I W A S away at the university. I lived in a house just outside of Durham with a bunch of other students. It was a communal thing. We shared our money with each other and we shared the chores around the house. We ran some chickens for a while but they never laid and finally a chicken hawk got them. That, or a fox.

"We used to hypnotize the chickens. One of the boys was good at it. He was a psych major. He'd hold their heads in one hand and do it with two fingers on his other hand. Sometimes he'd scratch a line in the dirt and hold their heads to it. After a while, they wouldn't move."

Asel pulls his chair closer and then bends to pick Phoebe's hair up off the floor where it lays at the foot of the bed. He holds it in his lap, curled up like a kitten. He strokes her head gently, trying to bring her sleep, trying to send it up through her hair.

"After you stroke my head, you're to flick your hands, like you're throwing the tension away. That's what a good masseur does."

Asel doesn't know what she means, so he keeps stroking her head the same way, stopping once or twice to look at his hands in the gray light.

"We ate health food and wore only clothes with natural fibers. We bought USA-made. Clothes with the union label. We ate a lot of cheese and eggs. Tofu and soybean. Jesus, that stuff tasted awful. I used to catch HoJo's on Thursday nights. All the fried clams you could eat.

"There was a boy there named Mike who got drafted. He didn't live in the house, but he hung around with us. He played ball. He was a beautiful thing to watch in the outfield, drifting in under a high fly ball, stepping back and forth and then catching it in his glove.

"He asked me to marry him before he left. I told him I would because he was going, but I wasn't ready to be his wife. I told him he couldn't make love to me because I might get pregnant and he might not come back. It was a beautiful wedding. We did it outdoors. A lot of people got married in meadows back then. The other girls put flowers in my hair and we all went barefoot. Some people had unusually big feet, I remember thinking. Mine were ugly, sticking out from under my dress.

"The young vicar did the service. It was a church wedding, only out in the meadow.

"We slept together for a week and toward the end he was the one who had to deny me. He wouldn't let me change my mind.

"I wanted him too, Asel. I was twenty years old and I wanted him to love me those last nights and I told him so, but he wouldn't. And then, he died over there."

Phoebe and Asel start at the sound of dishes shifting in the drainer. Then there's silence and they both settle back down. After a moment, Asel gets up to make sure it's nothing more. He comes and sits back down again, collecting her hair in his hands and arranging it on his lap. Bringing his wrist in against his ribs, he feels the frame of his revolver under his shirt, a habit he's gotten into these past few years.

"I like that story," he tells her. "It makes me sad when I hear it. You add a little something different each time."

"One night we went down to the union to see Richie Havens. He was the blackest man I ever saw, which isn't saying much because up to that time I hadn't seen many black people. I felt bad about that. I felt it was somehow my responsibility, but then again that's not true either. I felt bad because they were having a bad time of it.

"One time the Black Panthers came to campus to conduct workshops. It was after one of them got killed in Chicago. They came up from Hartford. Let me tell you, William Loeb went birdshit. The *Union Leader* ran red headlines.

"We smoked a lot of pot that night. I liked doing that. I liked it when the lights went down and Richie came out. People lit up all around us and before his first song was done you could see a cloud of blue smoke drifting up through the spots, making it hard for them to cut their way down to the stage.

"They didn't have the kinds of sound back then that they do now. The sound was more harsh and when he went deep, the whole place throbbed right down into the floorboards. Today with the digital stuff it sounds more pure, not like the way music really is.

"The country was different then. It isn't that way anymore. Carl and Leslie hitched up from New Haven and I didn't even know it until they sat down next to me. Halfway through the show, everybody stood up on their chairs and clapped their hands. I don't know if I could do it today."

Asel likes this part too. He tells her so. He settles in the rocker and puts his head back.

"Richie broke three strings on his guitar, but he kept playing anyway. A friend of Carl's and Leslie's came along with them; in the morning he moved on to Canada to keep himself out of the draft. I never saw him again. That was the last time I saw Carl and Leslie too. They're potters somewhere. They make sets of dishes and mugs. Carl had beautiful hair. He wore it in a ponytail that fell down his back. I got along better with him than Leslie. She was in a way more strident than he was. She was sometimes difficult to handle.

"People began to dance in the aisle and in front of the stage. People danced in a different way back then. They stepped a lot, keeping their feet out in front of them. They didn't shake their asses as much as they do now. A guy who was in one of my classes handed me a joint and smiled at me. He said it was homegrown and he was quite proud of it.

"Some friends of mine were doing acid. They wanted me to try it but I never did. Carl was doing it. He told me he was in love with me and he wanted to marry me too. He told me my hair was purple and blue sparks were shooting out of

it. Sparks that hung in the air, turned into stars and exploded.
He told me the walls were melting too. I think Leslie got
pissed off.

"It was after college I joined VISTA. That was in 1975.
The fall of Saigon. I'd been widowed for four years, but most
people'd forgotten. You know all about that. It's how I met
you. I worked in the Headstart program the church started.
I came in the summer. You and Cutler and Big George were
building the Reverend's garage. No, it was before that. It was
the fourth of July. I wanted you the first time I saw you. You
were quiet and your eyes were soft. I liked your shoulders.
I watched you out the window when I should have been
tending to the children. I went out of my way sometimes to
make sure our paths crossed.

"I think back on 1975. I think it was the happiest year of
my life. It made me sad when I decided you were the one I
loved. It made me sad because I really didn't know who you
were. I decided to give up a little bit at a time to see what
would happen.

"It makes me sad now to think how I have kept you. I
have been selfish, keeping you the way I have. I have not
been fair or honest with you and yet I'm not ready to be any
other way than I am right now.

"Even little things, like me telling you all of this. Some of
it isn't true. I know where Carl and Leslie are. They have a
studio in the Adirondacks where they make table settings on
commission. I am told they have an Apple computer and that
Leslie uses it to help her do designs. Carl goes to New York
City. He likes it down there.

"A lot of people I have known died in other ways. When
I was a freshman in high school, a senior died in a car accident.
His brother was in my homeroom. Some of us forged notes
so we could go to the funeral. I remember standing out in
front of the church while they carried him out. I didn't know
any of the family, just his brother, and I didn't even know
him that well. There were a lot of kids from school there.

To this day I've hated myself for going to the funeral where I had no right to be. I can still see myself standing on the sidewalk, wondering if I should cry or not while they carried him out. That one I just can't seem to shake, no matter how hard I try. And there were things I said to people. Unkind things."

"That was a long time ago," Asel says. "You should try to forget about it. I'm sure they have."

"I almost died too," she says. "When I was a little girl I was climbing in a tree. I slipped and got my hair caught."

"I know," Asel says, stopping her from telling the rest of the story because it pains him so much. "Tell me about college again."

"We used to drink tea in college. We'd drink tea and eat bread that we baked ourselves. The bread was always heavy with grains and seeds. The heavier it was, the better it seemed. The tea always ran right through me and the bread would lay in your stomach like a brick. I don't miss that very much.

"We lived in a house. There were six of us. We did everything together. Boys lived in the house too. When my father found out, he stopped speaking to me and hasn't since. He told me it was the first time in his life he was glad my mother was dead so she wouldn't have to suffer with what I was doing. He sold the farm and moved to Seattle."

"Where's that?" Asel asks.

"West of here. You go west for three thousand miles and then take a right at the Pacific Ocean."

He can tell she's making fun of him but he doesn't mind. He smiles and she does too, reaching up to touch his cheek. He thinks how nice it would be if he could get them back together.

"That was all right, though," she says. "Nothing happened that I was ashamed of. We did grow pot in the garden, but that was no big deal, or at least it isn't now. But you know, I guess it's getting to be a pretty big deal.

"We had some grand discussions. Some real knock-down, drag-outs, but they always ended on good terms. It was hard being a woman because nothing was required of you. The boys went off to war or off to Canada or somehow they beat the whole system. The girls stood by and watched it happen. Don't misunderstand me. For most people, things went on as usual. The Greeks were turning them away. They had so many. Greeks are fraternities and sororities.

"There were only a few who decided to take it upon themselves, and for them to end up looking like pitiful victims is now unavoidable. As long as I'm on the subject, I'll tell you what pisses me off to no end is the sheer disregard for history. Today, if history doesn't fit some sanitized, myopic view, it is rewritten. The only good history is the history that makes America great. If it doesn't do that, it was either a mistake or it didn't happen."

Phoebe stops talking. Silence comes to the room as if it were human and could cast a shadow. Asel can feel it expand until somehow it outgrows the house and stands over the land. It's a silence that has come before.

He looks down at her, calling up images of her in bed to help him find her, shape her face and trace her body under the covers. He's sad that she's stopped talking. He takes her words to fashion a past for himself. He always makes room in her stories for himself. Room where he can stand and be a part. If she talks about something she's done with two of her friends, he always adds room for another in his mind so he can be there too. Sometimes he brings Lion and Sal along with him.

Her eyes are open and wet. She holds the back of her hand to her forehead, breathing softly and then more deeply, her chest demanding more than she can control, until finally her mouth comes open and she weeps, her ribs rising and shrinking with each sob.

Asel reaches out from where he sits and places his open hand on her belly. She takes it in both of hers and brings it up to her face, where she holds it. He can feel her lips and teeth against his palm and with his fingers he feels the wetness on her temple and cheek.

After a while she stops and moves his hand down to her chest. Hunched over, on the edge of the rocker, he draws her hair from his lap and lays it on the bed. He starts at the top of her head and strokes its length as far as his arm can reach.

The shadow outside seems to fold and the moonlight makes its way back into the room more brightly than before. She turns her head to look at him.

"I was thirty years old before I learned that twelve million Russians died in World War II."

"Go to sleep," Asel says. "You have to get up in the morning. You can cry for one, but not twelve million."

"I know. It's foolish to get all worked up like this, to talk about these things. Over the long haul it doesn't mean anything, but in the short run it counts for something and that's where we're living and sometimes it catches up with you, here and now."

Phoebe rolls onto her side to face him. She draws her knees up and curves her back. The light of the moon is full on her face, coloring it blue and gray.

"I want us to get pregnant," she says. "Sometimes I worry because it hasn't happened yet."

Asel looks down at her.

"If you sleep facing into the moon, you can get moonstruck," he whispers. "It's almost as bad as a sunstroke."

"I'll take my chances," she says, pulling his hand under the covers and holding it to her body, feeling its roughness against her bare skin.

Asel thinks about the things she's said and he hopes she's wrong about the short run sometimes catching up with you.

She finally sleeps and Asel thinks about other things. He remembers them walking through the green fields at night, down to the river where they'd wade out and duck under, to come up blowing water and her hair wound about them, making soft water wherever they touched.

9

PHOEBE is in bed. It's now one in the morning. There's a woodstove in the living room. Asel has a second rocker pulled up tight to the hearthstone. He likes to sit there and read. He has a stack of *National Geographic*s he's working his way through. Phoebe brought them home from school. One of the mothers sent them in for the kids to cut up, but Phoebe held them back because they were issues from the years Asel spent alone in the woods, so she put them in the car and brought them home to him.

Asel checks on Phoebe. She has made the bed so that her feet are at the headboard. She makes it this way so she can let her hair fall off the foot of the bed and lie on the rug. Tonight, though, her hair lies beside her. It's coming over her shoulder and down her side to where it disappears under the sheet. Asel looks in on her to make sure she's all right. Outside, branches are ticking against the window under the dark blue light that comes into the room. He can see fields of snow that stretch a half mile to the farm next door. The lights are still on in the barn.

Phoebe says something in her sleep, but he can't make out the words. He goes to the window for something to do while he waits for her to speak again. He wonders why the lights are still on in Tut King's barn.

Phoebe stretches her arm, sliding it under her hair. She opens her hand and spreads her fingers. Asel looks out the window again. A truck is pulling out of the barnyard. Its lights sweep across the field as it makes its turn and begins down the road toward his house. He and Phoebe live at the end of the road, so he knows someone is coming for one of them.

"I have to step out for a minute," he whispers. She doesn't hear him, but she moves her arm until her hand is lying across her chest. He says it again.

"I'll be right here when you get back," she whispers.

Asel touches her head and then leaves the room. He stops at the stove, steps into his pac boots and then goes to the door and waits in the dark kitchen.

It's Bobby Vachon, Tut King's hired man. He's short and round and white whiskers spring from his face like the quills on a porcupine. His hands are black and cracked, always swollen from too much cold, water or heat. For the most part, he can only close them enough to get them around the handle of a shovel or ensilage fork. He's thirty years old.

"Robert, you old bandit. Come in," Asel says. He likes Bobby Vachon. He reminds him of one of the boys he grew up with.

"I'm not a bandit," Bobby says.

"I know you're not. It's just an expression people use."

Bobby wonders if Asel knows that half the stuff he told Tut he lost in the woods or fields ended up down to the auction barn to make him a little extra folding money—pin money, as he calls it. It was nothing much, a log chain, some hand tools, maybe an occasional roll of barbwire. Bolt cutters, socket wrenches, barn shovels, sledgehammers, salt blocks, baling twine, an eighteen-inch MacCullough and an air compressor that didn't work anyway.

"Hey," Asel says, "did I ever ask you if you were any relation to Mad Dog Vachon, the wrestler?"

"No, never did. But I'll tell you I'm not. My brother says he is, though, and I'm related to him. Why'd you ask?"

"No special reason. What brings you here?" Asel says, thinking about how he's related to his brother too.

Bobby Vachon stops to think. Asel often confuses him with his questions. He doesn't know why the lights are always on in the house. He does know Phoebe is teaching school and keeps regular hours, but Asel moves about at odd times, not seeming to pay much attention to the time of day.

"Jake's all busted up and Tut wants to eat him. He says

for me to come get you to do him in. Said you can have a quarter for your troubles."

"What's he want me for? Why doesn't he do it himself?"

"Can't find his gun."

"What do you mean, he can't find his gun?"

"What the hell's it mean when someone says he can't find his gun? He can't find his gun. Tut says you're a guide from the Maine woods."

Asel walks to the stove and stands with his hind end toward it. He only knows Tut to say hello, but Phoebe stops in to see him often. He takes him to be a nice enough man, someone who will mind his own business if you do the same. He's met up with Bobby many times in the woods and in the fields. When Phoebe bought the property from Tut, he sent Bobby over to show them exactly where his land ended and theirs began.

"You go back to the farm," Asel says, "and I'll be along in a few minutes. I haven't cleaned my guns yet tonight."

"Tut says for me to drive you back. Can't we shoot Jake with a dirty gun? He doesn't really give a goddamn. Use what you got right there," Bobby says, pointing to the Ruger under Asel's arm.

Asel shakes his head and silently curses himself for not thinking to pull a shirt on. He wants to take the anger he has for himself out on Bobby by telling him he wouldn't have the guts to watch how a .44 makes the eyes bulge and the head swell to the point of bursting and then does.

Asel keeps shaking his head and goes into the spare room, where he has his gear, and gets his .22, his cleaning kit, a leather apron and his set of knives and steel, which is in a leather roll with a drawstring. He gets his meat saw too. He knows the easiest way out is to do what he's been asked.

Bobby Vachon stands by the stove while Asel works at running rods and pads through the bore. He thumbs through a copy of the *Sportman's Guide Catalogue,* which comes in Phoebe's name. He thinks he'd like to get the fifty-eight-inch blowgun on page two. It's a reproduction of the original model used by South American jungle Indians. It's made out of aluminum and billed as being better than the original. He thinks it would be handy to have. He also decides to get a green shirt that says "Kill 'em All and Let God Sort 'em Out." For his wife Lillian, he will get one that says "All This and Brains Too!" The "All This" goes across the chest. Bobby is quite proud of his wife's chest. It's the kind that gets stains on it whenever she cooks, the kind that gets pinched when she rolls over in her sleep.

Right now the only shirts they have that say anything are a couple of sweatshirts that have "I'm with Stupid" printed over an arrow. The problem is that both arrows point in the same direction so when they wear them together, the joke is only on one of them and the person who happens to be standing around at the time next to them on their left. Once Lillian figured this out she refused to wear hers at the same time he did. She even threatened to cut the arrow out of his shirt and sew it back on, pointing toward his crotch.

Buying her a new shirt would be a way of getting in good with her. It's something he's felt he should do ever since the day the car wouldn't start and he had to take it apart. He'd told her, "Blow on that gas filter and see if you can get any movement."

"I'm not blowing on it," she'd said.

"No really, blow on it."

Lillian had put the pipe to her lips and started blowing.

"Don't gum it. There's been gas touching it. You'll poison yourself."

Lillian had curled her lips so the dry part was against the hose.

"Now blow, Lil," he'd yelled, and her cheeks puffed out, but nothing came from the filter. It was then that the phone rang and Bobby had answered, telling whoever was on the other end that Lillian couldn't come to the phone because she was blowing on his pipe and then hung up.

She'd crossed the room in a fury and cuffed him.

"What in hell are yóu telling that to people over the phone? Someone could be listening."

"What's gotten into you all of a sudden? You're like a madwoman."

"People could be eavesdropping. They'll think we're doing something sick."

Bobby Vachon had tried to get his arms around her, but he couldn't. Her chest, like a mountain ridge, kept them apart.

"You want to take that?" Asel asks, but Bobby doesn't answer. Instead, he folds the catalogue and slides it inside his coat and down the sleeve.

The phone rings, surprising both of them. Asel grabs it before it can ring again. He doesn't want Phoebe to wake up.

It's Tut King. He wants to know what is taking so long. Asel tells him he had to clean his gun and that he will be right along. Tut tells him he wouldn't be bothering him, but that son of a bitch of a hired man, Bobby Vachon, borrowed his gun and lost it in the woods. He tells him Jake won't mind if it's a dirty gun and to come along and then he hangs up.

Asel puts the phone back in its hook, now feeling a little bit like it's his fault he has to be helping Tut King. He can't figure out how Tut did that. He tries to forget about it, but can't. The man's voice was soft and rich, the voice of a man going out of his way to be nice and provide you with an opportunity whether you want it or not.

Bobby asks Asel about a brass belt buckle that holds a five-shot .22-caliber revolver. The ad says it could be a lifesaver.

"I suppose it could be," Asel says.

"Do you think it's worth a hundred and eighty dollars?"

"That depends on how valuable the life is," Asel tells him, applying lubricating oil to the gun metal.

Bobby nods. He would like to bring himself to trust Asel, but he isn't sure if that would be a good way to start a friendship. He does know it's a good way to end them. He thinks on what Asel said about the value of life. He decides his is worth the hundred and eighty but just now he's strapped for the cash.

Asel fills a Thermos with coffee and then goes to check on Phoebe. She's awake, lying on her stomach, a pillow bunched under her chest.

"I've been listening," she says. "You go ahead. I'll be okay. I think it's nice Tut thought he could call on you."

Asel doesn't say anything. He goes to the closet and takes out his shotgun.

"Don't," she says. "I wouldn't touch it anyways."

"Yes, you would," he tells her, loading it and leaving it across her dresser, hoping she'd remember his words if ever the time came.

A S E L follows Bobby Vachon through the barnyard to a machinery shed. Several men are standing around, bouncing from foot to foot to stay warm. Only one man isn't moving. Asel can see it's Tut. He is leaning back against a tractor tire that's taller than his head. He stands on one leg with the other bent over the crook of his cane.

Asel looks at the men, who stop moving once they see him. He doesn't recognize any of them. Tut King is the first to speak.

"Mr. Asel, I'm glad you could come by to help us. You go about your business and we'll just keep right out of your way."

Tut points to the back of the shed. An ox is sitting there on its hind end like a dog waiting for a bone. Water is coming from its eyes, and puffs of breath are condensing in the air around its nose. One leg is splayed out at an odd angle on the floor, the hide scraped down to the bone. The other is tucked underneath. It's a blue roan and Asel figures it to go at least eighteen hundred pounds.

A set of chain falls is cabled off to a steel beam that runs from one side of the building to the other and a gambrel is hooked to it, hanging over Jake's head. To the side is a band saw and a grinder. The ox is looking in Asel's direction, but it isn't seeing him. Its eyes are drawn and its breathing comes more even and slow than a man in a deep, peaceful sleep.

Asel then stops for a second and listens. He can hear the sounds of cows shitting and pissing. He looks around to see where the noise comes from. Bobby touches his elbow and points to a speaker on the wall.

"Intercoms," he says. "He has one in each shed and one in the house so he can hear if they're bullin' or calving or if one goes down in the night. I had one too, up to my house, but I lost it."

Asel takes off his jacket and puts on his apron. He un-cinches his knives and rolls them out on a stainless-steel table. His sticking knife has an edge on both sides and comes to a point. A blood groove channels through the center on each flat. He works it with the steel, moving both hands at once, sending rapid *snick, snick* sounds into the air. He then sheaths the knife in his back pocket and walks up to Jake, chambering a .22-long into the rifle as he goes.

Without stopping, he holds the gun with the buttstock high over his head and shoots down, into a point between the eyes and halfway to the poll. There's a burst of muzzle flash in the half-lit shed, followed by a thin red arc of blood that immediately mats in Jake's hair. By then, though, he's falling, tipping off his stiff front legs, and Asel is opening a six-inch gash in his throat, severing the carotid before he slams to the floor.

"Jesus Christ," one of the men says. "If I didn't know better, I'd say he genuinely liked doing that."

"Well, it's obvious you don't know better," Tut yells. "It sure beats shooting them in the head with a dirty gun and having them run through the barn wall and disappear for a week with the worst goddamn headache I can imagine."

The rest of the men laugh at this. They look down at the floor and scuff their boots. They light cigarettes and cigars and pack their cheeks with tobacco.

"Now you listen, Tut King. That wasn't any fault of mine. That bull had a double skull and you know it. The bullet couldn't penetrate. I sent it to Cornell and had it verified."

"That's right," Tut says, gumming his cigar. "Now refresh my memory. Was it one inside the other, one in front of the other, or were they side by side? Cornell, my ass."

This makes the men laugh even harder. Tut smiles. He swings his leg to the ground and swipes the other man with his cane across the seat of his pants and winks. The man looks at Tut and then he smiles too. They all step closer to watch Asel work. Already he's cut round the hooves and peeled the hide down using the curved blade of his skinning knife. While he works with that knife, Bobby Vachon sharpens another one for him so he doesn't have to stop, but occasionally he does, looks up at Bobby and shakes his head. Then he moves his hands in the proper fashion to show him how he should be drawing the knife across the steel.

Bobby tries it the way he's shown, picking up speed as he goes until he loses his rhythm and slices the skin off his knuckle. A patch of blood blossoms on the spot. He doesn't say anything, though. He sucks on it for a while and then goes back to sharpening knives, getting it right this time.

Asel works in the cloud of steam that rises from the warm flesh. The fat cakes to his knife and hands, forcing him to constantly wipe them on his apron. He has the hide skinned back evenly from the line he slit, crotch to brisket. Parts of the meat and fat are flushed with blood from injury and from where it pooled in the body while it lay on the cold floor. They'll have to be cut away later, but now he takes the meat saw and with four quick strokes severs the head from the body. After that he cuts off the front legs just above the knees and the hind legs just below the hock. With his sticking knife, he opens the tendons that run down the back legs, then inserts the ends of the gambrel and motions Bobby Vachon to work the chains.

As the animal rises in the air, Asel works at the back, skinning away what's left of the hide. It falls cleanly to the floor, its own weight pulling it free.

"I'll need a barrel for the guts," he says.

"Just bail 'em out, right on the floor. Bobby'll clean them up later," Tut tells him as he raps the side of an empty fifty-five-gallon drum with his cane, making Bobby look up and nod his head.

Asel nods and turns back to the carcass. It's pearl white in some places and in others it's traced with blood like the veins in a leaf. The steam has lessened as the carcass has cooled. He cuts around the anus and down along the urethra. He pulls them free and lets them hang while he cuts again from the crotch to the brisket, this time opening up the body cavity. A new steam rises. This one is sour, the sourness of fermentation, rank in the air. The men puff harder at their smokes as body gases fill the shed. They know it's a smell that'll get inside their own bodies, such that even a day later it'll come from them when they break wind.

"Roger, here, gets the liver," Tut says. "Tom the heart and Willard the kidneys. Cy wanted the blood, but you were too fast for him. So be it."

Asel peels the gall from the liver and slices open the heart to push the clotted blood from its various chambers. He thinks about how the heart can often be the ugliest part with all of its complications. He then hands out the organs to each man, letting them drop in plastic bags they hold out to him and then they use paper-covered wires to cinch them.

"I'm sorry about the blood," he says to the man named Cy. "I have a Thermos of coffee, though, if you'd like some of that."

"No, no," he says. "I wouldn't take your coffee, but I would like to have you do a beef for me this week. I've got some hogs too. Do you prefer skinning them or scalding them?"

"I never did a hog before."

"Scalded," Roger says. "If you do any for me, I want them scalded."

The men begin to argue about the best way to do a hog. Some prefer them skinned while others say the only way to do it is by scalding. They argue about the effect each way has on getting the hams and bacons smoked right.

Asel picks up his meat saw and goes behind the carcass to split it down the middle. Bobby Vachon offers to do it with the eighteen-inch Homelite Tut just bought, but Asel tells him no. When he's done, it takes two men to hold up each half so he can quarter them. These they put on hooks strung from the bottom cord of the roof trusses.

The men look at the meat and comment on how coarse and tough it'll be to eat, best for stew beef or hamburger. Tut tells them it will be flavorful and more lean, better for their hearts. Friendly bidding begins on each quarter. Asel agrees to let his be sold too and then packs his gear while Bobby Vachon drags the barrel over and tries shoveling the guts into it. Asel tells him to lay it on its side and just roll them in.

When an argument breaks out, Bobby taps him on the shoulder and points to the side door. Asel follows him out and into the milkhouse. There they pull up their sleeves and wash their hands and forearms in the long stainless-steel sink. The water is hot and makes their hands ache. They have to scrub hard to break through the thick fat that coats their skin. Bobby Vachon gives up after a while and wipes the beaded water from his hands, still slick and greasy. He leans back against the bulk tank and lights a smoke while Asel keeps scrubbing.

"Try that white bottle," he says.

The bottle has a black skull on it and says poison. Asel uncaps it and pours some of the clear green liquid on his hand. It's hot on his skin, but the grease washes away easily, leaving the skin on his hands and arms red and hot.

When he turns around, Bobby Vachon is climbing down the steel ladder attached to the tank. He has a glass of milk in his hand. Standing with his feet spread and pointed out, he drinks it down, tilting his head back until he almost tips over. It leaves a band of white that's spread over his lip and up to his nose. He drags his arm across his mouth, smacking his lips. Tut comes in.

"Mr. Vachon here will give you a ride home," he says to Asel, handing him several bills folded in half. Then he leaves through the door and goes to the house.

Asel dries his hands and arms. Bobby hands him a glass of milk he's dipped from the cooler. He drinks it down and they leave. Stepping out on Route 63 Asel stops so quickly Bobby Vachon bumps into him. He remembers it was on such a night in Maine five years ago that he saw a comet arcing across the dome of the sky in the early morning, the tail flared out like the contrail of a rocket. He imagined that if he'd been close enough he would have heard the sound and it would have been like a sled running across the snow in an open field.

"There is north," he says to Bobby Vachon, pointing to the sky over his house, the lights on in all the rooms except one.

"So what?"

"There's much to be said for knowing where north is. Not for the sake of going, but just to know."

"I guess so. Get in the truck and I'll drive you home."

"No, that's okay. I'll walk," Asel says. "I'll walk."

When he gets to the house he sees that the shotgun has been unloaded and put back in the closet. From the way she breathes, he knows she is awake but neither of them speak. He rocks quietly in his chair and only after she dozes off does he fully realize it's the first time he's left her alone at night.

10

A S E L   stands under the shower head with his eyes closed
and lets the water come down on his face and beard. The
spray comes hard on his cheeks and brow and against his lips,
draining into his beard and falling off his chin.

He's been slaughtering hogs for Roger and the stink of it
is on his body. He's been doing that kind of work for the
four men who were in Tut's barn the night he shot Jake. He
only does it late at night, though, when nobody else is around
except for Bobby Vachon, who picks him up and drives him
where he has to go. He's been helping with the slaughtering.
Phoebe doesn't seem to like the idea, but she lets him go
anyway.

"What time is the game?" he yells to Phoebe in the other
room, but she doesn't answer, and for a moment, he thinks
she didn't hear him, until he feels a draft of cold air against
his backside. He turns around and she's standing there in the
shower with him. He takes her in his arms.

"Were you calling me?" she says.

"You have your clothes on."

"They're dirty. I need to wash them."

Phoebe pulls her sweatshirt over her head and skins off
her jeans. Her hair spills out over her shoulder and falls down
her front. It covers her breasts and belly and most of one
leg.

"I need you to help me wash my hair," she says, stepping
in beside him so the spray falls on her too.

Asel gets the Herbal Essence while Phoebe turns around,
swinging her head to the side so her hair falls straight down
her back. Asel starts at the top of her head, working up a
good lather. She lies back against his body, her head just
under his chin.

"That feels good," she says.

Asel continues down her long tresses, separating strands and squeezing them back together. He can feel the bones of her spine against the back of his hand as he works. Her hair is slick and wet in his hand.

"Don't rub too hard," she says. "This water is hard. It makes my hair brittle. I'm afraid it will come out in hunks."

Asel lightens his touch, feeling a little foolish for not knowing better.

"What can be done about it?"

"A water softener, I guess. Or move someplace where the water's soft. It's no big deal having soft water, though; you get lead and that can poison you."

Asel puts his hands on her bare shoulders and walks her forward. He holds her under the spray while the suds rinse down her hair and then he walks her back.

"Once more," she says, "and that will do it."

Asel starts the process over again. This time he has her lean forward so he can fan her hair out across her shoulders. He works it against her skin, moving along her ribs over her back and down her legs. He works her hair gently, letting it slip from between his hands and against her body. He reaches around her into the space between her thighs and holds her. They stand quietly, listening to the water on the tiles. Phoebe leans her head back against his chest.

"We'll miss the game" she says.

"We'll be late," Asel whispers, "but we won't miss the game."

A S E L ' S damp hair freezes as soon as he steps into the cold. He starts Phoebe's car and then goes back inside. Keene is at Brattleboro tonight in the finals of a tournament. For Phoebe it's fun to go to the games. The parents and brothers and sisters of her students will be there. Sometimes she runs into an old friend from high school. Asel watches how she avoids some people if she can. She keeps it short and never introduces him, for which he's thankful, because he doesn't like for his name to be known by others.

He thinks how he's come to like being around people, though, people besides Tut and the men he kills for. This will be his first basketball game and his first time out since they went to the Latches Theater to see *Gone With the Wind*. They brought a sack of hamburgers and took turns putting their hands inside each other's shirt.

Asel gets in the passenger side and settles back. He loves to ride in the car, usually falling into a quiet sleep. He knows how to drive, but doesn't enjoy it as much as riding slowly over the road and being lulled by the gentle ups and downs created by frost heaves.

The game is a rout. A kid named Hamlin for Keene bombs them in from all over the court. Another kid named Waterson steals the ball at will and drives the boards hard. Asel expected to see black men playing the game, like in the magazines and on television, but there aren't any. The game seems slower this way, slower than he thought it could be played.

He has a good time, though, taking pleasure in the rhymes the cheerleaders make and in watching the boy dressed up like a giant blackbird go sliding across the floor. Phoebe buys him popcorn, candy bars and Cokes, and he eats until he thinks he'll get a bellyache.

"It's actually a good thing the game isn't close," Phoebe says, her face next to his so he can hear her words. "Otherwise there'd be a brawl. One year a guy got knifed."

Asel slides toward her and begins to pay more attention to the crowd. He doesn't want any trouble.

"Take your coat off," she says. "Relax. The sweat is sopping out on your forehead."

Asel pulls at his collar, but doesn't say anything. He can't take his jacket off because he's wearing his gun.

"You have it here?" she says. "I wish to hell you could leave that thing home once for a change."

He looks at her and can tell she knows she's spoken harshly.

She takes his hand and tells him she wants to go. The game
is almost over. Other people are leaving too.

On the way out, Phoebe stops and talks to a little girl with
her hands. They silently say how much they liked the game
and that they'll see each other in school the next day. Phoebe
moves her hands again and says they'll talk some more tomorrow. The girl's mother looks on, smiling.

Outside the air is cold. Sounds come like lead in the frozen
darkness. The snow crunches under their feet and the buses
can be heard with their engines running to keep them warm.

"Phoebe," a man says. "Jesus Christ, it's you. I heard you
were living around here."

"Hello, Phil," she says. "It's been a long time."

"This is Linda," he says, putting his arm around the woman
next to him. "Listen, a bunch of us are going up to the Putney
Inn. You come up too. Bring your friend."

Phil and Linda walk away laughing. He has his arm still
around her and he holds her close.

"What do you say?" Phoebe says. "Do you want to go?"

"That sounds fine."

"Will you leave that in the car?" she says, thumping him
in the side.

He tells her that he will and they get in the car for the
fifteen-minute drive up I-91. When they get there, Asel un-
straps his holster and slides it under the front seat. Then he
follows Phoebe into the bar. It smells of wool and smoke
and spilled beer. Phil and Linda are sitting at a round table
with some other people. The band wears cowboy hats and
the dance floor is full. Most are couples, but there are also
girls dancing together. When the song slows down some of
the girls sit down, but others hold on to each other and move
slowly about the floor. Asel thinks it to be a strange sight.

"Did you ever see anything like it," Phil says, and the
others laugh. He pushes glasses toward Phoebe and Asel and
fills them from the pitcher.

"Hello, Jerry," Phoebe says to one of the men.

"How you doing, Phoebe?" he says.

"I'm fine, Jerry."

Jerry and Phil talk about when they played basketball for Keene. They talk about how they pounded the hell out of Brattleboro every time they played them. Once they did it when they were high. They're able to remember scores and plays and who scored the most points. Asel listens to their stories, enjoying their happiness over kicking the shit out of Brattleboro.

A girl with short hair in tight curls leans over and tells Phoebe her hair is still beautiful. Phoebe thanks her and then tells Asel she'd like to dance. They get up and the band starts playing "Blue Eyes Crying in the Rain."

Asel holds her and they move slowly across the floor. He feels her hand at the back of his neck, her touch, cool and light. She sighs and lets her head go against his chest.

"What's the matter?" Asel says.

"Nothing. I'd just forgotten how much I disliked certain people."

Asel pulls her to him. He kisses her ear and rubs his beard against her neck. The band moves into "Angel Flying Too Close to the Ground." They do a good enough job to keep the people dancing.

When the song is done they go back to their seats. Two other people are sitting in them. A man and a woman. The man stands up and says, "Phoebe, the all-around girl." He goes to hug her but she holds out her hand.

"Hello, Gary."

"Phoebe, everybody. It's Phoebe," he says, and the others laugh at him. He's been drinking from the pitcher. His face is red and swollen and his sweater lies tight to his body. "You must be her husband," Gary says. "I thought you died in Vietnam. I admire a man who comes back from the dead and drinks with his wife. Tell me, she wasn't all used up, was she?"

Asel looks at the people sitting at the table. They are quiet and expressionless. Phoebe takes his wrist and squeezes it.

"Get the coats," she says.

He wants to punch the man and drop him where he stands, but Phoebe moves in front of him, squeezing harder on his wrist. He gets the coats and lets her head him outside, where she starts to cry.

"I'm sorry," she says. "I didn't want anything like this to happen. It's a small town, I guess. People get drunk and say things that aren't true."

"Take me for a drive," Asel says, "so I can sleep." He smiles at her and daubs her cheeks with the back of his hand. "Nothing to worry about."

They get in the car and drive for what seems like hours. Phoebe opens the glove box and finds a stale pack of menthols. She lights one and smokes it down. Then she has another. Finally they crest the hill and Asel sees what he thinks is the moon coming up on the horizon, but it's not. It's the dome of Tut's silo, silver and bright in the night. When they get to the house he sits with Phoebe until she falls asleep and then he sits in the dark weighing out the good and bad of finding the man named Gary and evening the score.

Outside he can hear something scratching at the door. He goes out and finds Bobby Vachon's dog sitting on the hard-packed snow in the driveway. He gets a handful of hamburger from the refrigerator, steps out onto the porch and holds it out. He bends down and the animal comes to him and eats it from his hand. When he stands it jumps up and puts its feet on his chest and they stand there like that for a while and then Asel begins to move his feet in slow tight steps, the dog moving with him on its stiff legs. They waltz across the driveway, under the moon, in the middle of the white fields that go all the way to the frozen river.

11

T H E next night, Asel takes Phoebe's car and goes to the Putney Inn. He stands at the bar and watches the drunks dissemble, their somnambulant bodies heavy with gravity, their movements timed to bad clocks. He hears a man say, "My ex is in Baltimore. I got a cash settlement." The drunks tread in place at the bar until the music starts and then they lumber out onto the dance floor, sawing the air with their arms and occasionally upsetting the gyroscopes in their heads.

On the television, men in camo silently slog through wetlands and cast decoys onto the water. He recognizes one of the men. He's Jim Carmichel, the shooting editor for *Outdoor Life*. He's seen him before on television, hunting pheasant in Wyoming. He thinks he'd like to meet him, maybe show him a few tricks. Asel laughs to himself, amused by this confession of willful competition. It is something he'd never thought about. He looks around for the man named Gary, but can't find him.

And then he thinks how foolish it is for him to be out like this and how running into Gary will only mean trouble. But he admits to himself he's drawn to the people, the colors and sounds, things he's been outside of his whole life. And as soon as he thinks it, he knows he's probably a little drunk himself, if there is such a thing as being a little drunk.

Someone punches money into the jukebox and Emmylou Harris sings "Making Believe." A girl comes up to him and stands at his elbow. She's tall and wears her hair like a thatched roof. She asks him to dance, but he tells her no. She doesn't listen to him and he doesn't know what to make of it as she leads him out amidst the other drunks who've now taken up with women too.

She puts her arms around him, but Asel stands there. He doesn't move until she puts his hands where she wants them, one at her waist and the other on her back, between her shoulder blades. She puts her face in his neck and then moves him about the floor in a slow circle.

Her scent is exotic to him. It's in her hair and on her face, and neck. Asel thinks it must be what the jungle is like after a rain, but then it's not. It's something he knows. It's more like spring otter or prime muskrat. Barkstone, castorium, musk, ambergris, assafoetida, oil of skunk or a compound of them all. It's a scent he's smelled before, Tink's No. 54 or Pete Richard's Original Indian Buck Lore, especially effective during the rut season.

Asel forgets about the woman, whose bones he feels moving inside her skin under his hands. He thinks instead about female muskrat and the scent they carry in a small bag near their passage. It holds thirty to forty drops of liquid that's prized by trappers and male muskrats. The scent gives him rise and he holds her tight to his chest.

She cocks her head back and smiles.

"You're a strong one, aren't you?" she says.

Asel looks down at her. Her smile makes her face look torn, her red lips uneven against her teeth. She lays back into him and he can feel her bones again, smooth and edged as they mesh together inside her body. He wants to ask if it hurts her to move, given the way her bones are like knives under her skin, but he forgets.

He doesn't know this woman, so he tries to pretend she's Phoebe. It works for a time, but then he gives up trying to fool himself. He feels bad about trying to pretend the way he did, but he knows that it was something he wanted to do. He holds her close and with a grand effort she becomes Phoebe again and he's mystified by how easily it could happen.

It will do for now, he thinks, and when he sees Phoebe, he will tell her everything he's done and he knows it will be all right with her, but then he doesn't want it to be all right. He thinks he'd like to have her cuff him in the head or slap

him across the face, the way Borst would've done. He looks
about the room again, trying to find the man named Gary.

He hears someone say, "I haven't seen you around here
before," and realizes it's the woman he's dancing with, talking
to him. He feels her breath against his ear.

"It's because," he says, "I haven't been around here in a
while. I haven't been around anywhere in a while." He hears
his words and he's proud of them. He looks at her and can
tell she takes them to be more profound than they really are,
and that she thinks she has found herself something valuable.
A real catch.

"I think I'll take you home with me. What do you think
about that?" she says, but he doesn't think about anything.

The song ends and another one comes on, a faster song,
one where people are supposed to flit about the room like
giant water bugs if they're to keep pace with the music. The
drunks come to life, shaking their heads and stretching their
bodies.

The woman takes her steps to the rear and Asel falls toward
her. She thinks he's out to grab her, but then she decides
he's a little drunk so she leads him over to her table, where
two other women are sitting. Setting him down to her right,
she sips her colored drink through a straw and then reaches
under his arm and feels the revolver under his shirt.

"What the hell is that?" she says. "Are you some kind of
narc or what?"

She looks to her girl friends.

"He's got the biggest damn gun I ever felt," she tells them.

"Good for you, Marsha," one of them says. They are both
happy for her. They nod and wink at her.

"No. I'm talking a real gun."

The other two women don't understand.

Asel smiles. He doesn't know what a narc is, but it certainly
appears to be something that impresses people. The women
have a conference. They decide that maybe he is not someone

they want sitting at their table. They yawn and feign interest
in their lighters, cigarettes, drinks and fingernails. They try
to ignore him, but he doesn't realize it.

Finally one of them says, "Why don't you take a hike?"

Asel tells her he has been hiking all his life and that just
for now he'd like to sit awhile. "Besides," he says, "my ex is
in Baltimore. I got a cash settlement."

The women get a kick out of this. They decide that whether
he's a narc or not, it doesn't matter because he's a little drunk
and he won't be a problem.

"Unless, of course, he's very good at being a narc," one
of them says, "the kind who can show drunkenness the way
he does, but really be sober."

They hold another conference and agree that he isn't that
kind, unless he really is very good at what he does. They
laugh again and then decide they'll take him home with them
and make him their pet. They each buy him a drink, something they would have liked for themselves. They believe
that liquor is an extension of their personalities. It's to be
worn in the hand, and gotten into the blood. It's a way for
them to each get inside him and guarantee their share of the
night.

Asel drinks them one at a time and then begins to alter-
nate—green, yellow, red—and they do get inside him as his
head fills with the dumbness of a traffic light.

He watches the women get up, swooping about the table
like big-assed birds, collecting water life from a pond or lake.
Two of them go for him while the third one manages the
pocketbooks. They hold him up under his arms and maneuver
him to the door and onto Flat Street.

"He does have a big gun," the one on his left says.

The one who hasn't felt it yet tells her to make sure it
doesn't go off before they get him home and they all laugh.

. . .

W H E N Asel wakes up, the room is dark. One of the women, the smallest of the three, hovers over him, her back a clipper bow, moving in waves to become soft, oppositely curved, scrollwork. She looks down at him and stops. He's not the man she started with. She sits back on her haunches.

"I'm Darlene," she says.

Asel nods. He can see the bones in her chest and shoulders, the deep hollow between her breasts. They shrug with her breathing, which now comes easily as she sits on top of him, the only light of the room coming through the open door. He smells again the scent of the woman, but now it's mixed with bedding, sweat and clothes in the hamper. It's now the cloying smell of store-bought perfume gone sour in the air, the smell that comes from inside the body.

"Where am I?"

"You're in Marsha's room," she says, drawing a line with her finger from his neck to his navel.

"That's very nice, but I have to go."

Asel rolls to his right but the woman doesn't. She clings to him like a wet leaf, laughing into his chest. He sets her aside and gets his trousers off the floor along with the rest of his clothes. He then gets his shoes on, but can't find his gun. He goes to the door and sees the other two women at the kitchen table. The acrid smell of bad pot fills the room.

Marsha is holding the gun. She points it at her friend.

"Bang, bang," she says.

Asel can feel Darlene's arms go around his waist.

"Jesus Christ," he says. "Don't do that."

Marsha turns toward him. Her whole body looks bleached in the light that comes from the two three-foot fluorescent tubes over her head. She turns back to her friend. They laugh together, the gun cocked and the barrel wobbling at the end of her hand.

She opens her mouth to speak and the gun discharges,

sending a round into the eighteen-cubic-foot Kenmore Side
by Side. Blue smoke rises from the point where she held the
gun before it jerked from her hand and fell silently to the
floor. They are deaf from the percussion inside the small
room, Asel and the three naked women.

He is the first to hear the sound of the liquids inside,
dripping onto the bottom shelf. He takes up his gun and goes
out the door, knocking over a plant stand, sending dirt, pots
and plants across the floor. He goes down the stairs, taking
three and four at a time, barely missing the headers above
each landing until he's on the street. A crowd stands outside
on the street but they are looking up at the wrong building.

Up the street he finds Phoebe's car. He doesn't let down
until he crosses the Connecticut River, a sober man. He
decides he won't go to town again for a long time.

A S E L   reaches out his hand and holds it against the window. He can feel his hand sink slowly into the sketch of frost
that has built up on the inside. Water seeps out from his
palm, catches the blue artery in his wrist and runs inside the
cuff of his shirt. He holds it there, listening to the dog on
the mountain while trailings of water drip onto the floor.

"Asel, what is that?" Phoebe asks, rolling onto her stomach
and tucking her arm under her chin.

Asel sits back in the rocker that's between the window and
the bed. She hasn't spoken to him much since his trip to
Brattleboro two days ago. Moonlight comes across his body,
making Phoebe's hair blue and her face white. The blankets
carry down the line of her back to her rump and then drop
off at the foot of the bed.

"It's a dog," he says.

"What makes it sound that way?"

"It's lost itself on a deer run, or it's been caught in a trap.
It's on the mountain."

"I can't sleep with it making that noise. It cuts through me. It's as if it were right inside my head."

Asel has been listening to the dog for two hours. He knows it's trapped. He drew a vector in his mind at the first sound. He knows it's within twenty-five yards of a caved-in cellar hole that has trees growing out of it, trees already a hundred years old. If the dog had been lost, it would have moved back and forth, mistaking its own trail for the way out. The first hour, Asel tracked it, from where he sat, between the mountains and over the hollow, south to north and back again, but it hasn't moved in a long time. It only cries.

"When will it stop?" Phoebe asks, somewhere between sleep and wake.

"People don't think of animals as making mistakes." Asel looks off in the direction of the sound. He takes a drink of coffee. "People don't think of animals as changing their minds."

Phoebe gathers up her hair and drapes it over the side of the bed. It falls at Asel's feet. She pulls the covers over her head.

"It will die," she says. "It's cold out, too cold for it to live out there. It will die."

Asel listens. The sound is now muffled. For a moment he thinks he has miscalculated. The mountains have a way of changing the direction of sound and the snow makes it even more difficult. He decides it's probably chewing off its leg, trying to get free.

"Go to sleep," he says, putting his hand on her head. "Go to sleep and it will be all right."

Asel finishes his coffee and goes to the kitchen. He straps into his holster and takes down his revolver from the cupboard.

The road to Tut's is clear. He'll go there first to pick up the Old Post Road, which runs over the mountain. He'll take the snowmobile trails that crisscross the drumlins and then halfway to where the road breaks out on Route 12 there's an intersection that goes over the top. The dog will be there, near the cellar hole.

W H E N Phoebe wakes up at break light the sound has stopped. She gets out of bed, catches her hair up in her hands and folds it in her arms. Barefoot, she pads quietly about the house, going from room to room looking for Asel, but she can't find him. She calls in sick and then makes herself some breakfast. The woman who took her call suggested she eat oranges and drink plenty of fluids. She told Phoebe to take care of herself. Phoebe feels bad about lying to her. She decides that tomorrow she'll find the woman and tell her she lied. She'll make up some other reason, a lie also, but at least that way she'll be able to make her confession. In the meantime, she will eat an orange and a glass of grapefruit juice and a cup of coffee.

Phoebe puts on one of Asel's shirts and then takes her glass into the room where the television is. She switches from one morning show to another. People on the screen seem very happy. They smile a lot. Their heads bob up and down. They move their cheeks and eyes. She stops listening and watches them. She turns to "Sesame Street." It makes her feel better to be in the company of Big Bird, Grover and Cookie Monster. They are talking about the color green. It sounds so beautiful. She feels as if she has never seen the color green before and now that she has an opportunity she will miss it, because the TV is only black-and-white and she's worried about Asel.

She goes to the closet and takes out her green corduroy skirt. She runs her hands over it and holds it to her face. She looks up and starts to cry when she sees Asel standing in the doorway. She looks at her hands and then at him. She holds them out and he goes to her. She's able to get her arms around him, sliding her right hand down into his back pocket and pulling him against her.

"You're wearing your green wool pants," she says, and then she tells him she wants to go shopping. She wants to be alone with him inside crowds of people. She wants to buy something pretty to wear.

"We'll go in a little bit," he says. "We will go to Brattleboro and go out for lunch at the Country Kitchen. We'll have a grand time."

Phoebe goes to the kitchen and makes him breakfast. She keeps him close beside her while she cooks. He knows she wants this and he keeps a hand on her, making it feel as strong as he can, and then he sits down and she brings him eggs, bacon, fried potatoes and coffee. She has another cup herself and she asks him about the dog.

He doesn't say anything, though. He doesn't tell her how he found a fresh deer carcass, hamstrung and chewed at the nose and Bobby Vachon's dog dragging itself back and forth because someone had shot out its hind legs and about the tracks of other dogs that were scattered into the woods. He doesn't tell her how he patted it on the head and scratched it behind the ear. He doesn't tell her the things he said to it before he shot it and she doesn't ask him about it again.

12

I T was the winter of '81. Things were slow on the farm. Tut got it in his head to send Bobby Vachon to Chesterfield to pick up sawdust for bedding, instead of having it delivered. It was a way to save a few dollars and to keep the man as busy as he could so he wouldn't get into trouble. It was a good plan too, because trouble stalked Bobby Vachon as it does most fools who are trying to get ahead in life when they don't have anything to begin with.

The snow was deep that winter. If it hadn't been so deep, Tut would have sent him onto the mountain to keep him busy cutting cordwood, but it was too deep to buck, drifted as it was wherever the wind could stroke it. The oxen they had were too young to breast the wind-driven banks and cross the snow fields, which were so deep they would've floated the pair right off the ground. There had been a road they could've taken at one time, but that was in December and now the woods and meadows were given over to the snow and wouldn't be seen again until spring.

So Tut took pity on his man and sent him to the mill in Chesterfield once a week for sawdust to use in bedding down the cows. He sent him in the International. It was painted yellow and had a snub nose with high fenders and West Coast mirrors that rattled at thirty-five, but seemed to seat themselves for a silent ride when the speedometer stuttered its way up to sixty, which had been only a dozen times in its life. The steering column came out of the floor and the dash was green steel. It had a two-speed axle and was on its fourth windshield, a special-order job that had to come out of Troy, New York, because the truck was so old.

Tut told Bobby Vachon it was the last windshield he'd foot the bill for and the next one would come out of the driver's pocket.

. . .

B O B B Y V A C H O N, in high spirits at the prospect of a day away from Tut and the farm, wants company to share his good fortune, so he takes a hard right at the road to Asel's house. He pulls into the driveway and leans on the horn, working the air in the brakes as only he knows how, making the ropes, chains and rings in the dump box clatter against the sideboards. The horn moans out low and painfully.

Asel comes onto the porch in his moccasins and wool pants. His suspenders hang at his sides.

"Want to go for a ride?" Bobby Vachon yells over the deep thrum of the engine, standing with one foot on the running board and the other on the brake, craning his neck across the face of the windshield.

"I'll get dressed and be right with you."

Asel turns off the radio and the Mr. Coffee. He throws a log on the stove and shuts down the damper. He then finishes dressing with layers of shirts and slides his feet into the shells of his pac boots. Bobby Vachon has the truck turned around and aimed for a run up the hill.

Before Asel has the door closed, Bobby's in second and revving for third, double clutching all the way. They crest the hill at forty and then back off, the snow so high outside their windows that the tops of the cedar fence posts are yet another two feet down.

"You get a hill like that, you have to take it fast."

Asel nods, picking up only a few of Bobby's words over the roar of the engine. He's come to like Bobby even more. He takes him to be hardworking and too simple in his way to be deceptive. Asel feels easy in his company. He was a big help back when Asel was killing hogs, but they haven't done it for a long time. Word was getting out and one day he got a call from someone he didn't know, so he quit that line of work.

Asel likes to watch him when Phoebe is around because of the way the man seems to come alive, making jokes with her and poking her in the ribs. The friendship is mutual. Each man usually keeps his mouth shut and they both like it that way.

The heater in the truck is busted. The wind licks in through the cracks in the window seals and gusts up from the holes in the floor. It sets in motion a great stirring of chaff and dust. Candy wrappers snap about the cab until they find something to plaster themselves against, making only ticking noises that can't be heard too well over the engine. The seats are hard as bone because Bobby let them get wet the night winter came and now the horsehairs and springs are frozen in a long slab.

It's work for Bobby to hold the wheel. The road heaves and buckles and the suspension on the unloaded truck won't give an inch, skipping from one hump to the next, and bouncing their heads near the ceiling.

By the time they've picked their way into the village, the cold has gotten to them. Bobby Vachon wheels in beside the Village Store, swinging down from the driver's seat while the brakes are still hissing, the engine idling.

He comes back with a case of Black Label, trying to keep his smile from breaking his face open.

"This will ward off the chill," he says.

Asel hasn't been around beer since the night he went to Putney by himself. He remembers the promise he made to himself about drinking, and thinks how much better a cup of coffee would taste.

Bobby Vachon handles the wheel with one hand and manages to rip into the cartons with the other.

"Boy that tastes good," he says, "you know something?"

Asel looks over at his friend. He's spilled beer down the front of his shirt, where it still foams white on the green-and-black-check plaid.

"I can't eat lunch on an empty stomach," Bobby says and

laughs, his teeth black and his whiskers bristling on his face.

Asel laughs too, but he doesn't know why. He tries to keep laughing as long as Bobby Vachon does, but he can't.

"I'd like a cup of coffee myself," Asel says, and then thinks about what he's said. It surprises him because he can't remember ever talking that way. He smiles as he thinks about what he's said as being something Phoebe would say. Saying what you want without asking for it.

"Asel, beer is good for you. Doctors say that one beer a day is good for the constitution. It's in books. Lillian's read up on it and she says it's all right. She says coffee is bad for you, but you still have to drink it because it has things in it you need."

Asel thinks of himself as a passenger, someone along for the ride. He'd like to sleep, but the ride is too rough. He takes a beer for himself, determined to enjoy it. Bobby Vachon's driving, so Asel relaxes, knowing he's been down this road many times before.

B Y   the time they get to the sawdust pit, it's noon and one of the six-packs is gone. Bobby Vachon wheels into the mill yard, skirts the mountain of sawdust and then stops the truck. He climbs out onto the hood, holding the bottom of his beer bottle against his thigh, his opposite hip cocked out at an odd angle. Asel laughs as he remembers pictures he's seen of ship's captains and cowboys, done while they scan the edges of earth, water and sky. Bobby Vachon jumps back in and slams it into reverse, gnashing gears as he goes. He pops out the clutch and floors the accelerator.

The old International coughs and lurches and then the fire inside the engine catches up with the surge of fuel, rocketing the dump truck deep into the mountain of sawdust directly behind them with a great thump that rattles the bottles and knocks their heads against the rear window, before the engine stalls.

Seconds later there's another great and swift blast of air, cushioning off the ground and sending shots of sawdust through every hole and crack as the wall they've rammed shears off and, like a great hand, fills the truck and then some.

Asel gets back on his seat, thinking he's gone blind for the darkness inside the cab.

"Might have overdone it a tad," Bobby Vachon says in full wonderment of his own act. He laughs and fumbles for another beer.

Asel watches him in the dashboard lights until Bobby turns the key and puts them out. He can then hear him settling back in the darkness. He takes a beer for himself and reaches to his heart to reposition his gun. Slowly his eyes adjust and he's able to see everything he needs to. He takes the baloney sandwich Bobby offers him and eats quietly, listening to the sounds of sawdust draining through cracks and filling voids like streams of heavy sand. He starts to not mind where he is and concentrates on enjoying his lunch, feeling the warmth that comes from inside the pile and breathing deeply the smell of pine and hemlock so strong it takes him back to the woods. He allows himself a growing pride in that he can make himself be this way buried inside the sawdust pile, here in New Hampshire.

Bobby Vachon turns the key on and then holds his sandwich in his mouth, letting most of it hang out. In the red light of the dash, it looks to Asel as if he has fat white lips and a rounded flat tongue where the sandwich yawns open and the baloney hangs free. Bobby feathers the choke with one hand and works the starter with the other. Asel hears the pedals thud as Bobby works them with his feet but he can't see how he's doing it. The engine cranks and grinds and finally comes alive, sending a blast of sawdust and fumes up through the floor.

"Must have tore up the muffler," Bobby yells over the engine noise as he builds rpms inside the block. "I hope we don't die of monoxide before we get her out."

He reaches to the visor, where the toggle switch for the windshield wiper is. He flips it on and the wiper starts down the glass and then breaks off.

"Oh, Jesus. Tut's going to have my ass now. He sees that broken wiper, it'll be all over but the crying."

Asel'd hoped for a little light to come through, but none was able to make the trip. He coughs in the noxious air and holds a hand to his nose. He tries to take a drink but the sawdust has found its way into the bottle.

Bobby sets her down into low and lets out easy on the clutch. The truck shakes and jerks and the sharp smell of burning pads joins in the air with the wood and exhaust as the drive shaft fights to gain torque. It heaves once and then hunkers down, plowing its way into the sun, where it stalls again.

Both men go for the doors, spitting sawdust out their mouths and noses. Asel stays on all fours until his face is clean and he can breathe again. He stands up and goes to where Bobby's standing with a beer in one hand and a cigarette in the other. He has one leg hiked up on the bumper. An open beer is perched on the front of the hood, waiting for Asel.

"I learned that trick from a fella who used to be one of Tut's hired men. It worked for him every time, right up to the day it killed him."

Bobby motions with his cigarette toward the beer he's set out for Asel.

"We'll drain these two, trim the load and then kick back for a while. We gained a few hours on the day. Tut thinks I load this by hand."

Bobby Vachon goes around to the cab and comes back with more sandwiches and the rest of the beer. The sun comes off to their right and for the first time in weeks it's bright and warm. The men begin to peel off their shirts, wanting the sun to be as close as they can make it, until finally they're down to their woolens. Bobby Vachon eyes the revolver under Asel's arm, but doesn't say anything.

They unclamp scoop shovels from the side of the truck and climb to the top by way of the hood and cab roof. Steam from the hot sawdust now broken out from inside the pile swirls around their ankles and up their pants' legs as they cuff off the overage. The sawdust smells heavy and sour and they breathe it in every time they bend over. Bobby tells Asel to make sure he picks out what crusts of snow he can so the bedding will be dry.

They finish their work, throwing down the shovels and leaping from the top. The front of Asel's shirt hangs off his chest, heavy with moisture. Bobby has a band of wetness down his back, and across his forehead where the skin is kept white by his hat. He retches and throws up his lunch. Asel watches his shoulders heave and then Bobby stands up straight, spittle at the corner of his mouth. He manages to find another beer and that seems to set him straight.

Asel can feel a dullness in his own head. He holds a cold beer to his temples and that helps.

"Drink that up and let it work from the inside out," Bobby says, his voice high from his throat still being drawn and tight.

The air begins to chill them, so they put their shirts back on, layer after layer. They climb into the truck and Bobby gets the engine to turn over on the first try but now its roar comes up from under them where the muffler is broke off.

He pulls out onto Route 9 and begins working his way up through gears, gaining sixty-five in no time at all, a billow of sawdust gusting out behind them in two sweeping sheets that swirl together twenty feet to the rear, dusting the highway behind them, the silent fumes from the engine coming into the cab, slowly poisoning them as they head for home.

T H E trip home is long because of one too many short-cuts. It starts to get dark with the sun setting in front of them, miles away. The loaded truck floats over the heaves and buckles in the road as Bobby takes both lanes for himself. The

yellow line begins to disappear, forcing him to slow to a crawl
until he thinks to turn on the lights.

Asel can feel a dullness coming over him. It's as if a net
has fallen and now he's trying to swim free of it. He opens
another beer and drinks deeply, trying to get a surge going
in his body that will shake off the lethargy. Beside him is the
lake, so close to the road it compounds his notion of gravity.
At any minute, he expects the truck to topple over onto its
ice, break through to the cobalt water below and disappear.
The only thing between him and the lake are stubby posts
and two strands of cable that tick by, no higher than the
running boards. Asel thinks back to the summers when he
and Phoebe drove over the same road and saw the boys and
girls lying out on the docks, wearing almost nothing and
letting the sun seep into their bodies, and then he thinks of
them there now, freezing and dying in the night. Something
that almost happened to him.

He knows Phoebe's home from school by now, cutting up
vegetables for a salad and telling herself not to worry. She
rarely shows it, but he knows that whenever she can't have
him close enough to touch, she lets his absence grow until
it becomes a thing that torments her. He doesn't take it to
be a normal feeling, but then again he won't use it in any
way to lord over her.

Bobby Vachon has slowed the truck to a crawl again because now it's snowing and the road is greasy. The ride takes
on the feel of walking in a dream, the tonnage of sleep, riding
through the night on the back of a blind whale out for a stroll.

"Damn, I need some air. I'm falling asleep," Bobby Vachon
says, trying to work the crank, but the windows are frozen
shut. Asel tries his too. Both men work the cranks until
they've spun them off in their hands. Bobby tries to break
out the glass with his elbow but can't. Asel finds a clevis on
the floor. Holding it by its pin as if it were a set of brass
knuckles, he drives his fist into the window, shattering it into
shards that flash in the dark. He reaches across Bobby's chest

and bursts the other window too, letting in another blow of clean air.

The men hang out the openings, their tongues lolling in their mouths like dogs on vacation. The new air brings life to the men, lifting them out of sleep and letting their stomachs go back where they belong. They realize it's late and they can't understand why it has taken them so long to get to a place they don't know.

"Jesus. I think we were dying," Bobby Vachon says.

"I didn't really consider it," Asel tells him.

"We did all right for ourselves, saving us the way we did. Fish around behind the seat. There should be something we can stuff in those floor holes."

Asel finds grain bags and stuffs them in the holes that open up to road under their feet. He thinks about Phoebe, drawing out a sheet of tinfoil and snapping it off across the saw teeth on the edge of the box. He can see her spreading it over the mouth of a bowl and crumpling the edges under the lip. She stands in the white light of the refrigerator that casts the colors on the shelves but doesn't go far into the room, only a few feet beyond the swing of the door, a light that's different from the light of the room.

Bobby takes a deep breath.

"Tut's going to have a conniption fit over those windows." He presses down on the accelerator, causing the broken muffler to trumpet at their feet, making more noise than speed or power, yet they are off, at a pretty good clip. He works the steering wheel to keep up with the four inches of play that has to be compensated for at every turn. He takes it up Park Hill in high range, peaking out the engine at the crest and making the down side before it can quit. "By God we came close to giving it up back there," he says, stiff in the cold they'll have to live with until they get home.

Asel, crossing his arms and jamming his hands into his armpits, hangs at the door, staring at the blue of night that's along the high banks and then turns off dark, deep in the forests of Butterfield Hill, which stacks up to his right like the back of a bear.

"It's funny how death can sneak up on you like that," he says, the words more a thought that found a voice than anything else.

Bobby Vachon makes his way down the narrow black road, straddling the yellow line, the engine too loud for a chance road kill, and too powerful to show any quarter if the chance comes. He points out his window into the darkness.

"That's the sand gully. It's the only one like it this side of the Mississippi. It goes to the river. It's moving this way," he says, as if it were something out there that even as he spoke was looming on its haunches, ready to come down. "I'm going to the auction barn and get a stereo cassette for this truck."

Coming down the home stretch Bobby turns to look at Asel, drawing the steering wheel along with the motion of his body. The right tire catches in the bank, blasting snow up over the fender and then the cab in a great white plume. The International goes twenty yards like that until finally it begins and finishes all at once the painful task of wrapping the front axle around a three-foot stump buried under the snow.

Both men leave their seats so fast they rip perfect tears from hip to hip across the bottoms of their back pockets. They hit the windshield together, cracking it, then bouncing back with a thud. Snow and sawdust wash together in front of them. Steam rises from the radiator and crossed lights shine deep beneath the snow. Bobby Vachon still holds the steering wheel and Asel holds a beer bottle with the neck broke off.

"By God. That new window glass is quite the invention," Bobby says. He daubs at a trickle of blood coming from his forehead, admiring the bowl-shaped impressions left by their heads in the windshield.

Both men laugh, Asel thinking about how much Cutler would love to hear this story. They get out and shake snow, sawdust and tiny squares of glass from their hats and shirts. Bobby Vachon goes back for the last of the beer. He gets halfway to Asel before he turns around and goes back to get the key.

"Old Tut would ream me a new asshole," he says, "if I went off and left the key."

Asel laughs again, but stops when he sees that Bobby Vachon doesn't think it's all that funny.

They strike off down the highway, leaving footprints behind them in the new snow that falls. Overhead the stars still punch through, giving off what little light they can. They see the barn lights ahead of them a half mile away.

When they get there, Tut and Lillian are in the milking parlor, starting on their second string of cows. They move quietly under the round glass weigh jars, the insides of which are awash in milk being pumped from the cows' bags. Tut sees Bobby and comes boiling up the concrete steps, a man on fire from within. Before Bobby can say anything, he cuffs him aside the head with an open hand and knocks him down.

"Don't you say one goddamn word. I know what you did. You got drunk and wrecked the friggin truck."

Bobby Vachon looks up at him, his face hot and red where Tut struck him. He pulls himself up to one knee, cupping his ear with his hand. After a full minute like that, he goes down the three steps to his place beside Lillian, and starts rinsing bags and setting milkers.

Asel looks at Tut. The old man's gaze is coming up at him evenly and without movement. For a second, he thinks he's being measured for a blow and in that second knows that if it comes he'll have to take it and that frightens him. Tut lets his hands fall and Asel can tell that Tut knows what he was thinking.

"You get home," he says quietly. "She's been up here looking for you. Take one of the tractors and bring it back in the morning."

Asel nods his head and leaves the parlor. He walks toward

one of the tractors, its block plugged in for the night to keep it warm. He starts to boost himself up the ladder, but then remembers he doesn't know how to operate it, so he goes off across the meadow, traveling by starlight until he can see through the falling snow the windows of his house yellow and warm.

When he gets inside, Phoebe is at the table. She has her earphones on and is correcting papers. She looks up at him, the need for an explanation apparent on her face. Asel tries to tell her what's happened, but doesn't do a very good job.

"Your supper's in the oven," she says when he's done talking. "I left it on warm. I hope it isn't all dried out."

Asel takes out the casserole dish and fills a plate for himself. He then plasters butter between two slices of bread and pours himself a glass of milk.

Phoebe watches him as he takes his plate and sits down across from her. She pulls her earphones down to her shoulders and holds the tip of her finger to her mouth while he eats.

"Tell me again what Tut said," but Asel can't, because he can't remember even telling her in the first place what Tut said.

"I am going up in the morning to help with chores," Asel says to her.

"Did he ask you?"

"No, but I feel I should."

"I'm happy you've made a friend in Tut," she says, nodding her head and smiling. The rest of the evening she talks about school and the things people said. She becomes buoyant, acting out the different teachers and putting her feet in his lap. When Asel stops smiling and looks at her she takes his face in her hands. "I'm happy because you've come home," she says. "I can't let it be anything else. I want you to always come home."

Asel can now feel the ache in his chest and the pain in his back from his day spent over the road and he feels better now that those things have happened. They turn out the lights and go to bed, where they hold each other until four in the morning, when Asel quietly slides out from under the covers, dresses in the dark and makes the hike to the barn, back up the road he's come down only hours ago in the same sweep of darkness that still covers the land.

13

A S E L works for Tut off and on the rest of that winter. The major project is rebuilding the International. They tear down the front end and then put it back together again with parts they salvage from the old wrecks lined up behind the barn. Tut claims it's one of Bobby Vachon's traits to break down machinery so he can have a reason to tinker.

Asel keeps his own hours and nobody seems to mind, but then again, he doesn't ask for any money and it isn't in Tut's nature to offer any.

L A T E in the spring, Asel decides to take a day to hunt turkeys. It's the only game he's never had luck with, but he figures he'll try anyway.

He hikes into the heavy mist early that morning, passing the ledges and climbing up through the pines and into the hardwoods. He comes out on a road that intersects the Old Post Road and moves south a quarter mile to where he'll go up the bank and into a stand of oak. He's headed to a spot he discovered the last day of deer season and wants to be there before sunrise.

Coming closer to his cutoff, he passes the cellar hole where he shot Bobby Vachon's dog. He slows down, beginning his approach in twenty-pace increments with a minute wait in between, the butt of his shotgun tucked to his shoulder and the barrel at four o'clock. It's unlikely he'll jump a bird, but if he does, he's ready. Mist rises from the forest floor and the abandoned roadbed as it does every morning. It holds at waist-high, cold and wet, and then becomes something else, disappearing into the air. The dampness of the ground makes it easy to be quiet.

Asel rounds a sharp bend, staying close to the trees. Ahead

of him is his cutoff and it appears as if someone is already
standing there in the shadows of an oak. Asel slides off into
the brush on his right, where he watches and waits. It now
looks like an out-of-season doe someone will be coming back
for. He steps back onto the road and makes his way through
the shadows.

It's a woman hanging in a tree. Asel goes back into the
brush again and hides behind a log. He can see her in front
of him. Her face is drawn and of a color he's seen the sun
make on only a few mornings when he was alone in the woods.
He counts nine turns around the rope above her head, and
at her feet he can see a bathroom stool kicked over on its
side.

Asel lies there for a long time, looking at the woman and
then not looking at her. After a while he hears voices in the
other direction coming up the road and from off in the woods.
They're coming in a sweep, the way some choose to hunt
deer. He crawls away on his belly to a place where he'll be
safe but still able to watch.

"There she is," one of the men yells.

"By God, I can see her. She's up in the tree ahead of us.
I see right where you're talking about."

"Jesus, look at her. You can say what you want, but she
did it by the book."

"She's got on the brown bathrobe too."

The men stand in a circle around the tree. The younger
fellows stay back, looking over shoulders when they dare to
look at all. Mostly they look at the ground and the toes of
each other's shoes, not wanting to look at what is inside the
circle of older men.

"This makes seven in my lifetime," an old man says.

"Six other? What six are you talking about?"

"Gilbert Hutchins, Lawrence Gray, Bertie Gilson, a man
and wife from when I was living in Rutland and a fellow in
the service, a boy from Connecticut."

"That's seven," one of the boys in the outer circle says.

"It ain't seven, it's six. The fellow in the service and the boy from Connecticut are one in the same."

A man across the circle steps to his left so he can see the old man. "I'll allow you Gillie Hutchins and Larry Gray, but those last three were from out of state and two of that three, I might add, were from Vermont."

"He's right, you know," another man says.

"You know, I wouldn't bet on it, but Bertie Gilson, I believe, was from downcountry too."

The man who stepped to his left puts one hand on his hip and pulls at his chin with the other one. "Now that I think about it, you're right. Her mother and father came up from Fitchburg just after they were married. It was during the Depression."

"It's still six," the old man says. "It's six in a lifetime and this makes seven and you ain't going to take that away from me."

One of the outer circle, more a boy than a man, turns on his heel and starts down the road. The others turn to watch him go. They watch him pick up his pace, but he just can't make it out of their view. He doubles over, heaving and puking at the edge of the road. When he's done, he stands erect and starts walking again. They watch him until he disappears.

"Kid's got moxie."

"Shit. They don't even know what it is."

"She had it," the old man says quietly.

"I'd be more apt to say she was crazy," the man across the circle says.

"What do you know about crazy? You all think crazy is or isn't. You think it's a thing, but I'm telling you, you don't know nothing. You ain't any closer to the truth of it than a rabid dog."

"Enough of this, we've got to get her down. Rodney, shimmy up there and cut her free."

The old man steps in close. He turns in his own tight circle, looking at the other men.

"You ain't gonna cut her down 'cause she'll drop in the dirt. Ain't one of you brave enough to hold her and I'm too old. You leave her where she is until one of these boys can run for a sheet. Even if you were to let her down, you'd have to lay her on the bare ground anyways. I won't let you do that to her."

"I'll get a sheet," the boy named Rodney says. "I'll run down and be back here in no time."

"You do that, son. You stop at Seely's and get a sheet. You tell them why."

Rodney takes off on the run, his long strides a blur of knees, elbows and heavy shoes. One of the boys says he'll probably trip and knock himself out before he makes it. A few of the men smile at this, so the same boy takes courage and directs himself toward the old man.

"What the hell's got into you? You have something going with her?"

Though most who were there swore they heard the last three or four words, they couldn't have, because before the boy can finish, the old man lashes out with a tiny fist, catching the boy square in the mouth. When he draws back, his knuckles are laced with blood where the teeth peeled back the skin before they gave way.

Another man grabs the boy by the back of the shirt to hold him up. He looks into his mouth. Some teeth are gone and others are folded in. The man holds the boy up with one hand and looks into the circle.

"By the Christ, he's my own nephew, but I would have done it myself if you didn't. I hope you can accept an apology from me on the part of my family."

"It was a young mouth," the old man says, wrapping his hand in a white linen handkerchief. He smiles and points to his own mouth, letting his dentures move in and out. "You go down the road too and get some first aid," the old man says, patting the boy on his shoulder.

One of the men steps up, pulling at his chin, deep in

thought. "You know something," he says to the men who are left, "I think we were just now saved from a big mistake. Last year, me and Tut drove out to Saratoga, New York, for a big dispersal. We left at five so we'd get there in plenty of time to have a look at the cows. They were good cows too. Big and rangy. Milky cows, if you know what I mean. Tut bought a mess of them. He sent half to Canada and half to Maryland. There were Arabs there too, but that's a whole different story.

"So we get there just as the machinery is starting to go. Tut's been looking for a conditioner, if any of you know where one's laying around, by the way. He doesn't want a new one. He wants an old one.

"So, I go for coffee while Tut's looking over the equipment. He's wandering around on the outside of the crowd when all of a sudden this young fellow up and keels over. Right on the spot. Not more than an arm's length from Tut.

"People don't move for a second, not knowing what the hell is going on. Then two of them jump in and go to work on him. It was a beautiful thing to watch, the way they pushed on his heart and blew him air. They went right to work like they'd been doing it all their lives."

The man stops talking and stares off toward New York, fifty miles away as the crow flies. His hands twitch and he tilts his head a little to the left. The others can see he's remembering how beautiful it was to watch them work on the man's heart. Asel cranes his neck. He can see it's Roger, the man he did some slaughtering for.

"So did he make it?" one of the others finally says.

"No, he died right there. It was a massive coronary. His old ticker just seized up at that moment and wouldn't be started again. It wouldn't be jump started and there was no ether to spray in the carb, if you know what I mean."

"I thought you said he was young."

"He was. Anyways, the point of the story and how it applies

to us is that they had to leave him there until they could get a coroner to declare him dead."

"He was dead, I thought," says the uncle of the boy who left with the busted mouth.

"Not really. He wasn't dead by law, so what they did was put a horse blanket over him and went on with the sale. People stepped over him and some of the latecomers even lifted the blanket to see what was underneath."

"That's the biggest crock of shit I ever heard."

"Well, now before you start disbelieving, remember it was in New York State and they have their own way of doing things."

To that statement, all the others nod their heads. Then they turn to each other and nod their heads again.

Asel can see Rodney huffing up the road behind them. Other men follow him. When they get closer, the others turn to watch them come. Rodney holds a sheet to his chest. It's white and stands against the world like a sign.

"Here's the sheet," Rodney says, handing it to the old man.

"Thank you, son."

The old man unfolds it, handing sides and corners to the others as they come out until there are four men to each of three sides. The ones to the open side hold their end low and the men to the top hold their end over their heads. They walk it toward her, taking her weight onto it as they go, raising her into the air.

The moments just before the low men lift, Asel can only see her, gently reclining against the square white sheet that's drawn taut and stretches out to all sides for what has to be only a matter of feet, but what seems to be an endless distance. The mist rises under her and in that moment it seems she's floating, hovering over the dark earth. Her eyes are on him and he doesn't look away, but raises his brow instead so if by chance she wants to say one last thing, she'll know that he'll listen.

The low men lift up and then the rest of the men lift up

until she becomes the sag in the middle of the sheet they hold over their heads.

Rodney's in the tree. He looks down into the sheet, and waves to her with the tips of his fingers, but only he and Asel know he does that. Taking the slackened rope in his hand, he cuts through it with his barlow knife and then lets it fall to one side so it won't hit her in the face.

They lower her to the ground, but don't let her touch. The side men take short steps toward each other until they touch hands. They fold in both ends and then begin to roll up the slack at the top, slowly raising her up again, not once letting her near the ground.

When the wrap is tight, each man reaches underneath and holds hands with the man across from him. The old man takes his place at her head. Rodney comes down from the tree and picks up the stool. He then takes his place beside the old man and they begin to walk. One or two men could have carried her out in shifts, but that isn't the way they do it. A boy moves in beside each man and other boys go ahead, moving fallen limbs from the path.

The old man says something Asel can't hear. The assembly pauses for a moment and then pivots to the left, reversing grips, and starts down the open road again, this time with the woman's head now higher than her feet. The last thing Asel sees is the old man's hat bobbing with each step as if he were going down a long, straight flight of stairs with no landing and no need to turn.

When they're gone, he rolls onto his back and stares up into the tree crowns just now coursing with the fluid that gives rise to the leaf buds that dot the branches as they web the sky. For a time he can see it all. He can see through the bark and into the sapwood and through that into the red heart that climbs like a spike from the taproot.

He closes his eyes to hold it a bit longer and then opens them, catching the world in its rush to reassemble and feeling better when it's able to hold.

He stands up and brushes himself off. His wool trousers are wet and in some places soaked through to the skin. He stretches and then goes to the spot where the woman was. He lays his shotgun against the trunk of the tree and then climbs to where she hung from. He cuts away the last loop that's knotted around the limb and comes down. He sits there, holding the length of rope in his hands, staring at it, and then he hears someone coming up the road. He doesn't have time to hide so he only sits with his gun across his lap, waiting to see who's coming.

It's the boy named Rodney. He's alone, walking with his head down, watching the ground in front of him. Asel thinks he might have to say something to keep the boy from walking into him, but the boy stops in time. He comes up short, his weight on one foot and the other ready to leave the ground. He squints at Asel and then slowly rocks back on his heels.

The boy looks like he's going to rub his eyes or turn to run but he doesn't do anything. He smiles instead and puts his hands in his pockets.

"She killed herself."

"Yes, I know," Asel says, tucking his chin in and looking down at the rope in his hands. He can feel his beard against his neck. When he looks up, the boy is still looking at the rope and then he looks up too.

"My name is Rodney. I live in the village. We only moved in a while ago."

Asel nods his head. He can see that Rodney's clothes are too big for him at the sides, but that he's outgrown them at the ankles, wrists and neck. The front of his shirt sticks out at the sternum, where he's grown pigeon-breasted, making his neck look corbeled and his head set back as if someone perched it there in preparation for knocking it off.

"My name is Asel and I live down on the meadow near Tut King's farm."

"I know who you are," the boy says. "You live with Tut's daughter, Ms. King."

Asel pulls his head back and looks hard at the boy, frightening him with his quickness.

Rodney takes a step to the side. In Asel's movement can be seen something more akin to a hunter sending home the bolt on a rifle or racking the forearm of a shotgun in an attempt to snap off the second shot. And in a way too it's like the quiet unseen movement inside a padlock receiving the thrust of the shackle. Rodney tries to think of all this to give him some handle on what he's seen, but he doesn't have time because Asel speaks again low and even.

"Phoebe King," he says, pausing between the first name and last name.

"Ms. King, the schoolteacher. Tut King's daughter."

Asel squeezes the rope, sensing the forest to be more of both alive and dead than he has known it.

"Her name is Ms. King," Rodney says.

Asel smiles and nods his head. He looks across the road and into the forest. He tries to remember what he saw before, when he was lying on his back but he can't. He feels the same way he felt when he first came out of the woods in search of his brother and then again the last time he went in to save Beecher. They were all the same, those moments that clear away entire memories, entire histories, bleaching away the words that were scratched inside the first set of bones, meant to be kept secret and passed along from one to the next.

Rodney kicks at the ground and then clears his throat.

"Are you going to keep that rope?"

"I hadn't thought about it."

"I have, but I haven't gotten very far. It seems important but I don't know how."

Asel looks again at the rope in his hands.

"It's only a rope. It's nothing more."

"My old man thinks she's brave. Do you think she's brave?"

Asel lies back against the tree and Rodney sits down on the ground. Neither one moves. They stay this way for a long time. A squirrel rustles so close Asel could have touched it.

A larger shape pokes its way out of the brush behind Rodney. It's a bearded tom with a deep red wattle and a plumage of reds, browns, greens and yellow.

"I think she knew something nobody else knows," Asel whispers, while he and the turkey stare at each other.

"But that doesn't answer my question."

"You would think that, wouldn't you."

The boy nods and stands up, causing the tom to duck back into the woods. Asel can see that the boy needs to leave but some want holds him back. Asel remembers the piece of rope he has in his hands.

He loops it around his fingers and then slides it off. He throws it to the boy, who holds it in his open hands as if it were a bird's nest he's brought down from a tree.

"We all kill ourselves in the end. Some of us need help. Some of us don't."

The boy doesn't say anything. He turns and leaves, disappearing down the road he came up three times that day.

Asel sits for a while and then pulls himself up. He looks for some sign that would remain to reveal the last of the woman's life that left soon after she made her short and abrupt descent through the air. Aside from those things that will disappear when the forest steps back in, he can see nothing. He considers blazing the tree, a small notch or slash that would scar over and climb a little every year until it was higher than a man's head and couldn't be found.

Asel shoulders his gun and leaves the spot by the tree. Holding his course to the road, he wishes he'd come to a clearing and Averell'd be there with a couple sports up from Boston or New York. They'd have liquor and food and fancy useless gear. They'd have some present for him, a compass or a knife or maybe a split bamboo rod from Abercrombie & Fitch. He'd pretend to look it over, put it to some test to gauge its flex or edge and then he'd give them a slight smile and say, "It's true enough," and they'd take him at his word and fill with pride he couldn't understand. He'd then say

good-bye to Averell and lead the sports back into the woods.
When he stopped walking, they'd pull up short, bumping into
each other, and he'd have to make sure he stopped smiling
before he turned around to face them.

Asel holds his course for twenty yards and then remembers
the last night he spent in the woods, chest-deep in a brackish
swamp, lying in ambush. He spoke no words to them and
saw no need to because they'd killed the man of the only
family who'd ever taken him in and shown him kindness. At
the time it was a simple equation, but now on the mountain
he stops. He stands between the woman who took her life
in the tree and the house he shares with a woman he realizes
he doesn't know.

He turns and, in one smooth motion, levels, aims and fires,
sending a tight pattern of copperplated shot into the trunk
of the oak, and then two more right after it.

W H E N   Asel gets home he broils a steak and makes a
salad, taking the time to rub garlic inside the bowl, sauté
mushrooms and warm the bread. The meal is ready when
Phoebe gets home.

"You must have read my mind," she says. "I am so hungry
I could eat a horse."

"No lunch?"

"I missed it. One of my kids got in trouble, so I spent it
in the principal's office. Leon is such an asshole. You would
think I was the one who messed up. You go to those people
with a problem and they screw it up. At the same time they
get you the message that they don't want any part of it. I'll
tell you who screwed up. It was Lib, the art teacher. She's
never in her room, so one of my kids started throwing
clay."

Phoebe talks on, eating with her mouth full. She eats her
salad with her fingers and mops gravy and dressing with her
bread.

"What about you?" she says. "It isn't like you to come home empty-handed."

"It happens."

"I don't believe it."

"It's true," he says, thinking about the tight pattern of shot he left in the trunk and the sap running down its side in the shape of a man's beard. "It's true," he says again, and looks at the woman who sits across from him.

A S E L doesn't say anything to Phoebe about what he saw that day and if she knows anything about the woman in the tree, she doesn't say anything to him.

He doesn't go back to Tut's either. He stays home, and works at weaving baskets. He figures he'll make up a supply and hit the flea markets when summer comes. He leaves his stack of magazines alone and keeps the television off. As he works he thinks about how Tut is Phoebe's father, and how she's kept him from knowing. He doesn't understand why. He decides that in a week, he'll pick up his studies again, reading, writing and math. He'll try to change himself into a better man. He will learn about another country, maybe Canada or Mexico, and he'll go there. He'll make the trip that the old man was never able to make. He'll find a country that isn't shutting down the way this one is, but one that's opening up. Whether Phoebe will go with him or not, he doesn't know. It's enough to know she's near her father, something that could happen to him, he now fears, given as so many people seem to know who he is.

The rest of the week, Phoebe's tired at night and they don't talk much. It seems one of the other teachers needs an operation and the school has put off hiring a substitute, so Phoebe and another teacher are picking up extra students. She's too tired to talk about it and Asel's relieved.

Friday afternoon, he sits on the front porch pulling oak splits across his thigh against the blade of a knife he holds in his hand. Stray fibers curl at his feet and stiffen in the sun. When he's finished with one he takes up his stone and sharpens his knife. It's important to keep the edge straight but even, so the splits will be flat. From up the road, he sees Phoebe's car coming.

She pulls in and gets out, closing the door behind her. She leans back against it and crosses her arms. She's wearing a white skirt and sandals. The skirt comes down to just below her knees. Her calves are white in the sun and she's looking at him.

"One of the high school students came to my building this morning. He told me to give you this."

She throws Asel the loop of rope. It's been braided into a bracelet. It looks to be a continuous braid without a knot holding it together.

"He said he was able to make two and he thought you would appreciate one of them. He said it was rightfully yours."

"It's nice work," Asel says.

"Asel, I'm sorry. I know you must hate me."

Her voice begins to drop away. He watches the shake come into her shoulders and then take over the rest of her. He doesn't realize how small she is until she holds her hands to her face and cries into them.

She goes down on her knees, her white skirt covering her legs and feet. She still holds her face, letting go only long enough to daub at her eyes and then start again.

"I left school," she says. "I told them I was sick and I had to go right home."

She cries out a second time and her hands go white.

"I never wanted to be alone again," she says. "I wanted to keep you however I could. I knew it wouldn't go on forever, but I didn't know that for sure. That's why I've lied to you."

"You've all lied," Asel says.

"Yes. Tut, Bobby, even Lillian. All of us. Only because I asked."

Asel goes to her and lifts her up. She's small in his arms

and through her blouse he can feel her ribs moving against the palms of his hands.

"I could never hate you," he says, but she cries harder and holds to his shirt.

Asel picks her up in his arms and takes her inside. He lays her on the bed and then sits down in his chair. He stares at the wall and begins to talk.

"I don't understand what's happening. I was content to not know any of this, but it won't leave me alone. At first I was left alone and that was fine with me and it was fine with everyone else but now it isn't. It can't be any other way, though. Things have happened and I can't go back and undo them." Asel stops and looks down at his hands in his lap, his fingers laced together like stitching. "I must go," he says. "There're things you don't know. Things that can hurt all of you."

"No," Phoebe screams. "Stay here and hate me but you can't go. I can't let you. I will die if you do."

Asel looks at her. Her face is drawn and colorless, her eyes like a deer's caught in a beam of light, blind with a fear he's never seen in her before.

"We will work this out," she says. "I know we can. We only have to talk. When two people have a problem they only have to talk it through. They only have to come to an understanding."

Asel touches her. She lies there feeling his hand and then she takes it in both of hers. She pulls herself to him until she's half off the bed and he has to hold her up. She curls up inside his arms and closes her eyes. He can feel her heart fluttering next to his own.

PART THREE

MISTS

Another method of hunting Deer is by what is termed "jacking." . . . I have often hunted thus, years ago, when game was more plentiful, and must admit there is a fascination about "jacking" or fire-hunting that is intensely interesting, and the strange weird sight of the glaring eyes with the unusual incident of the surroundings, and quiet amply repays for the watch and wait. Good marksmanship here is of course essential. . . .

—*Buzzacott*

14

IN Harrisville, New Hampshire, there's a steambath that's run by an old Swede, named Elmer, brother to Harvey, though, as most people say, it's always hard to tell just how old a Swede is because they take on age so easily.

The baths are in a two-story building with board walls, tucked into a steep side hill. In the cellar there's a boiler that heats up cast-iron radiators in separate rooms. A pipe comes out of the wall over their tops and a valve lets water through the pipe to sprinkle down on the iron, where it turns to steam. Most people go there when winter comes again.

The way to go there is to take Route 101 out of South Keene to Marlborough. Then you have a decision to make. You can take a left after you pass the truck that has been re-built into the shape of a giant muffler and go through Chesham or you can stay on 101 and head north when you get to Dublin.

Phoebe always makes the trip by way of Chesham. It's longer that way, but she'd rather take the time than go by way of 101 and pass a bend in the road where a boy died. It's a sharp bend. He missed it late at night on his way home in 1968. There's a green sign that's either before or after the bend, depending upon which way you're going. It says HAR-RISVILLE and points north.

After the boy died, they hauled his Volkswagen back to Trabold's Garage and left it by the fence. People went up to see it. They pointed at the places where the metal had taken on accordion shapes. The boy had long hair and there were places where some of it was caught up in the glass and steel. Phoebe knew the boy, but she didn't go to look at his car. It made the whole town sad because he had a way about him that everybody liked.

. . .

T H E regulars come up in the evening. They've spent the day ice fishing on Silver Lake or Nubamusit. They drag their shacks out onto the millpond that still backs up enough power to turn the wheels that run the looms, but now the looms are gone and the water goes about the business of ware-housing fish and looking pristine.

You can see their shacks set on skids that are now buried under the new snow that banks the sides. The woods are shut down for the season, the liquid in the trees frozen, so the men come to the lake to spend their days in the six-by-six huts, running hand lines down to where the yellow perch live. The men sit back on their benches, moving only to skim the hole, bring up a fish, quaff a beer or sip some blackberry brandy. Some leave the door open and throw seeds to the grosbeaks and chickadees that perch on their snowmobiles. Some do nothing.

Others come from the ski slopes. They are on their way back home. You don't get that many old-timers, just people who made the run from Keene or Swanzey when they were young and who are still holding on.

It's after Christmas but Phoebe brings in a bottle of Black Velvet for Elmer. He and some men are sitting at a picnic table playing cribbage and drinking beer. There's a boy there smoking a joint. It's something he grew himself, he tells everyone. The smell is harsh but the others don't mind. He sits with his back against the knotty-pine walls, close to sleep.

Phoebe and Asel stamp their feet to shed the snow from their boots and pants. They hover near the woodstove, smil-ing at each other.

"I haven't been here in years," she says, looking around the room. Since the time Asel found out she is Tut's daughter, she has been taking him everywhere she's ever been. She still keeps him to herself as much as she can, but she tries to give as much of her old life as possible.

The light from the bare bulbs is yellow in the smoke that hangs at the ceiling. The windows are black except for dots of milky light from distant houses.

Warmed by the stove they cross the room and sit down on a bench, their backs to the rail that Elmer built to keep the sweated drunks from tumbling down the stairs into the basement, where the boiler is.

At the picnic table there are six men, three with their backs to Phoebe and Asel, and three sitting opposite them. The men wear wool shirts with black-and-red- or black-and-green-checked patterns. They wear them half unbuttoned and their cuffs are ragged, showing the sleeves of their thermals. Suspenders cross their backs or hang at their sides. Phoebe takes the bottle of Black Velvet from her bag and goes to the picnic table with it. She puts a hand on one of the men's shoulders and leans into the center, setting the bottle down in front of the oldest man.

"Merry Christmas, Elmer," she says.

Elmer wears wire-rim glasses with lenses so thick they could be the bottoms of soda bottles. He takes them off to read the lable. When he's done reading, he turns the Black Velvet in his hands, studying it from every angle.

"That's a new experience, eh?" a man says.

"It sure is," Elmer says, and everyone laughs.

He sets the bottle behind him on the floor. Phoebe can see six others already there, lined up along the baseboard.

"Thank you, honey," he tells her, and then goes back to the cards he's been dealt.

Phoebe sits down next to Asel. She takes his hand up in both of hers and holds it with the fingers fanned out as if she's holding a hand of cards. She plucks at his fingers, pretending to discard them, and then looks up at him to see if he gets the joke, but he's not smiling; he's staring straight ahead at one of the men, who has turned around on the bench. The man is looking at Phoebe, his face tight and one eye half shut.

"Kurt," she says. "It's me, Phoebe."

"God damn," he says. "Phoebe."

Kurt smiles. It surprises Asel because he now sees him to be a different man, younger, with pale eyes that seem to have been cleared and brought to life. He swings his legs out so he's facing them.

"I saw Beverley at school not more than a month ago. She thinks you're in Houston. She's expecting you to come home," Phoebe says.

Kurt looks over his shoulder at the men behind him. He knows they're hearing the conversation, but he also knows they aren't listening.

"Not going home," he says. "She tried to kill me."

"Beverley tried to kill you? I can't believe it."

"Sure. Go ahead and ask her sister. She tried to kill her too."

Kurt looks back at the men. He catches the eye of the boy who's smoking the homegrown.

"It's true, isn't it?"

The boy nods so hard the ember of his joint falls into his lap, but he doesn't move. He spits on it and lights up again.

"Jesus, I wish you wouldn't persist in smoking that shit here," another man says. "It gives me a goddamn headache."

"That's no headache," the boy says. "It's a contact high."

"Contact my ass," the man says. "You give me any more sass, I'll show you some contact."

Kurt smiles and turns back to face Phoebe and Asel. He looks at Asel and his smile becomes one he might have been saving for an old friend.

"What'cha got in there anyways?" he says, pointing at Asel's wool shirt.

"I have a bad heart," Asel says. "It's a pacemaker that was poorly set."

The men behind Kurt smile and the boy with the joint laughs out loud. Kurt's face goes cold and again Asel sees the one lid close down and the skin under his eyes go dark. He gives the boy with the joint a look that Asel can't see but is enough to make the boy stop laughing. He turns back to Phoebe. He looks at her feet and starts up her legs, taking his time to get to her eyes. She squeezes Asel's hand to let him know she doesn't want him to move.

"Miss Phoebe," he says. "Me and Beverley's sister were laid out in a meadow the night of Chesterfield's Old Home Day last year. Beverley came looking for us. In her car. Young boy Kurt scrambled north to keep the radials off the backs of his legs, but sister girl took them across the shins. The ground was soft, though. They were clean breaks. It's one form of birth control, though quite effective, I would not endorse.

"So young boy Kurt hightails it for Houston, but becomes involved with the law in an altercation which I might add wasn't his fault. Something about a Mexican drowning in the channel.

"Young boy Kurt comes home and finds they've gone and changed the laws, making it easier to go to drunk school. He takes up sobriety. He does a good job in the classroom but fails miserably on the homework so he takes up with young Thaddeus here who lives off a trust fund and maintains a valid driving license."

Kurt swings his arm to the right in a grand sweeping gesture and points at the boy with the joint. The boy takes off his cap, holds it to his heart and then bows his head in a way that leaves his chin pointing toward his shoulder. Kurt turns back to Phoebe and Asel.

"We do good, me and Thaddy. We build custom shanties for your weekend fisherman flatlanders. We install bunks, fold-down tables for cards, shelving, casement windows and skylight. They are quite the rig."

Kurt reaches behind him without taking his eyes off Phoebe. He swings his hand back around holding a beer can.

"So what does your bearded wonder do when he's not playing bodyguard? Maybe you and I could find some time to step out and take a stroll, a promenade."

"Kurt," Phoebe says. "Your son. He's a good boy." Phoebe's voice is soft, so soft the men look up over their cards to see where it came from. Kurt puts his elbows on his knees and looks at the floor.

"He is a good boy if he doesn't have any problems," he says, the words sounding tight in his throat, sounding as if they hurt him when he spoke.

Phoebe gets up and goes to him. She places her hand on the top of his head. Everyone is quiet in the room. They listen to the sound of the water knocking in the pipes and the wood burning inside the stove. Each person thinks something private. Thinks of something no one else knows, something that was forgotten until now.

A DOOR bangs and someone yells out that number one is open. The men start to move again. Thaddeus gets up and goes for his coat. He gets Kurt's too and stands at the door waiting. Phoebe looks to Elmer, who says, "You go right in, honey. You and your husband are next," and then he reaches out with two fresh towels in his hands.

Phoebe turns and takes Asel's hand. She leads him into one of the dressing rooms and latches the door. She stands quietly, until she hears that Kurt and Thaddeus have left.

"It's all so sad," she whispers.

Asel takes her hand and kisses it. He wants to tell her something but he doesn't know what. He sees in her a way she has with people and he fears for her, but then she smiles and he lets it pass, knowing if only for a second that she's just done it to him also.

Phoebe bends down and looks into a peephole that someone has drilled through the wall. She looks back at Asel and holds her hands out as if she were telling him how long a fish she caught. He doesn't get it until she points toward his belt buckle.

Asel takes off his shirt and hangs it over the hole. Phoebe makes a frown and then she starts to undress. The room is small, not big enough for them to both undress at the same time, so Asel waits until she's done, then he undresses too. He wraps his gun in one of his wool shirts and tucks it under his arm, but Phoebe takes it from him and stashes it in the corner under her clothes.

"It will be all right," she says. She then takes a step forward and comes against him, the palms of her hands flat on his chest. Asel unwinds her braid from the top of her head and lets it tumble down her back.

"Are you ready?"

"Yes," he says and laughs.

Phoebe opens the door at the back of the room. They step across the hall, and go into number one. The smell of Ivory soap is full in the air. The room is white on all its surfaces. Nothing stops the stark light that lays itself about the space. For the second time in his life, he thinks about how small she is. It's a world apart from the tongue-and-groove knotty-pine boards that make up the rest of the building, a room outside the world if only for a little ways.

Phoebe takes her towel and Asel's and sets them outside the door. Then she closes it.

"It gets hotter the higher up you sit," she tells him. "You should sit on the bottom bench."

She reaches up to his shoulders and walks him to where she wants him to be, sits him down and then goes to the radiator. She turns the valve, releasing a sprinkle of cold water over the hot cast iron. It hisses and a whoosh of white steam billows to the ceiling. The room soon fills with a cloud so thick Asel can't see the wall across from him. His lungs burn and hot salty sweat springs out on his body. He licks it from his lips and it feels oily on his tongue.

Phoebe begins to slow dance about the room, in and out of the white steam clouds. Her body is still dark from last summer, except for thin white bands around her chest and hips. Her long braid shimmers as it runs the length of her body and licks about her calves.

"It's so soft," she says. "I can hold it in my arms."

The door opens and Elmer sticks his head in.

"Just checking the steam," he says. "It looks to be pretty good."

Then he closes the door and is gone before they can move. Phoebe and Asel laugh.

"That should keep him on edge for a few nights," Asel says.

They laugh again and Asel grabs her and pulls her onto his lap.

"Sometimes you seem so tiny," he says. "Sometimes I feel as though I could hold you in my hands."

"Go ahead and try," she says.

Asel stands up with her in his arms, close to his chest. He then extends his arms until he's holding her out in front of him like a child. She reaches around and grabs his beard in her fist.

"Put me down. I don't like it when you do that."

Asel sets her on her feet and then he has to sit down because it's hard for him to breathe when he's standing up.

Phoebe walks over to him. She stands between his legs and holds his face to her breasts. He licks their wetness and tells her how good she tastes. She tangles her fingers in his hair and rests her chin on the top of his head. She can begin to feel the heat rise up in her. She tells him to hold her up because she feels a little weak in the legs.

W H E N they've had enough of the steam, they turn back the valve and open the window. The steam cools and begins to settle about them. Asel points to the redness around Phoebe's neck and stomach and breasts and legs. She tells him his beard did it and for a time he feels pain over what he's done. She laughs at him, though, and tells him not to be foolish.

They turn on the shower and begin to wash. Phoebe steps across the hall and returns with shampoo. She has Asel unbraid her hair and then the two of them wash it.

"Somehow he has such soft water here," she says. "I don't know where it comes from, but it's something I've always remembered."

They finish their shower and then go back to their closet of a dressing room. Phoebe yells that number one is open. They can hear people move into the room beside them.

"We used to race through the rooms and jump in the snow when we were done," she says. "Elmer made us stop because the neighbors were complaining."

They finish dressing and go into the front room. Elmer is the only one left. He's playing a game of solitaire, the neck already drained from one of the bottles. Phoebe hands him a five-dollar bill and he tells her to come back soon.

They get in the car and skirt the lake, passing the great brick buildings that used to house the looms. Phoebe tells him a story about a Saab that came out of gear and rolled over the headwall. Then she tells him how happy he makes her. She begins to cry a little and Asel can't think of anything to say. She steers the car toward Dublin. Tiny lights can be seen on the lake where the fish shanties stand under the moon in the blue night air that rests over the snow and ice. Asel puts a hand on her thigh and squeezes. Phoebe pulls his hand between her legs, against the rivet at the intersection of seams in her dungarees. She still feels the wetness as she steers the car toward Dublin, where she'll pick up 101 and head for home.

15

W H E N the season comes, Asel and Phoebe load the car with pack baskets. They cross the river into Vermont and hit the flea markets, Putney, Newfane, Wilmington and Manchester. They sell them for forty-five dollars, but take less if someone wants to dicker. They stay out of New Hampshire because sometimes Phoebe skips school and they stay out of Massachusetts because of the gun laws.

Late on a Saturday afternoon, making their way back home, they stop in a tavern for a beer and a hamburger. Asel likes to sample whatever's behind the bar, Slim Jims, pickled eggs, ham hocks and pork rinds. He has one of each.

A trucker, come down off Route 91, sits at the bar too. Asel admires the fat double-clutch wallet he wears chained to his belt. The bartender brings the trucker his beer and sets it down. The trucker unbuttons the collar of his shirt and begins to drink the beer through his neck with a straw. Asel stares at him until Phoebe gives him a jab in the ribs and he looks away. The sound of hamburgers sizzling on the grill can be heard.

"You're a truck driver," Asel says.

The man nods and sets his beer down. Then he daubs at his neck with a napkin.

"Is it all it's cracked up to be?"

"Sure is," the man says, his voice sounding like a rake being drawn through gravel. "Just the other day, I had to haul a brand-new Corvette back to Detroit. The car got a hundred miles to the gallon. You see, it was an experimental design that somehow got sold on the lot. They give the fellow two brand-new ones in exchange to keep him quiet. I say it was me who hauled it, but it was really a buddy of mine. Is that your wife? I admire a man who drinks with his wife."

"Shit," the bartender says from the kitchen. "That story's a bunch of bullshit."

"You think that's something. I hauled one back that didn't work and there wasn't a goddamn thing wrong with it. Mint condition. I mean cherry. But it just didn't work."

"There must have been something wrong with it," Phoebe says, looking at the trucker from Asel's other side.

"You'd think that, but there wasn't. They brought in mechanics and scientists and engineers and they couldn't find one damn thing amiss. They said it was rare, but sometimes it happened. Sometimes they just didn't work."

The bartender brings out hamburgers for Phoebe and Asel. He flips them each a bag of chips and fishes dill pickles out of the jar too.

"Trabold, down in Keene, could have made it work," the bartender says. "He's a wizard."

"Well now, my buddy said they had one of them too and he couldn't do a goddamn thing neither."

Phoebe and Asel begin to eat their lunch. The bartender draws three more beers and sets them down in front of each person. Then he takes a glass of ice and goes down to the end of the bar to read the paper.

"If we hurry," Phoebe says, "we'll be able to go grocery shopping."

Asel nods and takes an extra large bite of his hamburger, bulging his cheeks and rolling his eyes. She laughs and slaps him on the back.

"Grocery shopping," the trucker rasps out. "By God, I'll tell you one I saw on the set I got in my rig. It's a commercial for pearls and it's got a close-up of this woman with long red fingernails stroking what turns out to be an oyster. Imagine a close-up of that, my friend. I'll tell you, by the time I looked back to the highway I was headed for the rhubarb."

The trucker's laughter can't be heard but he opens his mouth and his shoulders shake. He daubs at his eyes with the napkin.

"I'll be damned," the bartender says. "According to the paper, a man from Philadelphia was up to Tuckerman's Ravine, skiing. He fell down and when he did, the pint of whiskey he had in his jacket busted open and the broken bottle went right through his heart."

"That's bullshit if I ever heard it," the trucker says. "How the hell could that happen?"

P H O E B E and Asel walk the aisles of the grocery store until they get to the dairy case, where Asel bends and begins shifting the milk cartons back and forth. By tilting each one forward and craning his neck, he can read the names of the missing children printed on the backs. He looks to see if any new ones have come out since the last time he was there.

"Are they all the same as the ones you've got?" Phoebe says.

Asel answers by hefting two half-gallon cartons and holding them up for her to read. She tells him they are both five. One is from the Bronx and the other is from Decatur, Illinois. Both have been abducted by strangers. Neither has been seen for two years.

Asel turns the cartons back around so he can look into the kids' faces. One boy is black and the other is white. Both pictures are of the kind that are taken of kids just after they get out of the bath or come in from outdoors. They have big smiles and are missing a few teeth. Asel figures out that by now they are seven and look different.

He thinks about how Phoebe some time ago started bringing home milk cartons with pictures on the back. It began the year of the missing children. It was in the paper and on the news.

At the checkout line, they have posters from across the country. They feature a new child every week. Asel always looks for his own picture and Averell's, but it's getting harder to do because he hasn't seen Averell in a long time. He wonders about the idiot boys and the sister he had at one time, but for them he can only pretend. He has no memory of what they looked like.

Phoebe is getting to the point where she doesn't like to go grocery shopping with him. He dallies at the dairy case and stands at the missing-child display until people stare.

"It's nice to see they're not from Florida for a change," Phoebe says.

Florida is a state Asel has come to hate. It seems to be a place where children aren't safe. They're spirited away from their parents never to be seen again. It seems to be a place where Peter Pan and the Pied Piper work overtime, leading children to cast off from the windowsill, barnstorm the chimney and then disappear into the night. Sometimes the parents steal their own children.

He puts the cartons inside the shopping cart, positioning them so that the two children are facing each other amongst the celery, lettuce, tomatoes and carrots.

"There seem to be a lot of missing children," he says.

Phoebe looks at him. She hurts inside from the knowledge that when the carton is empty he will take up an X-acto knife and cut out the rectangle from the back before it can be thrown away. Three days later when the second carton is empty he'll do the same to that one, taking great pains to make sure the cuts are straight and continuous.

He will rinse each one off and let it dry overnight. He keeps them in a box. He has almost fifty. It would be cheaper to buy milk in the plastic gallon jugs, but he insists on the cartons. She wants to tell him that the children aren't really missing, that somebody probably knows where they are. Most of them are runaways and probably a little better off than they were before. Some have been snatched by a parent in a custody battle and are probably no worse off.

And then she'd want him to say something like, "It doesn't matter. Somebody cared enough to report them in. Somebody doesn't know where they are. We're all missing in a way and it's nice that something can be done about just a few of us." But she knows he wouldn't say these things. He'd only look at her, his eyes a long ways off from the thoughts in his head.

In the end, though, she doesn't mind. She lets him alone.

They weave their way back through the aisles, picking up the rest of their groceries. She'd rather get the milk last, but Asel takes them to the dairy case as soon as they've gotten their vegetables. He likes to set the milk cartons where they can be surrounded by the fresh vegetables. To him, it's like placing them for a time inside a small clean garden where it's cool and safe.

"Is there anything else you can think of?" she says.

"No. I think we have everything."

Asel pushes the cart toward the checkout. Phoebe holds his arm and walks beside him. People in the store who shop the same day they do smile and say hello. Sometimes Phoebe runs into the parents of her students. The father usually smiles and then looks down at the floor while Phoebe talks to the mother about reading scores. She refers to tests by their initials. This talking in code means something to the mothers. It makes them feel good about Phoebe as a teacher.

Since the missing children started showing up on the milk cartons, Asel has not enjoyed these conversations. He wants to remind parents to never leave their children alone, to keep their names off their clothes, to teach them to never get into a car with a stranger. He wants to give them an eight hundred number they can call if they see any of the missing children.

Phoebe and Asel come to the end of aisle five, crackers and cereal. He turns a hard right around a stack of Saltines that are on special and runs into a cart coming the other way. It's the woman named Beverley that Phoebe knows. He listens while they talk about her son, who had a chronic ear infection as an infant and now has trouble thinking. Phoebe explains to her how the inner ear works.

The conversation reminds Asel of the cuffs he took aside the head from Borst, a man he'd never consider killing, but one who certainly deserved it.

Beverley turns her body so she can rest a foot on the bottom rack of her shopping cart. Asel sees that she's missing her arm from above the elbow down.

"I've been meaning to tell you," she says to Phoebe, "you still have the most beautiful hair I've ever seen in my life."

Phoebe smiles and thanks her.

"How do you keep it so nice and shiny?"

"It's not easy. The water at the house is so hard you could eat it. Every week we unscrew the faucet and little pebbles are caught up in the strainer."

"I know what you mean. We have hard water too."

"How's Kurt doing?"

"He's still in Houston. He writes every week. I can't tell you how much we miss him."

The woman looks off past them.

"Where's your son now?" Asel asks.

"He's at my mother's," the woman says. "She takes care of him for me when I have to go out."

"You keep an eye on that boy," Asel says.

Beverley looks at Phoebe and then back at Asel.

"I will," she says. "I will keep an eye on him."

"You come for a parent visit as soon as you can get a little time off," Phoebe tells her. "I'd love to have you come in."

Phoebe smiles at Beverley and squeezes Asel's arm. He smiles too and then pushes the cart around her, where she stands next to the Saltines. Asel and Phoebe move to the checkout. Asel studies this week's children while the cashier drags their groceries across a green light and bags them. As soon as they get in the car, Phoebe turns to him.

"You had no right to say that to her. She works hard to keep her family going and she doesn't need you to make her feel worse."

"What about Kurt? What about these missing children?" he says to her.

"They are no reason to make one woman feel less of a mother. She tries hard without a hell of a lot to keep her going."

Phoebe puts the car in gear and pulls out onto the street. They drive down Route 12 without speaking. She holds the wheel with both hands and stares straight ahead. They climb the summit and descend into the valley toward the river. They pass through the east village and wind their way along Mill Brook. When they get to the iron kettle, Phoebe pulls off the road and stops.

A family has parked in front of them. They are filling plastic jugs with the spring water that runs into the great black iron potash kettle set there a hundred years ago.

"I'm sorry I yelled at you," she says, "but I feel awful for her. Her husband died in Vietnam and then she got pregnant by Kurt. It's a sad story. They were driving down Route 9 and rolled the car. That's how she lost the arm. She lost most of her face too. They put it back together pretty good, though, don't you think?"

"Yes," Asel says. "Her face looks good. They did a good job."

Asel and Phoebe watch the family load the plastic jugs into the trunk of their car. The man walks stiff-legged. The children are barefoot and built like little fire hydrants. One of the girls is growing out of her dress at the hips and under the arms.

"Tell me the rest of the story," Asel says.

Phoebe sits and thinks. She holds her free finger to her temple and her middle finger across her lips. She stares ahead at the children, who are helping their father put the plastic jugs in the car.

She begins to tell the story of the woman with one arm.

"We are the same age," she says. "She comes from a wealthy family, but she doesn't get along with her parents. They own a bank. I have known her since high school. She was a senior when I was just starting. She's a good girl. She tries hard. She used to live in a station wagon. She had a bad time with drugs, but now she's okay. Is that what you mean when you say you want to know more about her?"

"Yes it is. I've come to be interested in people's lives."

"I know you have. It makes me love you."

"What happened after that?"

"To tell you the truth, that's about when I left for college, but I heard that the boy she lived with came to work on the farm. They lived in a station wagon. It was in 1971. They lived up there, above the kettle, she and this boy. They would park there at night and then in the morning they'd drive down the train tracks to the depot. From the depot they'd drop down onto 63 and then drive to work. The constable tried to catch them because the car had no plates. It didn't have a muffler or a windshield either. The hood was gone and it was missing some of the doors.

"She was headed for a crack-up. Her parents wanted to commit her, but then he got drafted and killed. Now that I think about it, I guess they weren't married. Then she got tangled up with Kurt. He moved into the wagon with her and I couldn't bring myself to tell her he's in town."

Phoebe turns to Asel.

"Asel," she says, "I can't keep my stories straight. I'm mixing them up. I know that inside what I've said is the truth of it all. I'm trying hard to tell you straight."

"I know what you mean," he says, and he takes her in his arms and holds her when she starts to cry.

The father comes over to them and asks if everything is all right. The children crowd around the car trying to look in. He sends one of the boys to the kettle to get Phoebe a drink of water. The boy comes back and holds it up to his father. The man passes it in to her. She drinks it and thanks him.

Asel reaches into the backseat and fishes a box of cookies

from one of the bags. He gets out of the car and goes around to where the man is. He hands it to him and tells him it's for the kids. Then he gets in behind the wheel and drives home with Phoebe curled up on the seat beside him, her head on his lap.

P H O E B E   wakes up in the middle of the night. She reaches to the spot where she's come to expect Asel's hand, but it's not there. She rises up quietly as if weightless and pulls on one of his shirts. It's denim with pearl buttons and they're cool against her skin. The sleeves hang off the ends of her hands.

She goes down the hallway and looks in the kitchen. Asel's at the table. He has the leaves turned up, and the gate legs swept out beneath them. In front of him is a giant square made up of his missing-children cards. The reading lamp is directed onto them. She takes a step closer. If he hears her, he shows no sign. He's concentrating on the patchwork of cards in front of him, studying them in the yellow light of the reading lamp.

In the center she can see an empty space, room enough for two more cards, ones he needs to complete the square. She turns and goes back to bed. She makes herself fall asleep and later on she reaches out again and finds his hand. She takes it in both of hers and holds it to the wetness that is just now beginning at her eyes.

M O N D A Y   begins the last week of the school year. Phoebe is up early and on her way, trying to speed it along. Asel is anxious for it to come also. They are planning to do some traveling.

He sits at the table amidst the breakfast dishes and thinks about who he'd like to see. He gets out a pencil and a tablet of paper.

On the first page he draws a picture of Phoebe. He draws her thin and with long hair. He keeps making her hair longer until finally it swirls about her feet, spreading across the bottom of the page and up the sides. He tries to draw her face but can't make it come out as pretty as he wants it to.

On the next page, he draws Cutler and Big George. He gives them hammers and saws to hold. Cutler's smaller than Big George, made up of tight lines with sharp angles. Big George grows on the page until the top of his head touches the edge.

Page three is for Beecher and his family, followed by Averell, the Reverend, Malvine and then some of the sports. Asel tries to draw his mother and father after that, but can't remember what they look like, so instead he draws Tut, Bobby Vachon and Lillian. Then he does one of Lion and Sal.

When he's done, he goes back to the beginning and starts over, improving each sketch as he goes along. He draws in overalls with suspenders for George and he gives Bobby Vachon a cigarette. He gives Tut a cigar and Beecher a cardigan sweater. Then he draws his mother and father, again settling on shapes with the small details of what he can think up. For his father and mother he decides to include halos and wings because he doesn't know what else to do. They help, but he still isn't content so he sketches in an oak split basket next to his father, taking the time to accurately show how the weave intersects throughout the pattern.

After doing all that he can, he clears the table and lays his pictures out in two rows with the odd one being of his mother and father. That one he sets on top.

He begins to cite relationships, moving pictures around to get them next to the ones they are closest to.

"Beecher is Big George's cousin," he says. "Cutler is Big George's friend. The Reverend is married to Malvine. Bobby Vachon works for Tut. Averell is the son of my mother and father. Lillian is married to Bobby Vachon. Beecher is father to his children." He stops at Beecher and looks at him. Then he says, "Beecher is dead."

Asel looks at his picture. He takes a deep breath and holds on to it so long that he begins to get dizzy. He feels he's going to cry. He stands up and walks the room, holding furniture as he goes, then just touching it as he passes by.

He comes back around to his pictures. He takes up his pencil again and draws a halo and wings for Beecher. He draws them with fine lines, slowly and carefully, in one motion. The picture of the sports lies between the family of Beecher and Averell. Asel spreads his hand out over the face of it, presses down with his fingers and drags it into a crumpled wad of paper that he squeezes until his knuckles go white and the tendons in his arm begin to ache. He lets it fall to the table, where he leaves it.

The rest of the day he spends on the mountain looking down the river valley from inside a blowdown and then falling asleep, his back to a tree. It gets to be time to go home and get supper ready. He will go to the house and keep watch for what he doesn't know but fears must happen soon or he will go crazy. He tells himself to be patient. He tells himself he should leave and fills with hate when he knows he won't.

16

W H E N Asel wakes up, it's morning. The low-angled sun is on his face, bright and warm. Phoebe draped an afghan over him before she left for her last day of school. There's a note pinned to it. He reads, "I love you." It's written three times and at the bottom Phoebe has signed her name. She never wakes him when he's sleeping.

"Sesame Street" is on. Ernie is trying to put one over on Bert. Mr. Rogers will be on in a little while. When he first saw Fred Rogers he didn't trust him, but now he has come to feel safe around him. He's come to like him. He likes to lie back in his chair, close his eyes and listen to the man's voice.

Sometimes he watches Phil Donohue. He thinks Phil knows more than he lets on, but by no means as much as he thinks. He finds himself explaining stuff to Phil. Lately he turns off the sound and does Phil's voice for him. He says things like, "Now, I'm not the smartest person in the world. In fact, I can be pretty ignorant, but the thought of one man sleeping with another man. Well, I just can't imagine it."

When Mr. Rogers is over, it's hard for Asel to get up. He feels like he wants to go back to sleep, but he figures he's already slept for three or four hours and it's time to get going. He's hiking to Keene with his basket money, to buy presents for Phoebe and surprise her on her last day of school.

He washes up and brushes his teeth. He trims his beard with the razor Phoebe uses on her legs and then puts on the clothes she got him for Christmas. He puts together a day pack and checks his gun.

The sun is up and he can feel it on his head as he hikes the road out of the hollow. In the air is the smell of cowshit. To his left, a quarter mile away, he can see a tractor and spreader. The bucket on the front-end loader raised straight over the cab and the back wheels spinning around send a rooster tail of mud up behind them. The tractor isn't moving. Bobby Vachon is bent over next to the wheel, shoveling away in front of it.

The barn is a shorter walk so Asel goes there first to find Tut. He walks through the aisles and into the milk house that went out of use when Tut built the parlor. He's standing on the loading dock when Asel gets there, looking across the meadow, where he can see the whole show. Asel doesn't know what to say so he tells him what's happening in the meadow as if they can't see it from where they are.

"I know what he's doing," Tut says. "I told him to. If you can get those wheels to bite just a little, she'll pop right out of there. Then she lugs down for a second and the load catches and that's when you jump on. I didn't tell him that part, though, so if we're lucky, he'll jump when she surges and get run over and killed."

Asel smiles and waits for Tut to do the same, but he doesn't, so Asel walks away.

"You and me should talk sometime," Tut says, still looking out onto the meadow, but Asel doesn't reply. He keeps on walking.

B Y the time Asel gets to Keene, it's cool and feels like spring again. Caddis flies are somewhere between larvae and wing. They're in stones, sand, water and grass. The earliest ones will die when it turns to night, but for now the season has set in again and, with the rush of waters, it's as if snow can be heard melting out from under itself.

His first stop is at the Hair Plant on Water Street. He stands outside the door and looks in. Someone has painted the picture of a woman with a bouquet of flowers for a hairdo. Asel reads the black lettering on the window, PERMANENT WAVING, HAIR COLORING, FROSTING AND HAIR LIGHTEN-ING, HENNA, REDKEN, ZOTOS, NATURAL MAN. This is the place he wants, so he goes inside.

A young girl sits at the desk doing her nails.

"Do you have an appointment?" she says.

Asel stands with his hands folded in front of him. He feels his clothes to be rough and unkempt in this place of stainless steel, ceramic tiles and Formica.

"No I don't. I'd like to buy something for a friend. A hair clip. A nice one. Maybe two or three."

The girl points to a cardboard with hair clips held to it by elastics.

"Those are tortoiseshell. They're really nice. What color is her hair?"

"It's black, but when the light hits it, it takes on different colors."

Asel takes one from the top row and sets it on the counter.

"She says our water is hard and it hurts her hair."

"Oh yeah, tell me about it. Mine's ruined. You take some of this. It's a Redken product. It really helps."

Asel pays the girl and goes out the door. When he gets on the sidewalk, he puts the package inside his pack. He then starts down Main Street. He has other stops to make and it's already noon.

A family of small people walk past him. They're what looks to be kids, a mother and a grandmother. The mother is pushing a steel shopping cart and it's loaded with bags. Each one of them looks up into his face as they go by. The kids are all wearing some kind of plastic headgear, like hockey players do, only these have weaponry attached to tops and sides. After they pass, Asel turns to look at them. They've stopped too and they're looking at him. He waves and walks away.

The bloodmobile is parked by the Salvation Army. Asel stops to watch. It seems to make the people happy to give blood. He thinks that if he has time, he'll come back and give them a pint in someone else's name. Giving is something Mr. Rogers talks about.

Asel finds the place he's looking for, Goulds Pumps and Water Systems, Chester Gayman Plumbing and Heating. Inside, he asks the man what can be done about hard water. The man tells him to thaw it out, but when Asel doesn't laugh, he goes into an explanation about dissolved rock turned into calcium by hot water. Soap products turn it into a real mess, bathtub ring and film on the skin. Dry and brittle hair falling out of your head. Asel asks him how much he gets for a rig and the man tells him he doesn't sell them, he rents them. Asel takes a brochure and leaves. This one he'll have to talk over with Phoebe. It was going to be his best surprise.

Asel crosses the street and goes into the Crystal Restaurant. He sits down in the Thoreau Room and the waitress comes over with water and a menu. She calls him honey. He tells her he wants french fries and two hot dogs with mustard, relish and onions.

"Two dogs," the waitress says, "run 'em through the garden."

"Yes," he says, "run 'em through the garden. A beer too. A Budweiser. And celery salt if you have it."

Asel drinks his beer down and orders another one when she brings him his food. He puts salt and vinegar on his fries, then gently rolls each hot dog until the toppings fall down into the bun. He sits the hot dog back on top. He figured this out as a way to keep his beard clean even though he still gets mustard on his moustache.

Asel enjoys his food. Phoebe doesn't like to eat hot dogs and french fries, so they don't have it in the house that much. From where he is, he can see the bloodmobile still across the street. When the waitress comes back with the check, he asks her if she gave blood yet. She gives him a strange look at first, but then figures out what he's talking about.

"Oh no," she says, "I've been on medication and it's not out of my system yet. I think you're out of luck, though, after drinking that beer. Unless you already gave."

"No I didn't, but I was going to."

"Try again tomorrow, honey," she says, patting his shoulder and then leaving to attend to another customer. Mr.

Rogers didn't say anything about not drinking beer before you gave blood. Asel thinks that his big day is going to hell. Not too much has worked out for him. He drinks another beer at the bar and leaves.

At the corner is Miranda's Veranda, a store with ladies' wear. Asel stops and looks in the window. He can't see customers, so he goes inside.

"Hi," the woman behind the counter says. Asel looks at her. It's Beverley. She's wearing a long-sleeved blouse, the right arm folded back and held with a safety pin. "You're Phoebe's husband, aren't you."

"Yes, I am," Asel says, smiling and nodding his head, not wanting to explain they're not really married.

"You two make such a cute couple. She just radiates. I'm happy for the two of you."

"Thank you," Asel says.

"How are she and Tut getting along? Is he speaking to her?"

"Yes. They are doing fine," Asel tells her.

"That's good, because between you and me, he can be a real bastard if he wants to. I can't complain, because he treated me like a daughter, but I tell you, he can be a real bastard."

"There's trouble sometimes, but it usually blows over."

"Well, I'll tell you. He was a real shit to her after her mother died. He's one man you just can't read."

Asel looks at where her arm should be. The sleeve of her blouse is folded up to her elbow in neat tucks. He feels sorry for her and then thinks he shouldn't be so foolish about it. He looks at her other arm. Her wrist and hand are strong. For a moment he thinks he'd like to hold hands with her, maybe kiss her on the forehead. He figures it's the three Budweisers he had for lunch.

"My son does it for me in the morning. It's something that's pretty important to him, folding Mom's sleeves. He's my baby."

"Is your husband still in Houston?"

"Yes he is and you know what? We're better off, a lot better off. I get checks every month, insurance checks and government checks, and he's not around to drink them up. It's awful to say. I don't know why I'm telling you all this."

Asel smiles and shrugs his shoulders. He tries to put on a little boy's appearance and this makes her laugh.

"I'd like to get something for Phoebe. Something special."

Beverley's eyes go bright and she gives him a big smile.

"I'll tell you what I'd like you to get me if you were my man. Come with me."

She leads him to the back of the store where the lingerie is. She begins taking things off the racks and holding them up to herself and then handing them to Asel. She tells him she's the same size as Phoebe and any of these things will fit her.

"I think we're a little different in the bust, but not much. This is a camisole and these are matching tap pants. This is a chemise. I really like the teal, and take this too. It's a silk teddy. It has the oriental paisley print. And this is real neat. It's a bustier. It's real popular in Europe."

Asel's hands fill up with clothes, but they don't weigh anything. He catches a look at price tags and knows he's going to have to put most of the stuff back.

"It'll be a real trip, when she wears these under her school clothes. It'll give her a real rush."

"I don't have enough money," Asel says. "I could get maybe one of these for her."

Beverley puts her hand on Asel's arm. She tightens her grip and looks up at him. "I don't want anything," she says. "I want you to have these."

Asel starts to speak, but she gives his arm a shake. "A lot's happened. Things have been fucked up for a long time. What goes around, comes around. Let me wrap these."

Beverley takes the clothes to the counter. She snips the tags and then with a quick move folds them into a box, her hand traveling lightly, doing a better job than most two-

handed people. She sets the cover and tapes it. She hands
Asel his parcel and after he takes it she reaches up to the
back of his neck and pulls him down to where she can give
him a kiss and then she asks him if he ever thought about
getting an earring. She tells him he'd look great with one and
that he should think about it.

A S E L walks into the school building. A janitor tells him
which room is Phoebe's. He goes there and looks in the
doorway. She's reading them a story. When she sees her
students staring off over her shoulder, she turns too and sees
him standing there. They all look at him for a long time until
the bell rings.

"That's it," Phoebe says. "Time to go home. Make sure
you remember everything. And don't forget, have a *great*
summer."

While the kids are getting their lunch boxes and jackets,
Phoebe goes to him.

"What're you doing here?"

"I came to surprise you," he says, but he knows he's made
a mistake.

"You've been drinking," she says.

Asel looks at her. He doesn't understand why she is so
upset with him. It doesn't seem fair. He turns away to
the kids, who are sneaking looks at him while finishing the
job of emptying their desks of papers, pencil boxes and
crayons.

"They know who you are," she says. "They talk about
you all the time. They talk about the man who walks in the
woods."

"I'm sorry. I didn't know."

"Here are my keys. Please go to the car and wait for me."

"I didn't know."

W H E N they get home, Phoebe cooks ribs on the grill. She makes a three-bean salad and does up a pan of steak fries. She doesn't let Asel help.

"I owe you an apology," she says while they're eating. "I get scared when things happen that're out of the ordinary. I think I was afraid something was wrong."

"What is it they say about me?"

"They say you found the woman in the tree. That you saved her life. You're a great hunter and fisherman. They want to know about everything you do. Your story grows and is passed down through the grades. I ignored it for a long time, but now when they ask, I make up stories to tell them. I say they're not true, only made up and of course that makes them believe all the more."

Asel goes back to his food and Phoebe does the same. They finish eating and then he washes the dishes while she cleans up. He stands at the sink and she keeps reaching around him and sliding dishes and silverware into the water. One time she stops and presses against him. She says, "I know you did it for me even if you didn't."

Later, when it's dark, he shows her the things he got for her and she realizes why he came to Keene. She tells him how foolish she feels.

He tells her, no, not to feel that way and then he makes her try on her new clothes.

"You look beautiful," he says, and she smiles. Then he says, "How do you think I'd look with an earring?"

"I think you'd look great, but we have to figure out which ear. One means one thing and the other means another thing."

"Oh," Asel says, "I didn't know that. We'll have to make sure we get it right."

"Yes we will," she says, and they both laugh.

17

P H O E B E   and Lillian plunge their arms into the hot water of the stainless-steel basin. They cup handfuls of it and draw it up to their shoulders, rinsing off what's left from milking, the black and white hairs, the shit and piss, the sticky milk and the brown teat dip that has run down the backs of their hands.

Outside they hear the clatter of a thirty-two-foot skeleton elevator, lifting the bales of hay into the mows. The boys yell, "Faster, keep them coming," and then a minute later, they yell, "Slow down, you crazy son of a bitch! What are you trying to do, kill us?"

The women hose off their rubber aprons and hang them by the door. They step outside into the dusk. A half mile away they can see a caravan of farm implements coming up from the meadow. Tut leads with the big Ford, pulling the baler and a hayrack, half full. Bobby Vachon is next on the 5000 with a rake and Asel follows on the 7000 with two loaded racks jouncing along behind him. The falling dew makes the tires wet and shiny. The night is coming fast. Phoebe can feel it through the wetness of her T-shirt.

The boys bucking hay into the mow are almost finished. The one working the load is the Highway Preacher, at least that's what it says on the side of his black station wagon. He showed up two days ago and asked for work. He said he was from Keene but none of them had ever heard of him. Tut told him he could give him work but not money. "Work I have," he told the Highway Preacher, "but money I don't."

The Highway Preacher told Tut that was quite all right and that he'd share in whatever was most abundant. This made him the ideal hired hand in Tut's mind. Tut let him park his wagon behind the barn and provided him with a horse blan-

ket. Lillian took it upon herself to feed him his three squares
a day, for which Tut gave her extra money.

The elevator shuts down. Two high school boys come skittering down its frame to the ground.

"Now, you lads come back in the morning and we'll unload
the last three racks then," the Highway Preacher says.

One of the boys is Rodney. His father has been sick for
a long time. He works because the family needs the money.
Tut always gives him a little extra. The other boy is one of
his classmates. The Highway Preacher takes them to be his
crew, though both know more about bucking hay than he
does.

Rodney looks at Phoebe and then looks away, dropping
his head.

"Now, Rodney, why don't you ever look me in the eyes?"
Phoebe says, putting her hands on her hips.

"Just shy, I guess," he says.

"Now tell me, how's your father? Have you been down
to see him?"

"No I haven't. Alvin went and so did Gloria."

"You better go see him. You may not have many more
chances."

"I know it. It'll be my luck that he'll die during Cheshire
Fair and we won't get to go."

Rodney's friend laughs at him so he slaps him on the back
of the head. They both run for their bicycles, jump on them
and begin the race home.

"Preacher, you go to the house and get cleaned up for
supper. We'll help get the tarp over the rack," Lillian says,
giving him a strong enough push to get him on his way.

"You go too, Lilly, and then you come back to the house
for supper," Phoebe tells her. "Bring some tomatoes."

Lillian hesitates for a bit. She has never sat down to Tut's
table.

Phoebe watches her go trundling off to her house, her

breasts like giant sacks on her chest. Phoebe loves her, maybe more than any other woman she knows. She'd been Phoebe's wet nurse when Phoebe was born. She'd raised her as her own the first years, but Tut put a stop to it the day Phoebe snuck out of the house and crossed the highway to the barn to see her. Tut went into a rage and banished Lillian from the farm. He didn't let her come back until years later and when he did, it was only because she had a son who could work.

Lillian often goes loony. She's convinced that animals in the woods are out to get her. She claims fisher-cats run up her clothesline and try to jump on the roof so they can get down the chimney. When she goes wacky, she locks the doors and windows and turns up the heat. It gets so hot at times they worry the house will go up from spontaneous combustion. Fortunately she's been pretty sane lately. The only thing she does do is save her hair in shopping bags. She has three of them, Bobby Vachon claims. She keeps them by the bed.

Phoebe goes back inside the milk house and finds a shirt. It's one of Asel's. She puts it on and rolls up the sleeves. She pulls the front together and knots it at her stomach. Back outside the roar of the cavalcade becomes all she can hear.

They pull into the drive, swinging to the right as they run parallel to the barn. Each tractor sits side by side with their trains of equipment stretched out behind them. They idle down and cut the power.

The haying is over and Tut is happy. His face is black with dust and grease. There are watermarks across his forehead and under his eyes. He looks at Phoebe and smiles. His dentures are white and his eyes show pleasure.

Bobby Vachon and Asel come over to help him get down. He reaches out so they can take his arms, all the while telling them to get the hell away from him and leave him alone because he doesn't need any of their help.

Asel goes to Phoebe and gives her a hug. She lets him lift

her off her feet. His beard is soft against her neck. After he
puts her down, she makes him bend over so she can brush
the flecks of alfalfa and dust from his hair.

They'd planned on traveling this summer, but Tut asked
them to help on the farm and they both agreed to, a decision
neither has regretted.

Bobby Vachon and Tut begin to yell at each other.

"You wouldn't have hurt your goddamn hand if you'd been
just a little patient," Tut says.

Bobby Vachon tries to speak, but he can't. Rage has come
up from his heart and he can only whip his hand in the air
and make the half sounds of words.

"What's that all about?" Phoebe asks Asel.

"The baler plugged and Bobby had to crawl inside. Tut
hit the PTO by mistake and Bobby got some skin ripped off
the back of his hand. He's lucky to be alive."

Phoebe turns on the two of them.

"You two stop it," she says.

"Don't yell at me," Tut says. "If he knew how to rake hay,
it never would have happened."

Phoebe holds Bobby's hand. A flap of skin from his wrist
to his knuckles has been peeled away. It's black with dirt and
clotted blood.

"Go get it cleaned up," she tells him, "and then you and
Lillian and the Highway Preacher are to come over to the
house."

Bobby walks away, dragging his feet close to the ground
in the same rolling gait as Lillian.

"You two go in the milk house and wash yourselves off
after you get the hay covered. Lillian and Bobby and the
Highway Preacher are coming over for supper."

Tut starts to speak, but Phoebe holds up her hand.

"No," she says. "Go wash up and then come to the house."

Asel and Tut watch her go. Then the two of them heave
tarps to the top of each rack. Asel climbs up the sides and
rolls them out. When the straps drop down, Tut hooks them

on the bottom boards. Asel shimmies back down and the men go to the milk house.

They rinse off their upper bodies and find dry shirts. Tut checks the milk gauge and seems satisfied, so they go to the house.

Trays of food are already set out on the picnic table. They are party trays, the kind the grocery store puts together. There're cold cuts, cheeses, vegetables and potato chips. There's a basket full of rolls next to it and tubs of slaw and potato salad.

Tut and Asel sit down. They make thick sandwiches and slather them with mayonnaise and mustard. They take handfuls of chips and pickles and begin to eat. Phoebe comes out with a pitcher of lemonade.

Bobby Vachon, Lillian and the Highway Preacher are coming across the road. Phoebe waves and tells them they'd better hurry up before it's all gone. Bobby Vachon has on his red-and-white-checked western shirt with pearl buttons. His hand is wrapped in a white bandage. Lillian wears a lime green pants suit and the Highway Preacher has on a fresh white shirt that he wears buttoned at the collar. Each one carries a sack.

"Lilly, I love your outfit," Phoebe says. "Sit down. Sit down and start in."

Lillian hands her sack of tomatoes over to Phoebe.

"They're Beefsteaks," she says. "They're a little ingrown but they're still good. They say the strain is going out of them. I'll have to change next year."

"Strain's going out of everything," Tut says, his mouth full of sandwich.

The other two sacks contain six-packs of Black Label. It's cold. Phoebe passes them around. Asel hesitates, but Tut tells him to go ahead. He says he believes he'll have one too.

"God dammit," Tut says, "if we're going to eat together, we're going to enjoy it."

"Oh shut up," Lillian tells him. "We're doing fine."

"Good enough, then. Just don't crunch on those goddamn potato chips. If there's one thing I can't stand, it's the noise they make in people's mouths."

They finish their meal in silence. No one touches the bag of potato chips and they all leave what's left of them on their plates except for the Highway Preacher. He seems to have a knack for letting them get soft in his mouth and then swallowing them. Tut gets up from the bench and goes to his chaise lounge. He stretches out and lights a cigar. The rest of them settle back and breathe in the smoke that rises from it.

"Bobby," Tut says softly. "How's your hand?"

"It'll be all right."

"I cut up an old diaper I found in the rag box and made a compress," Lillian says.

Tut nods his head and smiles. Phoebe reaches out to the tray. She picks up a slice of ham and dangles it between her thumb and forefinger. The Highway Preacher passes another round of beer to everyone. Outside the land is wet with dew and pockets of it rise in the air and hover off the ground. Fireflies torch up their rear ends, bringing small green lights to the evening.

"It's just like the old days, Tut," Lillian says, but Tut doesn't answer. He rolls his cigar between his fingers and thumb, moving it around just inside his lips.

"What were the old days like?" the Highway Preacher says.

"Teams of men," she says. "Big meals that come out of one kettle. Cooking all day and then laying plates out on planks for tables. Big crews. All of it done by hand."

"There sure were some beauts," Tut says.

"I remember Perley White," Phoebe says. "He was afraid of cats. He said they attacked him, so one day I was in the barn walking behind him and two of them sprang out and jumped on him. It was the funniest thing I ever saw."

"Perley White used to be Lillian's man," Tut says. "He was Bobby's father, weren't he, Lillian?"

"Hear you talk like that. No he weren't and if you don't take it back, I'm leaving right now."

Phoebe puts her hand over Lillian's. The woman turns and looks at her. Phoebe sees how hurt she is.

"He didn't mean it, Lilly. He's only trying to cause trouble."

"I don't know why he likes to hurt people so," she whispers.

"Hey, Tut, what about that Freddy Chibeault fellow?" Bobby says.

"Jesus," Tut says. "Now Highway Preacher, there's a story for you. That man was the best breeder I ever knew. Every time a cow'd come in heat down at the county farm, they'd send out an all-points bulletin to have him arrested. That's a fact. Finally he went off the deep end. He cut a cow's head off with a chain saw right in the stanchion."

"I didn't know that," Bobby says, holding his bandaged hand up in front of his face so he can study it. "What kind of chain saw was it?"

"I believe it was one of those Swedish saws, a Husqvarna or a Jonsered."

"I could see a Jonsered, but I don't know as I'd try it with a Husqvarna."

Tut takes a puff from what is left of his cigar and then throws it out onto the lawn. They watch the small ember burn and smoke in front of them until it goes black with moisture. Tut pulls at his face with his left hand, rubbing hard from his forehead to his chin.

"That's the last of the hay," he says, staring out at the black mountain that looms up behind the calf barn.

"We did well this year," Phoebe says. She looks at Asel and smiles. He reaches over and takes her hand.

"It's the last," Tut says again. "The very last."

The rest of them are quiet. They want to ask him what he means by the very last. They don't push, though, because they know it won't get them any more than he's already said, but they know he meant more by it. Even the Highway Preacher knows he's stepped into one of the seams in the lives of these people.

"Asel and I saw Kurt over in Harrisville last winter. Remember him?" Phoebe says.

"I sure do," Bobby Vachon says. "He still owes me forty-seven dollars."

"He was the one who lived in that station wagon up behind the iron kettle, wasn't he?"

"Yes, he was," Bobby Vachon says. "One day they showed up as black as soot. They blew an oil seal and the thing spewed all over them. It didn't have a hood or a windshield, you know."

"I think he was the one who sugared my gas tank," the Highway Preacher says.

"She's a good girl," Tut says.

They all smile and settle back down. Night has come. The red sumac have turned black and the separate stems of goldenrod are now shadows beside the barn.

Tut speaks up in a voice so soft and hollow they have trouble hearing him.

"Kurty and another boy drowned last winter when their ice shanty sunk into Silver Lake. I guess they were pretty drunk at the time." Tut pauses for a second and then sits up. "I'm going to bed, but you people can stay if you want."

18

A MONTH later Bobby Vachon comes to the door and asks for Phoebe. It's late, past everyone's bedtime. She gets up and the two of them step outside.

"It's the old man," he tells her. "He's up there crying tonight. He's got himself stuck in a chair. He says he can't move and he wants you."

Phoebe looks up at Asel. He's standing in the doorway with a book in his hand that he holds against his chest.

"Go ahead. He needs you."

She smiles at him and then grabs her coat. She goes out the door and gets in her car. She leaves the two men standing on the step. The sound of her car disappears when she clears the knoll, but they can still see the lights, bobbing in the night. When they go out of sight, Asel walks back inside and Bobby Vachon follows him.

"Hadn't you better go too?"

"I probably should, but Lillian's there and between them they should be able to handle him. When I'm around, he takes it out on me."

"Has it happened often?"

"About twice a week lately, but this is the first time he's asked for her."

Bobby Vachon goes back to the door. He swings open the screen and looks up the road.

"He'll have my ass now," he says.

"What's the matter?"

"He wanted me to tell her he said she was a peach, and I forgot to."

"What do you mean, a peach?"

"I don't know. It was just something he wanted me to tell her. He said make sure I don't forget."

Bobby Vachon sits down at the table. He picks up Phoebe's

cassette player. He turns it over in his hands, looking intently at the buttons and the small lettering next to them. Then he sets it back down. "He'll have to tell her himself. He probably will too, when he sees her."

"What's the matter with him?"

"Nothing. He just can't do what he used to do. He lames up and can't move. It bothers him. He doesn't like to be outstripped by anyone, especially me."

Asel goes to the faucet. He runs water into the urn that goes to the coffee maker. He then pours it down into the machine and fills the basket with Maxwell House.

"You want coffee?" he says.

"No. I just had some."

Asel nods and sits down where Phoebe usually sits. He puts his elbows on top of her magazines and stares at Bobby. He has trouble figuring out how old he is. His eyes are those of a young man but his face has a permanent burn left by the wind, sun and cold.

The two men sit there without talking and Bobby picks up the cassette player again. Asel knows he wants to try it, but he doesn't say anything. The coffee maker begins to hiss and gurgle, pushing hot water through the tube and letting it sprinkle into the basket. It sets up a steady stream into the pitcher. It is black and the aroma floats out to mix with the rich smell of cowshit and ensilage that comes off Bobby Vachon's clothes.

When the coffee is done, Asel pours out two cups. He sets one in front of Bobby and takes the other for himself. They drink it slowly, holding the cups not by the handles but with their hands wrapped around them, a habit that men who spend time outdoors pick up. The cups are warm in their hands. They even hold them when they're on the table, under their chins, so the steam will come up into their faces.

"I'm afraid that if he don't get off it, he's going to kill himself."

"People kill themselves," Asel says, trying to make it sound like a question, but in the end knowing that it doesn't because Bobby looks up at him and then takes a sip of his coffee.

"Sure they do. People kill themselves all the time."

"Why do you think they do?"

"I figure it's none of my business."

Asel fills the cups again. He thinks about the woman he found in the tree. He tries as hard as he can to think of her as not being beautiful, but he can't. He sits back down across from Bobby. He holds his cup in his left hand and holds the wrist of that hand in his other one, expecting to feel the rope bracelet that has long since gone.

The knot came undone in the woods and it fell away. He didn't realize it was gone until he got home and he didn't go back to look for it.

He now holds his wrist until he gets back the feel of it and then he lets it go. He wonders about Rodney, the boy who made it for him. He realizes how often Phoebe has traced the bare spot across his artery with the tip of her finger.

"I'm her brother, you know," Bobby Vachon says, looking into his cup.

"No I didn't. What's that like?"

"Tut denies me, but I know he's my father."

"How long have you been her brother?"

Bobby Vachon looks at the ceiling. He cocks his head and closes one eye. Asel can see him moving his lips as he tries to compute the number of years. Finally he looks at Asel.

"Only since I've known," he says.

"How long is that?"

"Ever since my father died. Not that I knew then, but when he died, Tut used to come over to the house. He was good to my mother and to us kids. It was after Tut's wife died. They'd send us up to bed and then sit in the kitchen. We could see them from the staircase. We'd roost there like a bunch of birds and watch them. We couldn't hear what they said but we could see their mouths move and he'd touch her across the table until her head went back and her mouth would hang open. Her eyelids looked soft as if you could reach out and they'd feel like an animal's when you touched them."

"How does that make him your father?"

"One time we could hear them and he asked her how his boy was. They all looked at me because I'd come out different. That was the last time I watched them and then later when my mother moved away, she left me behind. She told me he'd come for me."

Asel listens to his story. He doesn't know why but he believes it's true. He wants to leave this place where people are trying to get ahead a little bit. He thinks that he will leave Phoebe here with her family and take whatever awaits him down the road to another town and when it's done, he'll come back if he can. It would be for everybody's good. He laughs at himself and it gives him courage. He looks up at Bobby. He has the earphones on and is playing the song "Easy from Now On." He's smiling and his eyes are closed.

T U T sits in the grain room. He's in a lawn chair, his weight leaned over on one hip. His face is red and bloated. It's wet and his bottom lip covers the top one. Phoebe stands with one hand on his shoulder. She looks out the door. It fills with the red brightness of taillights as Lillian backs in the pickup.

"She's here," Phoebe says gently, reaching her hand under his arm and lifting.

Tut pushes himself up and stands there. He doesn't move until he feels Lillian take his other arm. They direct him to the tailgate, where he hikes one leg, catching the edge under his buttock. Both women then move to his other side and lift the rest of him onto it. His eyes are closed so tight that his cheeks are almost drawn up into his eyebrows. Phoebe hops on next to him. She holds the tailgate chain in one hand and pulls him to her with the other. Lillian gets in the cab

and drives them to the house. She backs across the lawn to
the front door and then shuts down the engine.

They help Tut out onto the piazza, where he has a daybed.
Lillian tells Phoebe that Tut had it screened in so he wouldn't
have to climb the stairs at night. His eyes are still closed.

Phoebe steps back and looks at him. Lillian has him on his
stomach with a pillow under his middle.

"Is she still here?"

"She's right here," Lillian tells him.

That seems to make him feel better, but he doesn't open
his eyes. He lifts his head and tucks his arm under it.

"I'll make some tea," Phoebe says to Lillian.

"You do that, honey, and I'll get him into bed."

Phoebe walks through the house, turning on lights as she
goes. Antimacassars rest on the backs of chairs, stained yellow
from the heads of sleeping men that have lain against them.
She gets to the kitchen and finds the tea where she always
remembered it to be. She puts the water on to boil and then
she stops for a second and listens. Lillian must have switched
on the intercom. The house fills with sounds from the barn.
She hears water surging into buckets. A cow coughs and
another one stands up. She can even hear the swish of tails
as they snap at flies.

There are dishes in the sink. The cups and saucers are ones
they used when she was younger and lived at home. There's
a griddle with batter caked to its edges and a plate, sticky
with syrup. Phoebe runs water into the sink and then washes
them. On this night she is surprised at how small the basin
is and how easily she can reach everything.

When she's finished she stands with her hands in the warm
water letting the feel of it rise to her elbows. The pot on the
stove whistles so she pulls the stopper and lets the dishwater
swirl down the drain. She watches it sweeping to the right
and remembers telling her students how water does that in
this hemisphere. Before she gets the teapot, she reaches into
the sink and stirs the water back against itself, changing the

direction of the vortex. The new motion takes hold and it disappears down the drain in a way it doesn't usually go.

Phoebe carries the teapot and cups to the piazza. When she gets to the doorway, she stops and watches Tut and Lillian. He's now on his back and naked from the waist down. His legs are spread wide and in between there is almost nothing left. His skin is mottled in reds and grays. Lillian is rubbing bag balm from his knees to his crotch and out to his hips. His head is back and his eyes are still closed. The smell of menthol and eucalyptus is in the air. Lillian sings to him a song that Phoebe can't make out. She lolls her head on her neck in rhythm with her hand, the sounds of the cows in the background.

"Is she here?" Tut says.

"Yes, it's her. It's your Phoebe," Lillian tells him.

"Ask her for me."

Lillian looks up at Phoebe and smiles at her.

"Don't be afraid," she says. "He's old and he's getting more so every day. He loves you and he respects your man."

"What does he want?"

"He wants to see your hair. He talks about it quite a bit. He hasn't seen it since you left to go away."

Phoebe walks into the center of the piazza. She sets the tray down in a chair. She looks out through the screens in the direction where she knows Asel is. Moths tick and bat against tightly woven strands, threads of steel. She imagines she sees the phosphorescent glow of a lightning bug somewhere in the night. Its luminosity grows as she reaches to the back of her head for the butterfly clip that holds it all up. She squeezes the wings together, releasing its grip and letting her hair cascade to the floor.

"It's down, isn't it," Tut says, his eyes still closed.

"Yes it is," Lillian tells him.

Tut lies there, not moving. He breathes slowly and evenly, his white belly moving under the tails of his shirt. He now has his forearm across his eyes.

"It's beautiful, isn't it."

"Yes it is. It's the most beautiful hair you can imagine," Lillian says, looking up and down its length, her mouth open and her eyes almost shut.

Phoebe smiles at them and then takes her hair up in her arms. She cradles it and comes to believe what her father said years ago when he told her that her mother left him months before she was born.

T H E   room is dark. Asel sits in his chair by the bed and Phoebe stands next to him. Her body is blue in the light that comes through the window.

"I need you to love me," she says.

"I do," he tells her. "I do."

"I want my own children. I want them with you."

"We will," he tells her. "Soon."

19

P H O E B E wakes up to the shrill sound of cicadas already vibrating the morning air. The dew is burning off the meadows and hanging heavy up and down the valley. She can smell the hay that someone down the river mowed yesterday and that would need tetting in a few hours. Phoebe pulls on a dressing gown and goes to find Asel. He's in the kitchen drawing rawhide through the frame of a snowshoe. One he completed during the night is on the kitchen table. He's just now finishing the tail on this one.

His hands are orange and smell of hide. Phoebe holds one to her face and kisses the palm.

"What's for breakfast?" she says.

"I don't know. Coffee and something else."

"I'll cook you pancakes," she says, going to the cupboard for the mix.

Asel looks up from his work. When she stands in the light, he can see her moving inside her gown and he smiles because he knows he's seen it before. His hands work the rawhide into patterns of diamonds and triangles while he watches Phoebe mix the batter.

"What are you staring at?" she says.

"You. Do you think Tut will be all right? Maybe we should spend the day up there. Bobby Vachon started knocking down hay again."

"Not today. He has the Highway Preacher and the boys to help. We've been up there a lot. Besides, you and me have a date today."

Asel tries to remember what he agreed to, but he can't. It's been a long summer for them. They spent most of it up to the farm, where they worked all day, and then at night they'd walk through the woods to Sheep Rock, take their clothes off and slide into the brook water, so cold their tanned bodies went pink.

Asel mops at his brow and beard. Phoebe turns around and looks at him.

"Today is Old Home Day and we're going. We missed the Firemen's Barbecue and the Strawberry Social. We're not missing Old Home Day."

"What's Old Home Day?"

Phoebe tells him how every year the town holds a special day to welcome back its sons and daughters.

"We haven't been since we moved back and I want to go. I want you to come too."

T H E sons and daughters have been coming back the third Saturday in August since 1900. Phoebe and Asel set aside the whole day. In the morning they go to the horse show and skeet shoot. Then the parade and the ball game where the married men play the single men. The men play hardball but some of the newer people want to switch to softball and some of them want to cancel it altogether in favor of water soccer, using fire hoses. One of them even suggested that women play, but more temperate heads prevailed and it's hardball, married men against single men.

A guy shows up with an aluminum bat. The men stand around admiring it and then they make him put it back in his car. The high point of the game is when the left fielder for the married men dives after a ball and dislocates his shoulder. The injury gets blamed on sobriety, a condition that must be remedied because he's supposed to be Mortimer in the play that evening. Everyone offers to help.

Late afternoon the old-timers gather under the oak tree next to the red brick church. They tell stories about the Old Home Day parades of '32, '41, and '52. Three of them were George Washington and two of them Marthas. One was a

Negro footman and a group of them were Abenaki Indians. Some were soldiers and some danced the minuet for six miles from the depot into town. The Negro footman has been catching shit for over fifty years now.

A T seven-thirty, Phoebe and Asel take seats in the balcony of the town hall for the first one-act play. The people fan themselves with programs but it doesn't stop the sweat that soaks the fronts and backs of shirts. Asel rests a hand on his jeans pocket where he carries a small 9mm Iver and Johnson, something he has taken to in hot weather. There are six rows between him and the back wall. They're filled with young kids, some sitting stiffly, some holding sweaty hands and others kissing. The braver ones are still up at the ball field sneaking beer and sharing a joint.

The first play is about Mortimer and Evangeline. The ball-player comes on in a nightshirt, his arm and shoulder trussed tightly against his body. Evangeline is batty over the lightning that's being produced offstage. She tells Mortimer he should be ashamed of himself for not sharing her concern. When he wants to know how a man can be ashamed when he's asleep, everyone laughs, the men nodding their heads to confirm the question and the women shaking theirs over how preposterous it is. A hayseed comes in to find out what the brouhaha is all about. He tells them he only wants relevant details and salient facts, but he screws up the line and the audience laughs again. When the laughter dies down, he tells Mortimer—who's standing on a chair with his galoshes on and an umbrella over his head—that it's only the cannon going off to mark the country's centennial. Evangeline has the last word but nobody hears it because they're all laughing so hard.

Asel stiffens as he feels a hand on his shoulder. He smells the sweetness of whiskey and antiseptic.

"Asel," a voice whispers, inches from his ear. "Don't move. Listen to me."

Asel feels the hand tighten and then it goes weak. It rests there, the tips of the finger hooked against his clavicle to keep from sliding off.

"Wait ten minutes after I leave and then meet me behind the town hall, next to the firehouse."

Asel sits back in his chair. He knows it's Averell. There's something wrong, but he feels a contentment come over him. Knowing Averell is alive diminishes the threat that has surrounded him for so long.

He waits ten minutes and then tells Phoebe he has to take a leak. He kisses her cheek, letting his hand slide up her leg. She pushes him away and smiles.

"Hurry back," she says, "the next one is about two sets of twins, a case of mistaken identity."

Asel makes his way down the back stairs and out into the night. He stands next to one of the huge white columns that holds the portico roof over thirty feet in the air. Across the street on the common he sees the old people still sitting in lawn chairs. There's a couple holding hands near the war monument and some of the men who shot skeet and played ball are standing just out of the light, drinking beer. He wants to stop and join them, learn their names and something about their families. He wants to ask the pitcher how he's able to make the ball curve the way he does. He knows he can't do any of these things right now, but sometime soon.

He goes to where the cars and trucks are parked. He jumps the culvert and stands with his back to the cinderblock wall of the firehouse. Voices carry to him in the night, snatches of laughter and conversation. To his right he sees the glow of a cigarette cupped in a hand. It's Averell standing next to a tree, a green felt hat pulled low on his head. He walks to the other side and stands with his back against it.

"Where did you go to?" Asel says.

"It's a long story, boy. To put it simple, I got home one day from rendezvous and there was a big truck loading out all my gear and furniture. Seems the bills hadn't been paid.

The bookkeeper spent all my money on farts and whistles. The sheriff wanted to take me too."

"Why didn't you come back for me?"

"There was a couple sports we handled, Roddy and Blaze, two Micks who felt like we had something of theirs. I suppose we did too. They showed up after the sheriff left. I gave 'em the slip, though. From what I'm told, they eventually got taken care of."

Asel makes a move to go around the tree. Averell tries to back around the other way but trips on a root and sprawls out on the ground under the light that comes up from up the street. His face is bloated with blood gone black under his skin. One hand's bandaged and the other is splinted and wrapped.

"Stay back," he says. "Stay back where you are."

Asel keeps going, though. He bends over and grabs him by the front of his shirt. He lifts him to his feet and pulls him in close to the tree, out of the light.

"The boys caught up with me in Worcester a week ago. Not them but their sons. I was working in a Velcro factory. They want what you got and they probably want you too. They sent me up here to flush you out. They know where you are."

Asel holds his brother up. He looks around and then he looks at his face. He can see white whiskers growing in where he couldn't shave. Asel knows he must leave immediately.

"What about you?" Asel says, reaching an arm around Averell's waist, making him groan and lose his breath.

"Easy, boy. The ribs have had a bit of a workout. Let me sit."

Averell goes down on his knees. He rests his hands on his thighs and then he reaches up to his smoke and gets it in the tips of two fingers. When he pulls, though, it sticks on his dry lips, and his fingers slide down to the ash. They stay there for a second until he realizes he's burning them. He lets out a moan and snaps them in the air, making them hurt even more from the breaks.

"I have to go," he says. "I hope I haven't been a Judas coming up here, but you had to be warned."

"Averell, wait."

"What is it, boy? Can't you see what we're into?"

"You can stay with us tonight."

"What are you, foolish? I can't do that. You'd be risking everything you got. It all could go down the tubes. You got something here. You got a good woman and a good family. Someday all that Ol' Tut's got will be yours and hers."

"How do you know all that?"

"I've been asking and them boys'll be doing the same thing. Leave for a while. They aren't interested in these people, but on the other hand, they won't let them get in their way."

"I've known you were coming. I've sensed it for a long time."

"You don't know nothin'. You're a goddamn fool."

"You don't mean that. I know you don't," Asel says, straightening himself and lifting Averell with him, being careful of his busted ribs. "I don't know you. You're my brother and I don't know you. You're not leaving until I do."

"We're all together," Averell tells his brother. "Our mother, she looked like your woman. When I saw you two, it took my breath. Down the side of her face, down her neck and to her shoulder, she looks just like our mother."

Asel starts to speak, but Averell holds his hand up to his brother's mouth. He holds it on his lips and then after a long time he strokes Asel's beard and pats him on the cheek.

"You go get her and bring your car around. I'll come out when you flash the lights."

Asel helps him to the corner of the firehouse, leaning him against the block wall and stepping back to look at his face bathed in the glow of the small red emergency light that's always lit over the side door. Under the low brim of his green

felt hat his eyes are black and purple. His whiskers come out
of his sunken cheeks like quills, elaborately dyed shades of
red and pink and black. With every breath his mouth twists
at the corners from the pain in his ribs.

"Wait," Averell says. He unbuttons his shirt and from inside the bandages he wears around his middle, he takes out
an object wrapped in cloth. "Take this. You might need it."
He thrusts the bundle into Asel's hands and then gives him
a push.

Asel turns, jumps the culvert and runs up the hill. He
walks quietly into the hall and then makes his way up the
back stairs and sits down next to Phoebe. One of the actors
has forgotten his lines and the audience is laughing. Asel sees
that none of the twins look alike. He wonders how people
can be made to believe. One of the men is much older than
his twin and one of the women is not only younger but has
brown hair and weighs twice as much as the other one.

Asel taps Phoebe on the shoulder. She catches his hand
and looks at him. He can see she's frightened and he looks
away, knowing that when he does, it serves to fix the fear in
her mind.

She gets up quietly and follows him down to the car. She
hands him the keys and gets in on the other side. Asel starts
the engine and pulls out onto the road. He swings down the
hill to the firehouse and turns on the lights, flashing them
once and waiting, but Averell doesn't come. He puts the car
in park and goes out behind the firehouse. In the dirt is a
patch of phlegm and blood. He knows deep in his heart he's
been traded in by his brother and he's afraid, not for himself,
but for Averell because he knows the bargain won't be kept.

20

A S E L   takes Phoebe's car that night and drives the back roads north, into the White Mountains and past, pushing on to Errol and crossing the state line at the confluence of the Swift Diamond and Dead Diamond rivers.

On the seat beside him is a Thermos of coffee and the bundle Averell gave him. With his right hand he slowly unwraps it, fold by fold. It's a loaded .44 double-action Redhawk. In the bottom folds are a dozen more shells. He runs his finger along the butt and where the numbers should be, he feels only the groove left by a grindstone. He unholsters the gun he's worn all these years and replaces it with the better one.

The fog drops like a curtain as the lights of the car crest the hills and sweep the trees at each bend. The roads still ripple from the frost that heaved them up winters ago. The fog contains the headlights in its envelope, making them yellow and dull in the gray darkness. The road runs out under the tires, and the limbs of trees lace the night sky high overhead. Trees, water and towns run by silently as he makes his passage. He thinks of the people inside the houses, caught in private seas of dream, unaware of him driving past their doors with danger following somewhere behind.

Out the window he can hear the high trill of crickets in meadows. Someone from Bristol, Vermont, requests a song on the radio. The sumac is red and further north the trees are shot with orange, scarlet and yellow. He drives in and out of the fogbanks that find a place in the pockets and dips, drifting across the high ground and suspending over the rivers in a long continuous furl.

North, back into the woods, the tires catch in the veneer of cold patch the road crews have lain down to fill the holes.

They throb against the yellow line that splits the highway that takes him further into the north country.

He makes his way east through the night into Kennebec County and then shoots up 201 to Jackman. A quarter mile from Beecher's he pulls in next to a log truck that has "The Olde Hoar" written on its side, a truck that looks like it hasn't hauled a log in at least five years. He locks the door and tells himself to keep his goddamn wits about him. Then he shoulders his gear and strikes out cross-country until he comes up on the backside of the house. The sun is just coming up behind him. Settling down in a stand of pine that points to the sky like minarets, he waits and watches under the rime of the needles. It's Sunday morning. He'll stay where he is a few more hours and then he'll stop in to see who lives there before making the hike into the back country.

S T E A M   comes off the black shingle roof as he skirts the house and crosses the yard. He walks between a new pickup and station wagon parked in the driveway and goes up on the porch. He can hear the sound of a skillet being set down on the stove and plates being set on the table.

He knocks once at the door and turns the handle at the same time so by his second knock, the door swings inward and he has his right hand at his breast pocket. Cutler and Big George are at the table. Ellie and Malvine are in the kitchen and the sound of kids talking comes down the stairway. Asel stands on the threshold looking at them, filled with a wish that he hadn't come. He reaches for the door and takes a step back, thinking how easy it would be to turn around and leave if only they didn't move, didn't say a word.

"Ace," Big George roars. "By God, it's Ace."

Asel goes inside the house he hasn't been back to in years. Big George gets up from the head of the table and meets him halfway across the floor. Asel sticks out his hand, but Big George doesn't take it. Instead he wraps his arms around him and lifts him in the air, squeezing the breath out of his lungs. He can feel the Redhawk under Asel's jacket.

"We have to talk," Asel says quietly, his mouth inches from George's head. "We have to talk now. It's important."

"Breakfast first, Ace. Join the big happy family."

Cutler is next. He raises his fists and starts to shadowbox. His punches come just close enough to snap at Asel's clothes. "Look at you," he says. "Fat and flabby. You've lost your reflexes. Ol' Cutler'll take you down and dance all over you."

Malvine and Ellie stand in the doorway to the kitchen. Malvine's hair is different. She's let it down off the top of her head and has it drawn back in a ponytail. She looks younger than when Asel last saw her. Ellie is smiling. Asel knows he's made a mistake coming here.

Cutler continues to skirt him, bantering away about how he deserves a good thrashing. Asel's arm shoots out to his right. He catches Cutler's right across in midstroke and holds it. He holds Cutler's fist in his hand without smiling and says quietly, "Let's eat breakfast and then you can kick my ass."

Big George claps his hand over Asel's and Cutler's. It's his right hand, the one he uses to swing his thirty-two-ounce framing hammer. Asel's hand, with Cutler's hand tucked inside, can't be seen with Big George's paw wrapped over the top.

"We always eat breakfast first," he says. "What's done is done. A man can't do anything without his breakfast."

The three men smile at each other and then sit down at the table.

Malvine and Ellie bring in plates of fried potatoes, pork rinds and gravy. Then they bring doughnuts, milk and coffee.

Cutler fills his plate and wolfs it down before Big George and Asel are half done. He then breaks a doughnut and sops at the gravy. When he's finished with that, he fills his plate again.

Ellie goes upstairs to get the kids. Malvine comes in the dining room and stands behind Cutler. She puts her hands

on his shoulders and looks at Asel. Asel looks back at her
and in her eyes he can see the fear that he has brought with
him. She opens her mouth as if to speak but can't. Asel wants
to tell her that Phoebe is fine and everything else is going
good, but he can't bring himself to do it.

Cutler tips his head back into her stomach. He rolls his
eyes to look at her and then he looks at Asel. He smiles and
Asel can see that all of his teeth are gone. He remembers
the old man in the woods who died on his way to Mexico
and it's as if he's alive again and in the room.

"Periodontium," Cutler says. "Too much foul language,
Malvine tells me. My mouth just all went to hell, so I had
'em yanked."

Cutler's grin widens, curling his lips back so Asel can see
his pink gums. His mouth looks new, like a baby's mouth.

"You know what I did, Ace? I took those teeth and pol-
ished them up, nice and white, with a buffer. Then I drilled
a hole in each one and strung them on a silver chain for my
woman. Sometimes she wears them, but she says the old
ivories tickle her."

Cutler slaps the table. Malvine moves her hands and Cutler
says, "She says, she and Ellie have to get the kids ready for
church and that it's good seeing you, Asel."

Asel nods and watches her leave. Cutler goes back to eating, mashing his food with his fork and soaking it in gravy.
Big George doesn't speak. He eats quietly and when he's
done, he sits back with his coffee cup.

"We got a good life here, Ace," Cutler says, his mouth full
of gravy and doughnut. "It's quite a nice family. With what
the Reverend left Malvine after he was called to celibacy,
Beecher's estate in trust and with what me and Georgie bring
in, those two kids are well provided for. You know what
celibacy is, don't you? It ain't a place. Big George told me."

Asel hears a car door slam. He turns his head sharply to
the left and at the same time his right hand goes inside his
jacket, where he holds it.

"It's the women and kids," Big George says. "They went out the back door. They're going to church. It's time we talk."

Asel tells Big George that things were good in New Hampshire. He tells them he made baskets and snowshoes and worked on the farm a little bit. Then he tells them he's only passing through and won't be staying long.

Big George and Cutler look at each other. Cutler pushes his chair back and stands up.

"What the hell," he says. "I'm about the most stupid son of a bitch that ever come down the pike, but you, Mr. Asel, are a lying sack of shit. Now, you tell us what's going on or I'll beat the hell out of you. And if I can't do it, I know who can. Besides, if I remember correctly, we've got a little unfinished business from the last time you were in town."

Asel stands up too and looks at Cutler. "It isn't your fight," he says quietly.

Big George's fist comes down on the table, rattling the dishes, cups and platters.

"You will both sit down. And you will tell us the truth so that we might decide for ourselves."

Asel and Cutler sit down. George pours coffee for each man. "It's good coffee," he says. "The water is hard. It makes good coffee."

Asel drinks from his cup and then tells the men about his brother Averell showing up. He tells them about the sons of two sports who are stalking him, and how they want him and what he stashed in the woods years ago.

"What about Beecher?" Cutler says.

"The sports are the ones who killed him when he was trying to give them the slip."

"And they're the ones you killed before you left."

"They're the ones I killed," Asel says, nodding his head as he hears the words spoken aloud for the first time.

"Ellie said he just disappeared. One minute he was in the shop and the next he was gone," Big George says, staring into the black surface floating in the coffee mug he holds with both hands. "Sounds to me like it's our fight too."

Cutler jumps up and goes to the gun cabinet. He begins taking out long rifles, shotguns and ammunition.

"Hold on, Mr. Cutler," Big George says. "The first thing we do is take our time. You made a mistake running the way you did, Ace. You can't watch your back when you run. We must slow down and be patient. You will work with me and Cutler this week and then Friday, we'll go into the woods. Sooner or later they'll show their hand. When the ladies and the kids get back from church, we'll send them to Old Orchard for the week. You call Phoebe and tell her where you are. Tell her you've gone camping and you'll be back at the end of the month."

"I never expected to find you here," Asel says. "I came to lead them off, but brought them to you."

"Maybe you didn't and maybe you did," Big George tells him.

Asel tries to speak again but Big George reaches over and holds Asel's face in his hands. Asel tries to move to one side, but Big George holds him. He can feel Big George's hand drawing off his strength, leaving him tired and ready for sleep. Finally, Big George lets go and Asel moves to the couch, lying down with an arm across his eyes. He falls asleep, warm and dreamless.

A S E L   doesn't wake up until it's dark. Big George and Cutler are sitting in corners of the room. The TV is on and across the men's laps are pump guns. They drink coffee, watching first the set, then Asel, then the windows.

Asel turns to look at the TV. Two huge naked men are running toward each other, their short fat legs pumping under their bodies. They collide in the center of the circle, muckle onto each other, and then try to muscle the other one to the floor.

"It's sumo wrestling from Japan," Cutler says. "I got a satellite dish rigged up in the backyard. I like to watch these fellows go at it. I leave the sound off because you can't understand a damn thing they're jabbering about anyways. There's cold chicken on the table and potato salad."

Asel gets up slowly. He feels tired and lazy from sleeping through the whole day. He flexes his muscles and arches his back, much like a cat would just getting up from a windowsill after the cold has set in.

There's another light on in the room besides the blue of the television. It's a small lamp that hangs on the wall and shines down on a painting. Asel goes over to it. It's a boy with curly hair, his face lit up and his blue eyes like sparks. At the bottom of the painting is a brass plate with the words, PICTURE OF CHRIST AT 12. Asel wonders who the hell could know such a thing.

At the table he picks up a chicken leg. When he gets it to his mouth, he smells the seasonings, the lemon, oregano and sage. His mind goes backward to the porch in Skowhegan and Phoebe is bringing out chicken, fried the way Malvine taught her. Her hair is still wet and it drips on the floor at her feet. It makes the back of her T-shirt wet and her body makes the wetness warm, so that later, when he puts his arms around her for the first time, he can feel her spine and the lift of her ribs as if she weren't wearing anything at all.

Asel puts down the chicken without eating any of it. He picks up the platter and takes it to Big George, but Big George shakes his head. He's wearing glasses and writing on a tablet of paper. Asel takes the platter to Cutler and sets it down next to him.

"Averell says he's been working in a Velcro factory," Asel whispers.

"Is that so? I wonder if he does the little hooks or the little furry part."

"I don't know. He didn't say."

Asel and Cutler both take chicken legs from the platter.

They bite into the meat and then start pulling it away at the bones.

"A man downcountry told me a story about cutting a cow's head off in the stanchion with a chain saw. Do you think it's true?"

"I don't know," Cutler says. "He didn't happen to mention what kind of saw it was, did he?"

"No. He didn't seem to know."

"Watch this, Ace. This big ol' boy's from Hawaii. It drives them Jappos crazy when he takes them down. He's the best."

"Cutler. How is it that you and the Reverend's wife have taken up housekeeping?"

"He left her and he never came back. Me and Big George moved up here and one day she shows up on the doorstep. Come here. Let me show you something."

Asel and Cutler walk through the dark house until they get to one of the back bedrooms. Cutler opens the door and throws on the light switch. The walls are covered with huge paintings of the Last Supper. Asel counts at least twenty.

"What do you think? Malvine got me started. They're paint by the numbers. Look at these over here. I'm starting to change colors and numbers. Let them slop over the lines a little bit."

"They're quite beautiful," Asel says.

"It's her doing, Ace. She's the miracle worker in the family. She's a dream come true."

Back in the living room, Cutler sits down by the chicken and Asel goes to Big George to see what he's doing.

"It's for Cutler," he says. "He wants me to write a letter to this fellow, Percy Ross. He has a column in the newspaper where he gives out money to folks who are in need. He gave one guy two hundred fifty dollars so he could buy a belt to become a window washer. Another person he rejected. She wanted seventy thousand dollars to go to medical school. Cutler claims it's all in the way you write the letter. He thinks

Percy Ross could help us out. Not with money, but with advice."

"Don't forget to order my electric socks and my head-lamp," Cutler says. "I had them up in the mountains before we got burned out and they come in awful handy."

Cutler starts to choke. His face goes red and then purple. Big George and Asel go to him, but he pushes them back. He falls to his knees, his eyes bulging in his face. He lets go of his neck and gets his hand inside his mouth. It looks as though he's reaching deep in his throat. Finally he draws his hand out and holds it up with a chicken bone between his fingers. Tears are running down his cheeks as he looks at Asel and Big George and smiles without any teeth.

"You better call Phoebe," he says, his voice no more than a whisper. "You haven't done that yet."

21

T H E next day, Asel goes to work with Big George and Cutler. They have a job on Moosehead, building a lodge for a group of Boston lawyers. Most builders won't work for lawyers, but Big George and Cutler aren't scared off by little things like that, especially since it's cash money with no need for signatures, and payments are drawn in advance. They take their weapons along with them.

At times, Asel forgets why he's come. The company of his friends and the work at hand serve to draw him in. Every small detail has its own rhythm, something that happens when good men are brought together with tools and material.

On Wednesday, just before coffee, the men wrestle forms into place. They speak to each other in fractions and directions, Big George waist-deep in the lake water, Cutler inside the web of steel that will reinforce the concrete and Asel walking the top, one foot in front of the other along three and a half inches of lumber.

The seawall, when complete, will anchor a thirty-foot dock one way and the foundation system the other way.

Cutler barks his shin on the steel and he curses himself. Big George can hear him on the other side of the plywood.

"Mr. Cutler," his voice booms, "I'd need a carbide touch-hole to do with this wood and steel what you're suggesting, wouldn't I?"

Asel starts to laugh. He looks down at Cutler, who has his pants leg rolled up. The skin's grated along the length of his white shin, halfway from his knee to his ankle. He looks up at Asel and smiles. The sight of his pink gums makes Asel laugh even harder and to keep from losing his balance he does a drunken dance, trying to stay on top until finally, unable to stop himself, he goes over the lake side. Big George tries to catch him, only to be taken under himself.

The two men come up spitting water; Big George blowing like a whale; Asel, his nose full and causing small pains in his forehead.

"By the Jesus Christ," George bellows. "Next time you decide to drop out of the sky, you'd better take your chances with Mr. Cutler and the cold steel."

George then lunges for him but Asel's already churning his legs to make shore, still coughing and spitting. George plows along after him, leaving a wake behind. On the landing, Asel grabs the Thermos and threatens to throw it into the lake if Big George doesn't back off. He knows that George values his Maxwell House at ten o'clock sharp above all else.

Asel stands laughing at George, the Thermos held back behind his ear, ready to heave it like a football. But George isn't laughing; he's looking past him. Asel turns to see two men, one so small he looks like a boy and the other as big as George, but square, and broad in the chest.

"Greetings from your brother," the little man says, standing next to their guns. He then reaches into his jacket and pulls out a green felt hat. He curls his arm and then snakes it out, flipping his wrist at the last moment to make the hat skim through the air to the ground at Asel's feet.

Big George crouches down, but the little man looks up the hill and points. In the trees is another man in a red-and-black-plaid coat with a deer rifle. Before the little man can turn, though, Big George is on the move, driving into the little man and the four of them roll over the lip of the cut, and down the hill to the edge of the water.

Asel pins down the little man and goes through his jacket, finding a 9mm he has still holstered under his arm. He holds it to the man's head and then swings around to see the square man towering above Big George and holding a knife at his throat.

"Let go of Tommy," the square man says, smiling, his teeth bare and white.

Asel loosens his grip, but still holds the little man's face in the ground and his gun out to the side. He watches Cutler come out of the steel behind the square man and jam the barrel of the nail gun into the base of his skull. The square man's head snaps forward, knocking onto the top of Big George's.

"Say your prayers," Cutler says, pulling the trigger and setting off the .22 load that drives a tenpenny spike point-blank into the square man's brain. He hovers above Big George for only seconds and then goes down, finished with dying long before he topples, and lands on top of him.

The man in the red-and-black-plaid coat makes the lip of the cut in time to see Asel holding the 9mm back against Tommy's head. He draws a bead on Cutler with the rifle, ready to kill him in an instant.

"We have a bit of a standoff," Tommy says, his voice muffled by the ground.

"Shoot him," Cutler says, looking up the barrel of the .30-06. "Shoot the little son of a bitch, now while you can. I'll take my chances here."

Asel backs up a step, still holding the piece in line with Tommy's head.

"Back off, Michael," Tommy yells, sitting up and brushing at his sleeves with the backs of his hands. "I believe we can have a meeting of the minds with these gentlemen."

The man named Michael lowers the .30-06 to his hip. The little man stands up and brushes off his pants. He stretches his neck like a bird would. He holds his hands in an odd position out in front of him and begins doing breathing exercises. He does this until he reaches what seems to be some internal sense of balance and then he starts walking about and speaks.

"For all of us here, we are now even. Michael will go to the Blazer for refreshment and then we will negotiate."

Michael goes up the hill and Tommy follows him as far as the landing. Asel and Cutler help Big George to his feet and then they follow. Michael, unarmed, is already coming back down the hill with a steel Thermos and styrofoam cups.

"What the hell," Cutler says, going to get the Thermos Big George brought. He takes three cups from Michael and pours out coffee for Asel, George and himself. Michael and Tommy light cigarettes and smoke while they sip at the coffee Michael has poured.

"You're doing a good job," Michael says.

"Yes, you are," Tommy says. "The partners will be impressed. I hope you continue on when we get this mess tidied up."

"We're working for you?" Cutler says.

"The firm, not us per se."

"Well, I'll be damned," Cutler says, and then he looks at George and Asel.

"Just what is it you're working on now?" Michael says.

Cutler shrugs and then begins explaining the project to him. He explains the complexity of the foundation system Big George has engineered. Michael admires its cleverness and then suggests several procedures that will be more efficient by unifying pours of concrete.

Tommy and Asel from time to time catch each other's eye and then look away. Big George holds his hand to his neck and keeps glancing over his shoulder. His fight with the square man has taken some of his nerve. He's never been manhandled like that before. He sucks down the last of his coffee and touches at his throat once more to feel it work.

"Enough shit," he says, crunching his cup in his fist.

"Yes, Mr. Big George. You're right. All things now being equal, we came to negotiate," Tommy says, holding his hands out in reconciliation.

"You keep saying that, but what the hell do you mean?" Big George stands up quickly and begins walking around, thumping his chest with the flat of his hand.

"We have lost our fathers and you have lost a brother and a cousin," Tommy says.

Cutler stands up too and smiles. "I don't know where you
learned your figures, but as I look at it, it's three for us and
two for you," he says, pointing at the square man. It pleases
him to have one up on them.

"Hired help," Michael says. "Just hired help. We knew
we'd need someone comparable to your Big George here, so
we picked him up. He won't be missed."

"Please, sit down," Tommy says. "Please, let's work this
out so we can get on with other more pressing matters."

Michael brings the big steel Thermos around to Asel, George
and Cutler. He hands them new cups from the plastic sleeve
and fills them up, catching the last drips in a handkerchief.
His hands are white. They remind Cutler of the Reverend's
hands, the way the blue veins marble the white skin.

"Thank you," Cutler says. He looks to Tommy, who's
standing too. Even on his feet, he's no taller than Big George
when he's sitting down. Cutler wants to ask him where he's
able to buy clothes that fit him so well. He especially wants
to know where he bought his shoes. He can't imagine shoes
so small being made for a grown-up man. Instead he looks
to Michael.

"That's a real snappy coat you've got there. I lost mine in
a fire. I didn't think they made them like that anymore. Mind
telling me where you got it?"

"It was my father's," Michael says, looking at Asel. "It was
my father's coat."

"Well, it's real nice," Cutler says, showing his pink gums.

"Gentlemen," Tommy says, stepping in between Asel and
Michael. "Years ago, our fathers were in the habit of sup-
porting the effort to reunify their homeland, to bring together
the north and the south. Our fathers, being poor men of an
ancient order, raised money in various ways. They held corned-
beef-and-cabbage dinners, raffles and they got a cut of what
the diocese brought in. They tithed what came through the
till and then matched it. And, when we were younger, still

in college, they came up here and disappeared in these woods."

Asel thinks to set the record straight by telling them it wasn't the woods but a cedar bog. He lets it pass, though, and instead remembers them through open sights and then after they died not wanting to look at their faces.

"So Michael and I took over the various businesses that the two of them started. A few years ago, it came to our attention that there were some two hundred pieces still on the books, clean pieces. Michael and I wish to clear the books. There will be a tidy profit, of course, which we are willing to share."

"And what do you mean by clear the books?" Cutler says.

"Well sir, given the current shift in, shall we say, spheres of influence, we have been approached by interests in the north, Belfast to be precise, who now feel the onus is upon them to maintain the status quo."

"Call me stupid," Cutler says, "but I don't know what in hell you're talking about."

"You don't know your history, Mr. Cutler. The Prime Minister, she has shifted the power game. Let us say, our hearts are in Dublin, but our fortunes are to be made in the north. Business, Mr. Cutler, business. We are engaging in an age-old endeavor. We are running guns."

Tommy smiles and sits down. He crosses his legs at the ankles and holds his folded hands between his knees. He looks pleased to be where he is.

"So what do you propose?" Asel asks. Big George and Cutler look over at him. It's the first time he's spoken since the scuffle.

"You and I will go in for the pistols while Michael stays with your two friends. A simple transaction. We should be back in a few days. Their families will be back by then, but they don't have to know anything."

"Fair enough," Asel says, strapping into his holster and then handing Cutler his shotgun and George his rifle. "Fair enough," he says again, looking to George, who slowly nods his head and it's only then that Asel hands back the 9mm.

"What about him?" Cutler says, jerking a thumb in the direction of the dead man.

"You have a truck coming at one o'clock with nine yards of concrete," Michael says. "You figure it out."

22

I T ' S dark in the cabin except for the fire, glowing in lines and points through seams in the cast-iron stove. The two men sit facing each other, Asel silent, his mind cut back to when staying awake was the only important thing. He has done it before and does not figure this time to be any more difficult. He can see Tommy sitting across from him and at times when a knot of wood flares inside the stove it's like someone lit a match in the room and he can make out the face and hands, but only for an instant.

In those moments the light goes blood red like the light of a furnace held behind a small black door. And then another knot flares, its pitch taking fire, and Asel can see that Tommy is holding a gun flat on his leg with his hand cupped over its frame.

"You're an outlaw," Tommy says, his voice coming out of the darkness, friendly and soft. "You have no birth certificate, no draft card, no passport, no driver's license."

Asel thinks of the years he has spent in this cabin, listening to the stories the sports told. He remembers Tommy's father. He imagines that he and Tommy's father sat just this way years ago. It was Tommy's father who gave him the .44 Blackhawk on his second year into the woods. He'd been a sad drunk, sucking on bottles of whiskey with names like Mist and Breeze. He regaled Asel with stories of his homeland. His words thick yet lilting as if they were syrup running out the small end of a funnel, or down a hose.

Another knot of pine flares and snaps in the stove. Asel can see how Tommy has crossed his legs to gain elevation, aligning the three-inch barrel with Asel's guts.

The little man speaks again. "You are an outlaw. I know because I am a lawyer. What do you think of that?"

Asel doesn't reply. He knows that the man wants to talk.
He learned long ago that people have a need to talk for the
sake of talking and that the sound they make is the only thing
they have. When you become a part of it, they own you.
They can then lay down the rules and at their gentlest walk
away, thinking you're a fool.

"Michael's a lawyer too. We are partners in the same law
firm. We're second generation. Our fathers made the money,
we make it grow and if we have any children, they'll spend
it. You kind of fucked that up, though. You broke the chain.
My suspicion is you're the one who kept them from seeing
their grandchildren."

Asel can now see Michael's father too. He came with Tommy's both times. He never showed signs of drunkenness though
he drank down his share of the bottle. The fire cracks and
flares and Asel remembers when he was still a boy and he
and Michael's father got an early start on fresh deer sign while
Tommy's father was still sleeping off the night before. And
as he remembers that day, he knows he has to get back to
Cutler and Big George as soon as he can or lose them forever.

T H E   second week in November of 1969 was reserved
for two hunters who'd been north the year before. Asel thought
of them as the Charboneau brothers because they lied a lot
and he had a vague memory of a family he once knew named
Charboneau, whose kids made up stories for the sake of
something to do. They began every story with "You're going
to think this is a lie," and the other kids would hear "This is
a lie."

The Charboneau brothers were good customers. Aside
from their obvious lies, Asel didn't mind having them around.
They always brought him something nice along with the crates
he wasn't supposed to touch.

The two brothers played a game of inventing names for
each other. Asel took them to be the names of real people

because each new one brought signs of recognition followed by joy, relief, anguish, pain or hate.

"I'll tell you, Ace. The tavern business is some racket. Isn't that right, Wolfy?" This was from the man who at the time was called Brian.

"It sure is. I got one guy who keeps stealing the deodorant stick out of the urinals."

"I put a scoop of ice in mine. I say the hell with 'em. They tell me it stinks and I say, 'Stink. By Jesus, I guess it stinks. What do you want me to do about it?' "

Asel could hear in their voices the gentle lulls that turned their complaining into storytelling and then back again. Each man seemed to wish more burden on himself than he allowed the other. The stories moved in and out of what could be taken for plausibility, but Asel didn't mind because he had never known so much about urinals, let alone ever seen one.

"So why do you put ice in them?" he asked from across the darkened room.

"Oh Jesus, Charlie, he wants to know why I put ice in the urinals. I tell you, my boy. I put it in for two reasons. The first is to keep the hot stink of used beer from smelling up the joint. The second is so all the lost sons can pretend their little peepees are machine guns shooting Migs out of the porcelain heaven."

The men laughed at that one and Asel smiled too. It didn't make him happy to see the sports get drunk, but he preferred this to quiet ones who came alone and never spoke. He liked the way they changed their names and played out parts for each new one. He didn't try to keep them straight. Instead, he enjoyed the many people who inhabited the camp that night, making checks on occasion to reassure himself that one of the men was small and slight while the other was taller with a body hung on what looked to be long fine bones. The taller one conducted his speech with clean, blue-veined hands and the smaller man jabbed the air as if he were snatching pieces of it to hold in his own.

"You know there, Mr. Blaze, I spoke to this guy who was taking the deodorant sticks out of my urinals and I says to him, 'What are you doing?' And he says to me that he takes them home and puts them in his toilet. He says his wife counts on them. So I says, 'What the hell do you do for toilet paper?' and he says, 'I get that at the shop where I work.' Well, you know what I meant. I meant that he got his toilet paper somewhere else, why the hell didn't he get his deodorant sticks there too? You know what I mean, the blue ones, that smell like lilacs. He didn't understand what I was talking about, I'm telling you."

"I know what you mean, the public just doesn't understand what it's all about."

"You know, Mr. Blaze, I was just now sitting here wondering why some one of these pinball wizards we hear so much about doesn't invent a game where these boys can sidle up to it and for a quarter shoot ice figures with their peepees."

The two men laughed again. They poured out tumblers of Irish Mist and sat back in their chairs. They held their glasses near the top with their little fingers out. Asel trimmed the wick on the kerosene lamp, letting the golden light float out from his hand against everything in the room

"Jesus, that's lovely," the little man said, his tongue thick in his mouth. He held his glass between the lamp and himself, moving it back and forth, making the shadow cross his face and neck as if to cool the light on its way to his skin. "I want to see a flight of geese. What's the chance of a flight of geese, Ace?"

Asel shrugged his shoulders, holding them up to look the fool. "They've been out of these parts for a long time now. We may see a few late ducks, but the geese are gone."

"Then swans, Ace. I want to see swans. I want to see a flight of long-necked swans crossing the channel into the white arms of the good mother."

The tall man sat up, perching himself on the edge of his chair.

"You're pretty old and foolish. Shut up your mouth and your talk of birds. The boy said they're gone, which makes them ghosts in your brain."

The little man began to cry. He dabbed at his eyes and flushed cheeks with the back of his hand. His friend took out a handkerchief, unfolded it in his lap and then passed it over. He clucked his tongue against the roof of his mouth, shaking his head back and forth.

"Now Roddy, be a good boy and don't cry."

"My mother had ten children and eight of them died. One of them lived and then there's me. I have a brother in New Zealand I'll never see. I heard about him from somebody else, a woman who said she knew him but it was only a coincidence because I know she didn't, but I let her talk and I kept feeding her information hoping she wouldn't stop nodding her head. I told her everything I wanted him to be and she kept telling that that was the way he was. She drank a whole fifth."

"Oh Roddy, that's a good story," his friend said. The little man sat up, his face wet and red. He looked into the light as if he were trying to see something.

"I'll tell you, Mr. Blaze, I'd take that man who was stealing your deodorant sticks anyday over the shaggy-headed sons a bitches I have to put up with. Why don't they get haircuts? Dress like men? Talk about stink. I'm telling you, these men stink. And their women too. She was one of them. She'd been on a sheep farm down there. She smelled like sheep dip in August. She stunk to high heaven, like an old dog stinks when it's dying from the inside out. They got lice and ticks. Why don't they shave and get a haircut? This woman had long hairs hanging under her arm. They don't know nothing. Their brains are gone on drugs and free love."

"I know what you mean, Roddy. They're no good."

The men filled their glasses again and sat back in their chairs. Asel hoped this would be their last big blow for the evening. He sighed and settled back himself. He could feel his revolver, tight against his ribs. He didn't want to have it on but the men insisted it was for him to wear.

"What have you got for us this year?" Roddy said.

"There's a stand of hardwood a half mile from here where there's good mast. They'll be in that general vicinity, looking to yard up for the winter."

"That's a good boy," Roddy said, staring up at the rafter. "What I said about beards and shaggy hair. Now, I want you to know that I don't mean for that to apply to you. You're a good boy. Clean. You've just had a run of bad luck. The whole world has for that matter."

Asel smiled and looked over at Mr. Blaze. His head was turned and he was staring at Asel.

"Don't mind him," Roddy said. "Sometimes he falls asleep with his eyes open." Roddy got up and went to Mr. Blaze. He had to grab the chair arms to keep himself from toppling onto his friend. When he'd finally arrested his forward motion, he gently reached out with his finger and pushed down the eyelids of Mr. Blaze. He draped a blanket over him and then sat down himself, pulling his own blanket tight to his throat and holding it there with the ends of his fingers folded over the edge.

Asel turned down the wick, making it seem as though he were calling in the light that at one time or another had flowed through the room, to a small point at his right hand where he could have held it in his palm if he wanted to.

Tiny white-footed, bat-eared mice came out from the wall and skittered along the floor.

Mr. Blaze began to breathe like a man who was asleep, making Asel finally feel comfortable in the cabin, alone with the men. He threw a bread crust at the mice, scaring them off to a place where they could watch it for a while before coming after it. He then settled down in his chair to wait out the night, the smell of Irish Mist, woodsmoke and kerosene mixing in the air.

He let himself play out again the last day he spent with Lion and Sal, feeling the ground rumble as they strode, smelling the earth their shod hooves kicked up as they surged at the traces. He stayed with them until the rolling thunder of Borst's gun dropped them where they stood and at that moment he turned quickly to see Mr. Blaze watching him in the dim light of the lantern, watching him for a few seconds longer and then closing his eyes.

T H E next morning Roddy stayed in his chair, nursing a virgin bottle of Old Bushmill. When he wasn't drinking from it, he held it to his breast, stroking it and speaking in a language that Asel couldn't understand. It was cold that morning with a dust of snow that would make it easy to pick up a blood trail if needed. The sun was just now being seen from Cadillac Mountain, rising up from the ocean. It would be only a short time before its light made it this far west.

Asel scraped bear grease from a can he kept by the door. He worked it into his hands and wrists. It was to keep them dry and warm. He offered some to Mr. Blaze, but he only turned away and walked out the door. Roddy had fallen asleep again. Spittle hung from his lip and ran down his chin. During the night he'd gritted his teeth, something Asel had never gotten used to.

Outside, Mr. Blaze had his pants down and was adjusting a wide belt that he'd wrapped around himself, high on his pelvis.

"I have a hernia," he said. Asel looked away, reaching into his pocket and fingering a few loose cartridges.

"If you must know, I got it lifting a keg of beer. Sometimes it feels like my whole insides are about to flush out."

"We'll go easy," Asel said. "A hundred yards in we'll pick up a run. You follow it and I'll come along twenty-five yards to your right. If you're sharp, you'll run head-on into one coming up out of the swamp. If not, we'll wait down there for them to come home this afternoon. Walk slow. Don't get ahead of me."

It was not a good plan, but Asel saw no point in letting the sports bag game this early in the week. He'd wait until Thursday or Friday and then he'd put them onto a sure bet. It was a lesson he learned his first time out when a man shot four deer in one week, leaving Asel with the headless carcasses to rot in the afternoon sun.

By eleven o'clock, they'd made their descent down into the spruce and cedar swamp. It fanned out for hundreds of acres, serving as a source for an unnamed branch of the Penobscot. In the summer it was flush with ferns, fiddleheads and skunk cabbage, but now they were brown and dry, crumbling under the men's boots.

It should have taken them longer to make the swamp. Asel had to keep motioning for Mr. Blaze to slow down. He'd been too impatient. Asel knew they'd passed deer several times along the way, but he let them go.

Fifty yards into the swamp, there was an island of oak and beech. It had good mast. The bark was rubbed down where the bucks had scraped their velvet and the grass trampled where the deer yarded up.

"You stay here," Asel said, handing Mr. Blaze a packet of cheese and crackers. "It will be a while, but they'll be back to bed down for the night."

"Where will you be?"

"I am going over there," Asel said, pointing to a height of land a hundred yards away. "That way we'll be able to triangle them."

Mr. Blaze nodded, taking a silver flask from inside his coat. He settled to the ground, his face red and sweaty from the morning's hike. Asel could feel the warmth too. The weather was different down where they were. The water of the swamp held what little warmth there was to have.

"Let's us have lunch together," Mr. Blaze said.

"It's not the best thing to do. Any time now, one could wander down for a drink."

"No, I insist."

Asel shrugged. He kneeled down in front of Mr. Blaze, cradling his .35-caliber Remington across his lap. The man looked to be in pain. He shifted around, all the time holding his fingers pressed into his abdomen, until he was finally comfortable. That accomplished, he unscrewed the cup on the flask and took a drink. He held it out, but Asel shook his head.

"So, how is it that someone like yourself avoided service to his country?"

Asel didn't know what Mr. Blaze was talking about. He didn't like it when the sports wanted to get personal. It rarely happened but when it did, it scared him. Usually they were drunk when it happened and it didn't bother him much. They'd ask a question and when he didn't answer, they'd back off and make their apologies by giving him something. This time was different, though. Mr. Blaze looked at him and waited. He smiled, poking at his abdomen as if he liked the pain.

"Me and Averell got a lot to do right here running this business," Asel said.

"A lot of boys have a lot to do, but they made time to fight for their country."

"I suppose if there was fighting to do, I'd do my share."

"There is plenty enough fighting, or maybe you don't believe in the war my son is risking his neck to win."

"To be honest with you, Mr. Blaze, I don't know anything about a war."

"You mean to tell me you don't know about the Vietnam War? I have heard it all now. I'd like to see you try that one on the draft board."

"What's the Vietnam War?"

"Never mind," Mr. Blaze said, staring off into the swamp. "You mind your business and I'll mind mine. That's the way I'm told it's to be."

Mr. Blaze didn't turn back to look at Asel. He kept staring to the west where the swamp opened and closed on itself like a hundred doorways down a mile-long hall. Grateful for the end of the conversation, Asel stood up and left the island, picking his way over hummocks of grass and walking the length of fallen trees back to solid ground. From there he skirted the swamp and climbed the height of land. He liked it better in the trees. Down in the swamp the wind often changed course. He didn't like places where the wind could come from different directions. He tucked himself down in the brush of a deadfall where he couldn't be found and let himself sleep for the first time since rendezvous, when he'd helped pack in the second load of fifty-pound crates with the men who called themselves different names.

Sometime late in the day Asel dreamed about men who wore turbans and helmets. They carried gatling guns on the backs of elephants. Some of the men wore skirts and leggings. The names for all of these people were about to become known when he felt something pulling at his boot and he woke up. He looked down to see the blunt face of a porcupine staring at him from between his feet. It had gnawed at the leather lacings on his right foot and was about to take on the rest of the shoe. Asel smiled and went to kick it away, when a shot was fired from down in the swamp.

The porcupine, scared off by the noise, waddled away into the brush. Asel knotted up what was left of his lacing and crawled out from under the deadfall. He brushed himself off and walked down from where he was. The sun was going off across Canada. The air was cold again. Steam was starting up from the swamp in singular and independent columns. At the edge he could see Mr. Blaze beside a deer that was still standing. Its head was down and it was breathing hard, blowing up leaves with the air that came from its nostrils. It was a good-sized ten-pointer, well over two hundred pounds.

"You'd better get the hell out of there and finish him off," Asel yelled, still twenty yards away.

Mr. Blaze looked up at him. Asel could see how hard and red his face had become from drinking all day on the island. Behind him the columns of mist were beginning to meld into a blanket of white air drifting up without intent or purpose.

"Shoot it, I say," Asel yelled again, but Mr. Blaze only smiled. He tilted his head and waved slowly for Asel to come over.

"Look here," he said. "The lights are on but there isn't anybody home."

Asel could see where the bullet entered the skull just under the crown of antlers. A miniature fount of blood was just now welling up in the hole. Mr. Blaze took his white linen handkerchief from his pocket. He ripped it down into two pieces. One he threw on the ground and the other he used to plug the hole. He then took a length of rope from Asel's day pack and fashioned a halter. He looped it behind the antlers, over the bridge of the nose and back under the chin. That done, he shouldered his rifle and started up out of the swamp, leading the deer behind him with Asel following.

W H E N they got back to the camp, Mr. Blaze banged on the door and yelled for Roddy to come out. The noise made the deer skitter off to the side and fall down on its knees. The knot of linen was soaked with blood that had turned black at the edges but was still crimson in the center.

"Roddy, me boy. Come see what I've got for you."

Roddy came out the door, stumbling over the threshold and going down on his knees so he was face-to-face with the deer.

"Sweet Jesus," he said, "what have you done?"

"I've brought you a deer to shoot. It was most agreeable not to die so as we'd have to pack it out, me with a rupture and all. I figured I'd lead it home so my good friend Roddy could finish it off. That way I'm able to kill two birds with one stone."

"Shoot him yourself," Roddy said, his face inches from the face of the deer. "Put the poor bastard out of his misery."

Mr. Blaze turned and looked at Asel.

"No, Roddy, you will go inside and get your gun and then you will come back out and you will shoot this deer."

Roddy looked up at his friend, who now held out a hand to help him off his knees. Without taking it, he stood up and went inside. Seconds later he came back out with his new deer rifle. He held the gun up to the animal's head and pulled the trigger. The hammer snapped against an empty chamber.

"Load the goddamn rifle," Mr. Blaze yelled, his mouth so close to Roddy's ear that the man fell back as if struck with a fist.

Roddy worked the bolt and held the barrel up again. When he pulled the trigger the muzzle flash leapt out the end, bathing the buck's head in an explosion of light, burning the brown hair from its head and singeing its rack. The animal went back on its haunches and then collapsed.

Roddy and Mr. Blaze looked down at the dead animal and then smiled warmly at each other. Mr. Blaze slapped his friend on the back and the two of them went inside to a new bottle of whiskey, leaving Asel to hang and dress what they'd left behind. They were asleep by the time he went in that night.

The next morning they packed their gear and hiked out, leaving behind them the three crates stacked along with the three they'd brought their first time into the woods the year before. For Asel they left another five hundred rounds of ammunition for his Blackhawk and the deer, hanging in the tree, its headless body gutted and open for anyone who wanted to look inside.

Seven years later when the summer does were dropping their fawns and the bucks were still in velvet, there was a morning the sky still held the arc of a comet and Asel shot the two men who kept changing their names. He weighted their bodies into the black stagnant water of a marshy poke-logan and watched them sink below the surface, being the last man to ever see them alive or dead

A S E L   gets up from his chair. He can see Tommy move quickly, to hide his gun, but at the same time keep the business end pointed in Asel's direction.

"The fire needs wood," Asel says, moving between Tommy and the stove. He bends down and opens the iron door, feeling the rush of heat on his face and neck. He looks into its belly, where he can see the point where a fire becomes light. Dropping to his knee, he picks up a stick with his left hand and pokes at the log, causing it to crumble into blocks that glow and pulse in the breath of air that comes in through the door.

"You were in the last war," he says, but Tommy doesn't say anything. Behind him he can hear the legs of the chair shifting as Tommy angles it around.

"Yes, I was there," Tommy says. "Michael and I were both there. We were both decorated. It was a good war. It's too bad you couldn't make it, but then again you don't exist so you couldn't have if you wanted."

Asel reaches inside his jacket with his right hand. He cranks down on the grip of his revolver, angling the barrel up and swinging it out from his side an inch.

"You're not an American. You're not anything. You have no history," Tommy says, his words happy like a song.

"Sometimes it works that way and sometimes it doesn't. And for that I'm sorry," Asel says, squeezing the trigger of the Redhawk, blowing out the back of his own jacket and sending two hundred and forty grains of hard-cast lead tumbling through the little man's heart. It's a lesson in the way things work he takes with him to the bottom of his own marshy grave long before daybreak.

23

B A C K in Jackman, Asel sits across the road in the dark and watches Beecher's house burn. Four bodies lie under sheets and the volunteers hold back people who know there are still children upstairs. The pumper roars and the hoses rain water down on the roof. Windows burst and jets of flame shoot into the sky. Some people cry but most only look on, their eyes the color of fire.

Asel moves from shadow to shadow, closer to the bodies, closer to the paramedics, a man and woman in fluorescent orange nylon jackets. They are talking to the fire chief. Asel hears they're waiting for the state police, so he knows he must go.

"It's the damnedest," the woman says. "It wasn't the fire. It looks like concussion." She walks away and sits down. She puts her face in her hands and doesn't move.

"She mean they were hit in the head?" the chief says to the man.

"No, like from a bomb. She said she's seen it before. In the service."

"I keep forgetting she was over there," the chief says. "Just one of those things, I guess."

He pushes his helmet back and rubs his blackened forehead. He recites the names of Asel's friends. Asel listens and stares ahead, unflinching as tiny explosions go off, ammunition, aerosol cans and another larger one that must have been black powder. He thinks about putting the gun to his heart and ending it all right here beside the road, but then he thinks of Mr. Blaze's son, Michael. He's filled with fear and hate. Standing erect, he surveys the crowd of people. He looks for the new pickup in the driveway and sees it's gone. He knows Michael's taken it and he's left for New Hampshire.

One last time he looks at the faces being swept by the

emergency lights coming from the cabs of the fire trucks, not more than a hundred feet away. He wants to get up on one of those trucks and tell his story. Tell them the children died in their sleep and to never forget them. He wants his words to take away their pain. He knows it's foolish, though. He knows he must leave this place and that either way, no one will ever know.

P H O E B E washes and Lillian dries. They've been working late again. Since Asel left, Tut has been talking about his own death being imminent and if the farm is to go on they'll all have to pitch in because Phoebe can't do it alone. She'll need their help. He has been working too, with a new vigor. Doing things he's too old to do, healthy or not. He tells them he thought he could rest his final days but now he knows he can't.

The intercom sits on the counter next to them. A heifer has come into her first heat and the men are in the barn trying to get her bred. Phoebe and Lillian listen while they finish the dishes.

"Dammit," Tut yells, his voice crackling from the box, "that boy Asel was worth twice the two of you. Hold her, Bobby. Hold her. Preacher, reach in there and help him find the hole. Guide him to her."

Phoebe and Lillian stop what they're doing. They listen intently to the sounds coming from the barn, the low, throaty moan of the heifer and the huffing of the bull.

"Jesus Christ," Tut yells, "what'd he do, go all over your hand? That's it, wipe it on your pants. It does a hell of a lot of good on your pants, Preacher."

The women can hear Bobby Vachon start to laugh, sending Tut into a rage.

"You laugh, you sonofabitch. You laugh. Here I am dying, trying to get this heifer bred, knowing full well I'll never see the calf, and alls you can do is laugh. What the hell do you think farming is? Romping through the fields saying 'Aw shucks, aw shucks'? You may as well be working in a factory. Get the hell out of here, both of you. I'll do it myself."

"Why don't you go ahead and die before you kill us too?" Bobby says.

Lillian drops the towel and moves to the speaker. She picks it up and yells into it.

"Don't you sass him. You hear me? You do what Tut tells you."

She says it again and then she hears a bucket being kicked and doors slamming.

"Good riddance to you," Tut yells after they've gone and then there's only the sound the heifers make, feeding in the mangers and sucking water from their troughs. Lillian puts down the intercom and then bends over, placing her elbows on the counter, her head close to the speaker. She listens. She can hear Tut talking to the heifers. He says kind things, even about Bobby and the Highway Preacher. She thinks how long it's been since Tut has had a kind word for any man.

"A few beers will cool them off," she says, turning to Phoebe, but she's not there. She's at the window looking out through the darkness across the meadow.

"It's him," she says. "He's back."

Lillian moves to the window. She can see the lights of a vehicle going down the road to Phoebe's house.

"Now, slow down," Lillian says. "Don't ask him where he's been. Don't yell. Just tell him you're glad he's home."

Phoebe takes off her apron and goes out the back door. She climbs the fence and runs out across the mowing. She sees lights going on in every room of her house and then she's into the corn and can't see anything except the stars overhead, pinpoints of light coming through the green leaves that scratch at her face as she weaves her way from one row to the next. When she breaks out on the other side, she sees her front door open and the driveway empty. She looks up the road in time to see taillights disappearing past the corn ground.

She wants to cry out but she doesn't. She goes down on her knees, her heart beating in her chest, her lungs tight for air. She stays there, taking up a handful of soil and working it in her palm until her breathing comes more evenly. She coaches herself. She says, "Slow down. It's all right. Just be happy he's back. Things will be better now. There will be plenty of time to talk. A whole lifetime."

When she's finally ready, she takes the road back to Tut's, walking slowly, enjoying the night, its pockets of coolness and the figures of mist that rise from the earth.

Pulled in next to the barn is a pickup truck Phoebe has never seen before. She goes in through the milk house to where the heifers are kept. Grabbing the handle of the four-teen-foot sliding door with both hands, she opens it a foot and then gets her shoulder into it.

She turns and, in the yellow light that runs in behind her, she sees her father sprawled out on the concrete, blood, bright and shiny, coming from his forehead, one arm under him and the other across his chest.

She takes two steps forward, and from behind she's lifted by her hair, until her feet leave the ground. It's one swift motion and she knows that's how it's happening but it seems to take forever, as every hair draws on her skull. The pain cuts out her voice, cuts out her wind, and she's up there, stiff in the air, her neck ready to snap.

"I think we're waiting for the same man," she hears, the words at her neck, and then she's thrown with only enough time to turn her head, to save her face from the concrete floor.

24

ASEL takes Route 2 through Lancaster and picks up 91 in Saint Johnsbury, where he stops for gas and oil. He thinks of Phoebe asleep in bed, her head on the pillow and her hair falling over the side and onto the floor. He tells himself he'll steal a car if this one doesn't make it back. He rides low in the night under a full moon, dropping south past Wells River and Thetford. Some ways below White River he hears her voice. She says his name and begins to speak, her words so clear in his head he thinks, for a moment, she's there in the car with him.

"I thought I've known it all but I haven't. You know, don't you? It's not over yet, is it?"

Asel reaches down and rests his hand on the gun next to him. Its frame is cool and dry, the sights true.

"Stay here and hate me," she says, "you can't go. I can't let you. I will die if you do."

He moves his mouth as if to say no, but can't give sound to the word. He pushes the gas pedal another half inch.

By the time he takes the Bellows Falls exit, crosses into New Hampshire and starts down Route 12, the engine is overheating and starting to get balky. He lays into it, though, dropping off 12 and on to 63 so fast his head bounces against the ceiling.

Passing Tut's he sees the lights are off and keeps going to his own house on the meadow. When he gets there the engine knocks and dies. He crosses the porch, swifty, silently, the gun ready in his hand. The door of the house is wide open and the lockset parts are scattered across the kitchen floor. The bed has been turned over and on the bureau is a water glass with an ice cube melting at the bottom. He goes back out the door and into the corn, his head down, and shoulders forward, cutting a path to the barn.

The buildings are dark except for a faint glow he can see coming from under the door of the machine shed and through the burlap bags somebody has hung over the windows. Asel gets up close and listens. Inside he hears the grinder at work. It lugs down and then speeds up, lugs down and speeds up. He holds the gun at his side and works his way along the wall of the building. Behind it he sees the front end of a pickup truck poking out.

He looks in where the corner of a window hasn't been covered. Bobby Vachon and the Highway Preacher are sitting on milk stools smoking Pall Malls while Lillian is at the grinder boning meat and feeding it into the hopper. He puts his gun away and slips in the side door.

"By the Jesus," Bobby Vachon yells. "Where in the hell have you been? Just the very night we need you and you're upcountry."

"Mr. Vachon, you shut your mouth," Lillian says, pointing her knife at him.

"Whose truck is that parked behind the shed?" Asel says quietly.

Lillian looks at him. She squints and rubs her lips with her thumb. She looks at Bobby Vachon and the Highway Preacher, who are trying to light new smokes off the same match. She motions for Asel to come closer by curling her finger.

"I was in the house cleaning when I heard on the intercom Tut and a man yelling at each other. He said he was looking for you, but Tut wouldn't tell him anything so they got to fighting."

She saw the look on Asel's face.

"Tut told him to get the hell off the property, but the man whacked him on the head. Your Phoebe's in the house with Tut now. She's all right. They're both all right. My man and the Highway Preacher weren't here at all. That left only me, so when he come out of the barn, I was waiting for him," she says, looking at the knife in her hand and then putting it down. "So now you know the whole story."

"What happened to him?" Asel says.

"Oh, he left, and he won't come around here ever again. You and me, we both know what's going on, don't we?"

Lillian smiles. She doesn't have her teeth in. Her mouth goes wide and black across her face. She looks back over her broad shoulder to the far corner of the room, where Asel can see the sleeve of a red-and-black-plaid jacket hanging over the side of the gut barrel.

"It's the craziest thing," she says, laughing so hard the sound carries high into the cold steel rafters and hangs there long after she stops, long after Asel steps out into the rising mist and watches Phoebe come silently from the house and into his arms, her long hair coming over her shoulder.

Asel holds her, then reaches down and gently moves back her hair. That side of her face is scraped and swollen. He whispers her name and her hands come up to his shoulders, where she grips them, more powerfully than he can remember. Then she loosens her hold and lets her hands rest there.

"Tut's all right," she says, speaking into his chest. "He's asleep."

He whispers her name again and her hands go strong and stay that way.

"I wouldn't change this in any way," she says, her voice soft and distant. "The darkness is all around and it's fine. I've come to like the dark."

"It was in the north," Asel tells her. "It will be different now. I know it will."

"No, it won't," she says, "but we'll pretend it is. We'll pretend it never happened."

ABOUT THE AUTHOR

ROBERT OLMSTEAD was born in
New Hampshire in 1954. His work has appeared in
Black Warrior Review, Granta and *The Graywolf An-
nual 4.* He is a graduate of the creative writing program at Syracuse University and is currently writer in
residence at Dickinson College, in Carlisle, Pennsyl-
vania. He has worked as a contractor, teacher, and
farmer. *River Dogs* was his first published collection of
stories, and *Soft Water* is his first novel.

VINTAGE
CONTEMPORARIES

"Today's novels for the readers of today." —VANITY FAIR

"Real literature—originals and important reprints—in attractive, inexpensive paperbacks." —THE LOS ANGELES TIMES

"Prestigious." —THE CHICAGO TRIBUNE

"A very fine collection." —THE CHRISTIAN SCIENCE MONITOR

"Adventurous and worthy." —SATURDAY REVIEW

"If you want to know what's on the cutting edge of American fiction, then these are the books you should be reading."
                    —UNITED PRESS INTERNATIONAL

On sale at bookstores everywhere, but if otherwise unavailable, may be ordered from us. You can use this coupon, or phone (800) 638-6460.

Please send me the Vintage Contemporaries books I have checked on the reverse. I am enclosing $ _____ (add $1.00 per copy to cover postage and handling). Send check or money order—no cash or CODs, please. Prices are subject to change without notice.

NAME _____

ADDRESS _____

CITY _____ STATE _____ ZIP _____

Send coupons to:
RANDOM HOUSE, INC., 400 Hahn Road, Westminster, MD 21157
ATTN: ORDER ENTRY DEPARTMENT
Allow at least 4 weeks for delivery.

VINTAGE
CONTEMPORARIES